A
Dangerous Affair

By Caro Peacock

A Dangerous Affair
A Foreign Affair

A Dangerous Affair

CARO PEACOCK

AVON

An Imprint of HarperCollins*Publishers*

HarperCollins books may be purchased for educational, business, or sales promotional use. For information please write: Special Markets Department, HarperCollins Publishers, 10 East 53rd Street, New York, NY 10022.

FIRST AVON PAPERBACK EDITION PUBLISHED 2009.

Designed by Diahann Sturge

Library of Congress Cataloging-in-Publication Data
Peacock, Caro.
    A dangerous affair / Caro Peacock.—1st ed.
    p. cm.
ISBN 978-0-06-144748-8
1. Governesses—England—Fiction.   2. England—Social life and customs—19th century—Fiction.   3. London (England)—Fiction   I. Title.
PR6116.E16D36 2009
823'.92—dc22   2008038014

09 10 11 12   OV/RRD   10 9 8 7 6 5 4 3 2 1

A
Dangerous Affair

Chapter One

Neither of us knew the rate for bribing a gaoler at the Old Bailey. My friend Daniel Suter was two steps below me on the way down to the cells. He'd fought his way through the crowd to get there, pushing aside men twice his weight with bruiser's faces, ignoring jeers and curses. In those two steps he'd crossed the boundary between the civilized modern building of the Central Criminal Court and the centuries-old misery of the passageway connecting it to Newgate prison next door. Freshly plastered walls gave way to damp brick and a smell of choked drains.

"I want to see her," Daniel said to the gaoler's broad back.

He looked terribly out of place there, a slim and elegant figure, top hat in hand. That was one of the reasons they were jeering at him.

"How much?" said the gaoler, half turning.

The gaoler had hair cropped like a scrubbing brush, a wart on his chin the size of a coat button. Even from yards away, I could smell the onion and tobacco on his breath.

"Very much."

Seeing Daniel's confusion, I whispered, "He means money."

Daniel's hand went to his pocket. His arm was shaking. I knew he never carried much money because he never had much to carry, and we'd already had to pay to get into the spectators' enclosure in court. The gaoler walked down a couple of steps, slowly. From the top of the staircase, the crowd went on jeering at Daniel.

"Your fancy, is she? Look out she doesn't poison you, like she did Columbine."

Daniel turned to me, all the world's misery on his face, holding out a handful of coins. A gold sovereign and a half sovereign, two half crowns, a silver sixpence and three pennies. It might have been enough if she'd been an ordinary prisoner, like a pickpocket condemned to transportation, but when the judge had put that square of black silk on his wig five minutes ago, her value had gone up.

I felt in the pocket under the waistband of my skirt and found a sovereign. It was payment that I'd managed to extract from a client some time ago for music lessons, but with everything else happening I'd forgotten about it till then. I took a step down and added it to the coins in Daniel's palm. The clink of it made the gaoler stop and turn round.

"Is it enough?" Daniel said, holding out the handful.

"It's all we've got anyway," I said.

The man bit each sovereign in turn, nodding reluctantly as his teeth closed on the soft gold, then continued on down the steps into a narrow opening between stone walls. Daniel went after him and I followed. Down there, the clamor of the courtrooms upstairs was muffled but the wagons outside in Newgate, grinding over the paving slabs on their way from Smithfield market, made a constant vibration you could feel in your stomach. The smell and dampness seemed to cling to your face, as if you were trying to breathe through a wet dishrag. The gaoler stopped and gave an echoing slap with the flat of his hand on a heavy door. A voice from inside said something I didn't catch.

"Gentleman to see the prisoner," the gaoler announced.

A man's hand came out and some of the coins were passed over, then the door was opened from the inside just enough to let Daniel in. I followed before the gaoler realized I was there. He pulled the door shut behind us and I suppose stood guard in the passage.

It was a big, cold room—far too big for the figure that sat in a rough wooden chair against the wall, with a plump gaoler on one side and a middle-aged woman on the other. Jenny had always been slim but after the weeks in prison she seemed to be on the point of disappearing altogether. The sleeves of her rough gray dress flopped around arms that looked no thicker than withy twigs. Only the jut of a badly fitting corset gave any shape to her upper body. Her red-brown hair that had floated like autumn leaves in the wind when she danced was streaked with black dye and dull from lack of washing, twisted into a knot that seemed to stretch her pale skin painfully tight over her cheekbones. Her big gray eyes had been one of her best features but now they were frightening. They were as large as ever, larger if anything, but blank as slate, as if the world had ceased to exist. Even when Daniel was only two steps away from her, their focus didn't change and she didn't seem to see him.

"Jenny."

The way Daniel said it was closer to a groan than a name. It was enough though. Something sparked in her eyes and suddenly she was on her feet, flinging herself at him. Before the gaoler could move she had her arms wrapped round Daniel, her head against his chest. She was a dancer, after all; still quick on her feet even when nothing else survived.

"No touching," the gaoler barked, lumbering toward them. I stood in his way.

"Why, is that extra?"

He stared at me as if the question puzzled him. I think he was at least half drunk. Surprisingly, the woman took my side. I didn't know if she was a gaoler too or another prisoner.

"You leave them be. It's not for long."

She'd probably taken a drink or two as well, but it must have brought out her sentimental side.

Jenny was talking as she clung to Daniel, low urgent words into his chest. He had his head bent to hear them.

". . . help me. You're the only one who can help me. There's not much time . . . they haven't told me when . . ."

That went to my heart for Daniel's sake as much as hers. Here she was, believing that one man without power, money or influence could somehow halt the millstones of justice that were grinding on in the courtrooms over our heads.

". . . choking there for half an hour. They had to pull on one woman's feet to strangle her and make her die. I can't . . ."

Murderers were hanged outside Newgate prison, just next door to the courthouse. She'd have heard all of the stories in prison. I was glad I couldn't see Daniel's face.

". . . in my basket . . . you could get it from them . . . done up in brown paper. I don't mind how much it hurts. Promise you'll send it. Today or tomorrow, if you can."

There was a double slap on the door from outside. The plump gaoler had retreated to lean against the wall, but now he sprang upright.

"Keeper's coming. Get them out."

He took Daniel by the shoulder, and the woman, alarmed now, caught hold of Jenny round the waist and tore her away. As the gaoler tried to hustle him toward the door, Daniel planted his feet and resisted. The man growled and tightened his grip.

"Do you want me to lose my job for you?"

"To hell with your job. I'm not—"

The man gave a whistle and the first gaoler came in from the passage. They each took an arm and dragged Daniel along in the opposite direction from the way we'd come. I followed, terrified that they were going to throw him into a cell. It was a relief when one of them opened a narrow door onto the gray March daylight and the other gave him a push. He went sprawling on slippery wooden paving slabs and the door slammed behind us. I helped him up. Daniel was so tense with anger that it was like propping up a log of wood. There were people shouting and laughing all around, but this time it had nothing to do with us. It seemed that a man had been found not guilty of some crime in the other courtroom and he and his friends had come outside to celebrate and shout.

"Higgins not guilty. Three cheers for Higgins. For he's a jolly good fellow . . ."

They drank wine straight from the bottle, splashing it on the pavement, and sang loudly and so off-key that it would have caused intolerable pain to Daniel in normal times. As it was, I don't think he heard. Even when one of the revelers urinated against the wall and some of it splashed onto Daniel's boots, I had to nudge him to move aside. He looked at me.

"Did you hear, Liberty?"

"Let's get away from here. If we cross the road we can find—"

"Did you hear what she was asking me?"

"Did she want you to help her escape?"

"No. Not in that way, at any rate. She wants me to send poison in to her so that she can . . . can kill herself before they . . ."

The friends of Higgins had managed to hoist him onto their shoulders after a struggle; he was as big and unwieldy as an ox carcass.

"Three cheers for English justice. Good old English justice."

Daniel drew back his arm, clenched his fist and swung with all his might at the stone wall of the Old Bailey. If I hadn't managed to grab his sleeve I think the contact would have broken bones. Even as it was, the skin of his knuckles was shredded and blood ran down his fingers. He stood, looking at the blood, then at me.

"Daniel, please come home. This won't help her."

"What will then? What will?"

I couldn't answer.

Chapter Two

The case of Columbine's murder started, as far as I was concerned, on a February Saturday morning in Hyde Park, just as the sun was rising, turning the mist to a silver haze. At that point, Columbine still had two and a half days to live. Frost was on the grass, beads of moisture on the sleeve of my riding jacket. I was riding my horse, Rancie, one of the finest mares in London, with the blood of Derby winners in her veins and the sweetest temperament—if you treated her kindly—of any horse ever foaled. Amos Legge rode beside me on a powerful but clumsy-looking gray called Bishop. We'd come in from Park Lane through the Grosvenor Gate and cantered northward along the carriage drive. This early, there were no fashionable riders out, only soldiers from the barracks or grooms exercising horses from livery stables. We slowed to a walk near the point where the carriage drive turned westward. Bishop jibbed, planting his feet and shaking his head from side to side, although there was nothing visible to account for his alarm. Rancie rarely jibbed at anything, so I gave them a lead and Bishop followed reluctantly, walking sideways and snorting. Within a few paces, he went as calmly as if nothing had happened.

"Horses know," Amos said.

It was the site of Tyburn tree, where the gallows had stood for hundreds of years, from the time when London was no more than a village. The gallows had been taken down fifty years before, because respectable people who'd moved to new houses by the park didn't care for hangings on their doorstep. Still, as Amos said, horses knew. As we turned back down the drive a couple of grooms on matched dark bays came out of the mist. Amos knew them and called out a cheerful insult about carriage nags. I looked ahead, conscious of their curious glances. Rancie was worth looking at and my outfit respectable enough not to disgrace her. My riding jacket was the most fashionable garment I owned, fine black wool with leg-of-mutton sleeves tapering to tight cuffs, rows of silk-covered buttons decorating the wide lapels, and a peplum at the back that flared out elegantly over the saddle. It was a bargain from a secondhand clothes shop, almost new. One of the advantages of living in Mayfair is the quality of secondhand clothes shops. The black skirt and top hat, from the same source, were passable but no more. Most of the nap had been rubbed off the hat, but I concealed it as best I could by tying a piece of black muslin round it as a scarf that flew out on the breeze.

"Get a lot of questions about you, I do, miss," Amos said.

"What sort of questions?"

"We've been noticed, going out early like we do. People want to know who the mystery lady is."

"I'm no mystery."

"They think so. Riding the way you do on a mare worth a small fortune, they reckon you're a rich lady with her own reasons for not wanting to be seen."

"If they only knew! What do you tell them?"

"Me, I don't tell 'em anything. I just listen to what they say."

"Oh? And what do they say?"

"There's some think you've run away from a husband that ill-treated you. Some reckon you're secretly married to a duke, and another one offered to bet me you're a Russian princess, in London for your health."

I almost fell out of the saddle from laughing. I knew Amos well enough to be sure that when he said he hadn't told the inquirers anything he'd spoken the literal truth. But he had a way of not saying anything that was as good as a nod and a wink, and I could just imagine the glint in his eye as he let every one of them believe that his particular ludicrous guess was on target.

"Who's this coming?" I said.

Even through the haze, the horse and rider coming toward us didn't have the air of a barracks or livery stables. They were moving at an easy canter, horse's tail streaming out like a banner, the rider upright but relaxed. As they came closer, we could see that the horse was a bright bay, Arab or part Arab. The rider's tall top hat gleamed as brightly as the hide of his horse, with dark curls flying from underneath it. He rode with the reins in one hand and an air about him that suggested he should be carrying a lance or sword in the other. Altogether, they looked as if they'd be more at home galloping across some desert wasteland than in Hyde Park. I was about to say something along those lines to Amos when I realized I knew the man. Before I could gather my wits he'd reached us, brought the mare from a canter to a walk and turned her deftly so that he was walking alongside us. He raised his hat.

"Good morning, Miss Lane. Are you enjoying your ride?"

I managed an answer of some kind, probably looking as surprised as I felt.

"You ride early," he said.

"It seems you do too, Mr. Disraeli."

Now that I was recovering from my surprise, I had to fight an urge to laugh with delight at the beauty and unexpectedness of him and the horse. This was only the third time in my life that I'd met him, and on the first two occasions the circumstances had been so strange that they might have happened in a dream. From the first I'd sensed a quality in him that made the world an exciting place, full of possibilities that most people couldn't imagine. I wasn't even sure that I liked him. For one thing, he was far too pleased with himself. He was a Conservative member of Parliament and my political sympathies were quite the other way. There was, too, an edge of mockery in the way he looked and spoke, as if he couldn't take anybody except himself quite seriously. Although he'd given me no reason for mistrust, I did not quite trust him. Still, being in his company was like breathing mountain air.

"It seems as if a man has to get up early if he wants to talk to you, Miss Lane."

On the face of it, this was ridiculous flattery. Granted, he'd only been a member of Parliament for a few months and a notoriously unsuccessful one until now, but he had influential friends and was so far removed from my world that he shouldn't have known or cared if I rode in Hyde Park or on the surface of the moon.

"To talk to me?"

He moved even closer, so that his stirrup iron was almost touching Rancie's side.

"When we last met, Miss Lane, I made you a promise. I have done my best to keep it."

I nodded, unable to think of anything to say.

"A certain person who did you a wrong has retired to his estates in Ireland. He no longer appears in the House of Lords and he most assuredly will not be received at Court."

"Thank you."

"Did you know that?"

"I had heard, yes."

I'd met Mr. Disraeli the summer before. My father had been murdered and my life whirled to fragments as if by a hurricane.

Through no fault of his own, my unconventional and good-natured father had become tangled in affairs of state that reached all the way up to the throne. Mr. Disraeli and I shared knowledge of events that might have disturbed the peace of the country had they become public at the time. But that was all over now, so why was Mr. Disraeli suddenly seeking me out to tell me he'd honored a promise?

Amos Legge had drawn back and was riding behind us, as if he really were just a groom instead of a friend. I was grateful for his presence. The conventional world would know exactly what to say about a lady who permitted a gentleman to approach her in the park, before most people were up and about. I was some distance outside the conventional world, but not as far as all that.

"How are you liking life in London?"

He asked it almost as if we were meeting over the teacups, but there was an edge to his question.

"Well enough, thank you."

"Perhaps time is heavy on your hands."

"Far from it. I work for my living. I give music lessons."

My voice sounded sharp to me, but I didn't want him to be under any illusions.

"You're a versatile lady, Miss Lane."

Certainly a hint of satire in his voice. When we'd last met, I was posing as a governess. I said nothing. His mare, impatient at our slow pace, tossed her head, flecking Rancie's withers with foam from her bit.

"I wonder whether you might consider doing a service for a friend of mine," he said.

"Does he need music lessons?"

He frowned, knowing that I was teasing him. When he spoke, his voice was harder.

"I understand you have connections in the theater world."

I bit my tongue to stop myself from asking how in the world he knew that. My father had loved music and the theater, and many of his friends were musicians or writers. So were some of my best friends.

"Do you happen to have heard of a dancer who calls herself Columbine?" he said.

I was about to say no, when something stirred in my mind.

"Wasn't she quite famous about ten years ago?"

Ten years ago I was twelve years old, trying to make sense of the adult world from hints and half understandings. Disraeli laughed.

"Heaven help us all, if fame lasts no more than ten years. I think the word you are looking for is 'notorious.'"

"Better known for her diamonds than her dancing," I said. The phrase came back to me suddenly in the voice of one of my father's friends, surrounded by male laughter.

"Yes. She must have used up all the diamonds, because she's still dancing. I understand she's heading the bill at the Augustus Theatre. It opens tonight, as it happens."

I was on the brink of saying that here was a coincidence, because a good friend of mine was directing music at the Augustus. I stopped myself because, glancing at Disraeli's face, I thought perhaps he knew that already. We were nearly back at the Grosvenor Gate now, where Amos and I should be turning out of the park.

"So, what of her?" I said.

He hesitated a moment, then spoke, quickly and softly.

"She's done some damage to a friend of mine. We're concerned because that may not be the end of it."

"What kind of damage? And who are 'we'?"

"People who care for the good order of society."

"Politicians?"

"You sound skeptical," he said. "I'd forgotten you were such a radical."

I was sure he never forgot anything.

"You don't need to be a radical to be skeptical about politicians."

"Believe me, this goes beyond party politics."

"Are you implying that this Columbine is a danger to society? She must be a formidable femme fatale."

"A somewhat faded one by now. That's not where her danger lies."

"Why is she dangerous, then?"

"In all honesty, I don't know. I only suspect certain things which I'd rather not talk about at present. If you should happen to pick up any backstage gossip about the woman, I'd be grateful to hear about it. Particularly any gentlemen she's associating with."

I knew what my answer should be. A cold *Do you take me for a spy, sir?* Followed by a sharp turn of the back and rapid canter away. Rancie would go straight from a walk to a canter at one twitch of my heel. My heel didn't twitch. The trouble was, on the previous occasions when we'd met, a spy was precisely what I had been.

"We should be very happy to pay any expenses you might incur," he said. "You can always send a note to me at the House."

"I must wish you good morning," I said. "We turn off here."

In spite of his slow pace, we'd come to Grosvenor Gate. I nodded and Amos picked up the signal and came alongside me, cutting out Mr. Disraeli with the precision of a cavalry maneuver. I didn't look back as we went through the gate and into Park Lane.

"He's thinking of buying that mare," Amos commented. "They're asking twenty guineas too much for her and she's a devil to shoe."

He led the way across Park Lane, going carefully because at this time of the morning carts came in with vegetables for Covent Garden from the farms north of the park, their drivers still half asleep. As we rode along Mount Street, Amos carried on talking about Mr. Disraeli, not put out by my silence.

"They say he's got a mountain of debts already, and he's looking for a rich widow to marry."

Was that intended as a warning to me? If so, Amos was a long way off the mark for once. He was usually a totally reliable source of gossip. His success in adapting to life in London astounded me. A year ago, he'd never set foot outside his home county of Hereford-shire, far away to the west, and he still spoke with an accent that carried hayfields and apple orchards in every syllable. He'd been caught in the same hurricane that had blown me into the life I was leading. When Rancie and I came to London he'd talked about stay-ing a day or two to see us settled. Days had turned to weeks, weeks to months, and here he still was. With his strength and knowledge of horses, it was no surprise when he found work at a livery stables on the Bayswater Road, the northern edge of Hyde Park. He even solved for me the problem of how I was to keep Rancie (or Esper-ance, to give her her proper name), my father's last gift to me. She was given board and lodging at the livery stables, in return for being ridden by some of the more skillful and light-handed lady clients. What was surprising was the extent to which this country giant, standing some six and a half feet in his riding boots, had become a source of knowledge about fashionable London life, all without the slightest hint of snobbery, more the way a boy might study the habits of birds or animals.

At first I wondered how he came by this gossip; then one day when I happened to be crossing the park on foot I saw him, though he didn't see me. He was riding out behind a well-dressed and beautiful lady. His boots and the cob he was riding shone like ma-hogany, he wore a black hat with a silver lace cockade on his light brown hair, and his blue eyes gleamed with good humor. I saw the glances he was getting from riders with less impressive grooms and the complacent smile on the face of his own lady, and could hardly keep from laughing out loud. I'd heard since that he was so popular with lady customers that his stables had to increase his wages to stop him being poached by rivals.

We turned into South Audley Street, nearly home. It was al-most full light now.

"I'll come for you on Monday then, shall I?" Amos said.

"Yes please."

Most mornings of the week I rode out on Rancie with Amos. Even on days when I didn't see them, the thought of them less than a mile away across the park was enough to raise my spirits.

He rode in front of me into Adam's Mews, then through the opening into a kind of appendix to the mews called Abel Yard. At the mounting block by the open gates he slid off Bishop to help me down, then, taking Rancie's reins, vaulted back into his saddle. He touched his crop to his hat brim as they rode away, Rancie letting herself be led as quietly as a children's pony.

There was a cow on our doorstep, a Guernsey, being milked into a quart jug.

"Hello, Martha. Hello, Mr. Colley," I said.

The cowman looked up from Martha's stomach and grinned a hello at me, baring a set of toothless gums. He and Martha, along with his three other Guernsey cows, a dozen chickens and one cockerel, inhabited the end of the cul-de-sac that was Abel Yard. Mr. Colley, his wife, daughter, daughter's baby and daughter's bone-idle husband lived above the cow barn. If I woke early enough, I could look out of the window and see Mr. Colley leading his first cow of the day out by lamplight on the start of his milk round. He sometimes took the cows to graze on the long grass of the burying ground behind Grosvenor Chapel round the corner near the workhouse. The authorities tried to stop him and it was a frequent sight to see Mr. Colley sprinting along the mews, a cow trotting beside him and the parish beadle uttering threats as he puffed along behind.

The other business in Abel Yard was a carriage mender's. The owner, Mr. Grindley, made a reasonable living repairing the springs and other metal parts of carriages in his workshop, which took up two brick-built coach houses on either side of the entrance, with living quarters above. Our two rooms were over the one on the right-hand side as you came in.

Mrs. Martley was standing inside our door, watching to see that Mr. Colley was giving good measure. She wore a white cotton apron over her usual dress of navy-blue wool, her faded brown and gray hair firmly pinned under a starched white cap, her face reddened from stirring saucepans over the fire. My riding habit made her frown. She didn't approve of my morning rides, or very much about me at all for that matter, but I was the one who paid the rent, so she couldn't do anything about it. Until quite recently, Mrs. Martley had been earning her blameless living as a midwife; then that same hurricane had picked her up and plumped her down beside me like a ruffled hen. With the help of my father's and my dear friend Daniel Suter, I'd rescued her from kidnap and imprisonment and was now saddled with her, like the man in the fable who saves somebody from drowning and has to support him for the rest of his life.

It was Daniel Suter who had looked after us when I was too dazed to do anything. I strongly suspected that it was Daniel too who'd found some money for me. Soon after Mrs. Martley and I moved into Abel Yard a messenger delivered a banker's order for fifty pounds, made out to Miss Liberty Lane; he wouldn't say who'd sent it. It was a large amount, as much as a laborer might earn in a year. As a hardworking musician and composer, Daniel could never have spared such a sum himself, but he might have got up a collection among my father's friends. He'd denied any knowledge of it and put on a good show of being puzzled, but I couldn't think of any other possible source.

When Daniel told me he'd heard of a place that might do for Mrs. Martley and me near Hyde Park, I'd wondered how we could possibly afford such an expensive neighborhood. I had forgotten that expensive neighborhoods must have people and animals to support them: grooms and horses, sweeps and grocers, chickens to lay their eggs, terriers to kill their rats, and men to cart away their rubbish. So while the great houses showed their fine fronts to the park, a whole community of us lived in the mews and streets behind, like birds and squirrels in mighty oak trees. Four shillings a week bought us the use of a parlor with its own fireplace and an attic bedroom. It was no more than a temporary refuge, for the landlord had other plans; but since everything else in my life seemed to be temporary, that was the least of my worries.

Mr. Colley squeezed out the last creamy drops from Martha's udder and Mrs. Martley bent with a sigh to pick up the jug. Maybe I should have offered to carry it upstairs for her, but I didn't want to spoil my only good pair of black gloves. I went ahead up the stairs and opened the door to the parlor.

"There's a letter come for you," she said. "It's a foreign one."

My heart bounded. The only person likely to be writing to me from abroad was my brother, Tom—or Thomas Fraternity Lane, to give him his full name. He was two years my junior and, since our father's death, my only close relation. It was the grief of my life that we hadn't seen each other for four years and weren't likely to do so until we were old. Since my father could provide no fortune or proper profession for him, Tom was sent away to India when he was sixteen years old to work for the East India Company.

The letter was lying on the table; I picked it up and thought I caught a whiff of salt from its long sea voyage, and an even fainter one of spices.

"It came yesterday," Mrs. Martley said, "only the boy delivered it to the coach house by mistake."

By then I was halfway up the stairs. A letter from Tom was precious and I wanted to gloat over it on my own. I pushed aside the curtain that divided my share of the attic room from Mrs. Martley's and sat down on my narrow bed by the window to read.

The first part of it was entirely satisfactory. He was still, like me, trying to recover from the shock of our father's murder, but life in Bombay was a wonderful distraction. He was working hard, learning the language, living in a fine house with three other fellows, each of them with his own servant to stand behind his chair at mealtimes. His chief was pleased with him and hinting at promotion.

Then, on the turn of the page, he had to spoil it with a passage that flung me into that state of fist-clenched fury to which only your nearest and dearest can reduce you, wanting to yell at him over those thousands of miles of ocean as I'd once yelled across the nursery floor: *How dare you tell me what to do?* Service with the Company might be doing wonders for his prospects, but it was evidently making him pompous.

> *As to your own domestic arrangements, I understand what you say about their complete propriety but I am very concerned to hear that you have chosen to live on your own in London. Is this Mrs. Martley you mention a housekeeper, or what is her status? In any case, it will hardly do. You mention that you frequently see Daniel Suter, and that he has been helpful to you. I should have expected no other from one of our father's dearest friends and know I can rely totally on his sense of honor and your own. Still, we live in a world in which people are all too ready to impute their own bad instincts to even the most virtuous. If Daniel were to make you an offer of marriage, you would have my complete support and approval in accepting it. In the circumstances, I don't think you need wait until the year of mourning for our father ends in June. If Daniel wrote to me asking for your hand, I should give it most wholeheartedly, knowing Father would have approved. I have written to Suter to hint as much.*

That letter made up my mind for me, although not in the way my brother might have hoped. The day had hardly begun, and already two men had tried to tell me what to do.

As the world would see it, my brother's instructions were entirely reasonable. Of all the men on earth, Daniel Suter was the one I liked best. He was ten years older than I was, but young in heart, blessed with great musical talent and part of our family circle for as long as I could remember. Nothing could be more suitable. And yet there was something stubborn in me that made me rebel against what was merely suitable. Tom and I had been brought up to question everything. My very name, Liberty, was a token of my parents' belief in a world where women as well as men could make their own decisions. Here I was, healthy and well educated, in the greatest city in the world. I was mistress—for the while, at least—of my rackety two-room household. I had money in my purse—albeit diminishing fast. The events of the past few months had given me unusual freedom for my age and sex, and it seemed to me that it would be ungrateful to waste it.

Mr. Disraeli's suggestion—unlike my brother's—was entirely unsuitable, and yet the mystery and unexpectedness of it made my heart lift and tickled my curiosity. I wanted to know more about this Columbine and how she could possibly be a threat to people in Disraeli's comfortable rank of society. Later that day, as I walked down Piccadilly heading for the theater district adjoining Covent Garden, I felt as if I'd accepted a challenge.

Chapter Three

On the way to the theater, I called at the house in Bloomsbury Square where Daniel lodged with half a dozen other bachelor musicians. If Daniel had read his letter from my brother, I wanted to make it clear that the embarrassing hint about marriage had been dropped without my knowledge. The household's maid-of-all work, Izzy, answered the door with a duster in one hand and a harassed look.

"He's gone to the theater already. We don't see much of him at home these days."

It struck me that it had been two weeks or more since I had seen Daniel. He must be working even harder than usual, and yet the Augustus might be considered a step down for a man who regularly played at both Covent Garden and Drury Lane. I knew the theater from earlier times when I'd lived in London, and I had been backstage several times. It was a barn of a place, at the Covent Garden end of Long Acre, built ten years earlier by a man who had hoped to convert London audiences to the delights of classical drama and gone spectacularly broke in the process. It had passed through several hands since and was already showing signs of shoddy construction, with plaster flaking from the walls and rust blistering the supports of the canopy over the main entrance.

When I got there, just as it was beginning to get dark at four o'clock, a few loiterers were reading the bright new playbills plastered to the walls. THE RETURN TO THE LONDON STAGE OF MADAME COLUMBINE topped the bill in large black letters. She was to perform two ballets: *The Court of Queen Titania* and *Diana the Huntress*. Among the other attractions were a new comical domestic burletta entitled *The Hoodwinked Husband*, Signor Cavalari and his arithmetical horse, twin boy acrobats ("Peas in a Pod"), and the murder scene from "Shakespeare's Famous Tragedy" *Othello* performed by the renowned tragedian Mr. Robert Surrey. Daniel's name was near the bottom of the bill as director of music.

The main doors were locked so I went in at the side entrance. There was nobody in the doorkeeper's booth except a fat tabby cat, blinking at me from a stool. A long corridor with dressing room doors off it led into the depths of the building. The air was colder than outside and a smell of damp plaster hung over everything. With three hours to go to curtain rise, the place seemed deserted and quiet as a church.

Then somebody started singing. It was a simple song, "The Lass of Richmond Hill," to piano accompaniment. The soprano voice was sweet and true, but it seemed to me not strong enough for a big place like the Augustus. I took a right turn and walked down a flight of steep wooden steps into the orchestra pit.

There were just the two of them: the man at the piano and the woman standing beside it. It was almost dark in the pit, apart from one candle in the holder on the piano. By the light of it, the first thing I noticed was the girl's beautiful red hair, the color of a beech tree in autumn. Her pale face, eyes wide, was intent on the song. The man sitting at the piano was looking up at her, his fingers stroking out the accompaniment so tenderly that it seemed to make a cave of music to shelter the two of them. He was Daniel.

I knew I was intruding so turned to go, but must have made some sound because she stopped singing suddenly and looked scared, as if they had no right to be there. The accompaniment stopped as well.

"Is that you, Mr. Blake?" the man at the piano said, not able to see outside their halo of candlelight.

"No, it's me," I said, wishing I were a thousand miles away.

"Liberty?" From the sound of Daniel's voice, he wished the same. "Is something wrong?"

"No, I'm going. I'm sorry."

"Wait, Libby." He'd recovered himself now and spoke in his usual gentle voice. "Come over here. There's somebody I'd like you to meet."

The girl looked as if she wanted to run away. He touched her hand quickly and gave her a nod, as if to reassure her that I posed no threat.

"Liberty, may I introduce Jenny Jarvis. Jenny, this is Liberty Lane, one of my oldest and dearest friends."

Her bare hand met my gloved hand. I could feel her pulse beating like a trapped bird against a window. She was wearing a plain cotton dress, not warm enough for winter. Daniel picked up a gray woolen shawl from the top of the piano and adjusted it carefully round her narrow shoulders.

"Jenny, would you go to the dressing room and keep warm if you can. I'll come soon."

She went without a word, picking her way among the shadowy chairs and music stands as gracefully as a deer in a hazel copse.

"She's a dancer," Daniel said. "I'm teaching her singing, when we have time."

"You shouldn't have sent her away for my sake."

"She needs to rest before the performance. In any case, I wanted to talk to you. It's providential in a way, your being here."

I thought, but didn't say, that he hadn't felt that way a minute ago. He was keyed up and nervous, far more than a man of his experience would be for a first night in a second-rate theater.

"Jenny's nineteen," he said. "She's only been in London a few months. She comes from a village in Kent, near Maidstone. Her father's a farm laborer. Her mother died and he married again."

"She ran away from a wicked stepmother?"

I didn't like the flippancy in my own voice. In fact, I didn't like myself very much at all. Only minutes ago, I'd been angry that my brother was trying to press me into marrying Daniel. Now here I was feeling shocked and miserable because he loved somebody else. I'd guessed the moment I saw them together, known for certain when his fingers rested on her shoulder just a moment longer than needed to settle the shawl. Why should I be shocked? Daniel had made no promises to me, nor I to him. If I'd assumed, too easily, that I'd always be the woman in the world who mattered most to him, that was no fault of his.

Daniel gave no sign that he'd noticed my tone.

"She ran away to London because she wanted to dance. She saw some traveling troupe at a fair and that was all she wanted to do. I honestly believe she thought London was full of happy people singing and dancing."

I bit my tongue to stop myself saying that nobody should be that naïve, even a country girl. Daniel must have picked up on my thoughts.

"I'm making her sound like a fool, Liberty. I promise you, she's far from that. She's quick minded, a talented dancer, and has an excellent ear for music. And the sheer courage of her amazes me. Here she is, a little thing with no friends and no experience, managing to survive in London. Can you imagine what that must be like?"

"Yes."

"She's sharing a room with two of the other dancers in Seven

Dials. One of them brings men home. There's only the one room and two beds in it. You understand?"

I imagined two girls huddled in one of the beds of a slum room, listening to the sounds from the other bed a few feet away.

"She's only just begun trusting me enough to tell me about it," Daniel said. "It makes me sick even thinking of it."

"How long have you known her?"

"Three weeks. I must do something, Libby. But I can't bring her to lodge with me in a house of men. Her reputation would be entirely gone."

I thought, *Unless you married her.* I didn't put it into words in case it tipped him into something he'd spend the rest of his life regretting.

"So you can guess what I want to ask you. It was in my mind in any case, but when you arrived just now . . ."

Ironic, I supposed, guessing what was coming.

"I wonder if she might come to live with you and Mrs. Martley. Only for a while, of course, until I can make some other arrangement. It's a lot to ask, but . . ."

He looked me in the face, wanting this more than I'd ever known him want anything. I hoped my horror didn't show. The two rooms in Abel Yard were a tight fit for me and Mrs. Martley. Having to take in a girl I knew almost nothing about would be a burden, even without this feeling of hollowness round my heart. But Daniel had found me the rooms; even paid for them, if my suspicions were correct.

"Yes, very well," I said.

He grabbed my hand and squeezed it, face bright with relief.

"Bless you, child. May I tell her?"

"Yes, if you like."

"She could come straight home with you after the performance tonight. I'll find a cab."

Worse and worse. I'd hoped for a day or two's breathing space.

"I'll have to warn Mrs. Martley."

"We'll send her a note." He was buoyant now, glowing with relief. "Now, what was it you wanted to see me about?"

"My brother's written you a letter," I said. "I think there may be something impertinent in it about me. He shouldn't have written it; please disregard it."

He looked blank for a while.

"Oh yes, a letter from India arrived yesterday. I'm afraid I haven't had time to open it yet. Is it important?"

"No. Would you tear it up, please."

"Yes, if you want me to." He smiled like his old self. "Child, you're a constant surprise. You walk from Mayfair to Long Acre to ask me to tear up a letter."

"There's something else," I said.

"What?"

"What do you know about Columbine?"

His good humor was gone in an instant. He thumped his palm down on the bass notes of the piano, producing a sound like an elephant stepping on a stack of plates.

"That she has the temperament of a cobra, the rhythmic sense of a lame cow and a belief in her own importance that would make Cleopatra look like a shrinking violet."

I laughed.

"Seriously," he said, "she is the most infuriating person it's ever been my misfortune to work with. In two weeks, she's attended rehearsal just four times and then walked out the moment it suited her. She won't hear the faintest word of criticism, and the other dancers spend most of the time trying to keep the wretched woman upright. Why in the world are you interested in her?"

I took a deep breath and told him about the meeting with Disraeli, knowing he wouldn't like it.

"That puffed-up dilettante! He had no right to approach you. You should have snubbed him."

"He's not easy to snub."

"I'm sure he's past caring about his own reputation, but he should have more concern for yours."

That sounded so like my brother that I began to suspect he'd read the letter after all.

"I can take care of my own reputation, thank you. I know he's a Conservative, but what else is to his discredit?"

"Apart from the most ridiculous maiden speech in parliamentary history?"

It had been the talk of the town for days. Within a few weeks of taking his seat, Disraeli had made his first speech on the Irish question, with so many high-flown theatrical flourishes that he'd reduced even his own side to helpless laughter.

"That's beside the point," I said. "Apparently he has friends who are prepared to pay money for backstage gossip about Columbine."

"I hope you told him you'd have nothing to do with it."

I didn't answer. He drew the correct conclusion from that and sighed. He wanted to argue, I knew, but was too grateful to me at the moment.

"Be very careful, Libby. I don't trust that man or anything to do with him. Do you mind if I go and tell Jenny now?"

He ran up the steps toward the dressing room corridor, leaving me sitting at the piano, fingering out some tune and trying in my head to talk sense to myself. I didn't want to marry Daniel, did I? I'd been almost sure of that. So I would be an ungrateful dog in the manger if I did anything but wish him luck with all my heart in this affair with Jenny.

In the background, I was aware of things coming to life up on the stage behind the red curtain—bumpings and screechings of scenery being moved around, the swish of backcloth coming down. A deep voice with a West Country accent shouted instructions to the men up in the flies, as loudly as if he were in a Cape Horn tempest. He probably had been. Most scene shifters are ex-sailors, hired because of their skill with ropes. Somebody must have lit gaslights onstage. Even though I couldn't see behind the curtain I could smell the acrid reek of them.

Hearing footsteps hurrying down the stairs to the pit, I thought it was Daniel coming back, but it turned out to be a tall, plump man of forty or so, with a paunch that filled out his waistcoat.

"Suter, have you finished the music for the burletta?"

His voice was rounded and actorly. He had that air of professional dignity with panic showing through that seems normal with theater managers. I told him that Mr. Suter would be back in a minute. He gave me a harassed glance, not bothering to ask who I was.

"Has he finished the music, do you know?"

"Yes, I'm sure he has."

I was far from sure. Daniel would probably be scribbling notes for his musician friends up until the curtain rose and beyond.

"Tell him the business with the bucket is in. Cymbals when Charlie signals with his elbow. And in the *Othello*, the drummer's to go on until he's finished strangling the woman, however long it takes."

He hurried back up the steps out of the pit. Daniel returned soon afterward and I passed on the message.

"Who is he?" I said.

"Barnaby Blake, the manager. Big ambitions for this place, but he's trying to do everything on a small budget. He's relying on Columbine to bring in the crowds, which is why he's so patient with the confounded woman."

I told Daniel I was going for a walk outside and would come back in time for the performance. The gas fumes were making my eyes water. The doors along the dressing room corridor were still closed, but sounds and voices were coming from some of them. A distant smell of dung suggested that Signor Cavalari's arithmetical horse had arrived.

Outside, drizzle was falling, smearing a greasy gleam over the pavements under the lamplight. I put up the hood of my cloak and strolled to Covent Garden. At this time on a winter afternoon, the main business of the day was over, but the place was still teeming with people. Ragged women and children gleaned cabbage leaves and crushed potatoes from gutters by the light of public house windows. Sounds of loud voices and singing came from inside the public houses, while gaunt horses dozed in the shafts of empty carts outside. A few porters were still at work, collecting up empty baskets and stacking them, ready for the morning. They carried half a dozen of them easily on their heads. Some of the porters were Irishwomen, calling out to one another in their own language. There was one I noticed particularly, a woman who must have been nearly six feet tall, face brown as leather, thick dark hair with streaks of gray hanging in damp waves over her broad shoulders. She wore a man's tweed cap and jacket and a red printed cotton skirt with as many petticoats under it as a grand lady's. Her muddy bare feet were firmly planted on the cobbles and she was shouting the odds at a male porter who'd offended her in some way. She was surrounded by other women, yelling their support, jeering at the man until eventually he slunk away. I thought, *There's a woman who can look after herself*, and felt somehow comforted.

I bought a beef pie from a man selling them from a tray and took it to a bench outside St. Paul's Church on the west side of the market. I ate it with my fingers, getting gravy on my second-best gloves, as I watched a man juggling with flaming torches. A young woman walked past him into the church. She was tall and confident, wearing a purple cloak and feathered bonnet. Her hair under the bonnet was as yellow as an artificial daffodil and her pretty face had a hard, intent look in the flickering torchlight. I should not have put her down as a churchgoer.

Having finished the pie I walked back to the Augustus. Under flaring gaslights people were queuing for the gallery. This time there was somebody on duty in the doorkeeper's room, a plump, bald-headed man with tired eyes. He watched me walk in without inquiring who I was. By now, with less than an hour to curtain-up, the dressing room corridor was noisy and crowded. Some of the crowd were artistes. Twin boys in harlequin suits who looked no more than twelve years of age had their heads together in serious discussion. A man in a satin doublet with a handsome face and grizzled hair put his head round a door and yelled, "Honoria, where are my breeches?"

Some half dozen of the people cluttering the corridor were gentlemen about town, elegantly dressed and all with that air of condescending boredom, as if this would do as well as anywhere to fill the gap between card games and supper. They were clustered round the half-open door of one dressing room, leaning against the wall or on their canes, top hats tilted over their foreheads. Girls' laughter came from the room, along with a whiff of face powder and stale sweat. I glanced inside as I pushed my way past the dandies, collecting a hurt yelp as I trod on a fine leather boot. Gaslights and mirrors took up one wall of a long and narrow room. Piles of outdoor clothes covered most of the floor. Seven girls in green muslin dresses with low-cut bodices and short skirts showing ankles and calves were crammed into the room with hardly space to turn. Some of them were pretending to disregard the men, leaning into the mirrors to apply color to their lips, patting powder onto their bosoms. Two or three were talking to them, giving and receiving cheerful insults as if they were old friends. The men had probably spent most of the afternoon drinking at their clubs, and when you came close to them their breath fumed stale claret. Only one of the seven girls genuinely seemed to want to avoid their notice. At the far end of the room, a head of copper-beech hair was turned away from them all.

A blast of damp air from outside blew along the corridor. Barnaby Blake came running from the direction of the stage.

"Madame's arriving, thank God."

He dashed out to the pavement and returned as part of a small procession. First came the doorkeeper, struggling under the weight of an armchair with a gold wooden frame and damask seat. After him came a woman in her thirties, dark-haired and trimly dressed. She had an ivory silk cushion under one arm, a bag hooked round the other elbow and a glass bowl with a silver cover in both hands. Behind her Columbine floated in a swirl of plum-colored velvet and white fur, dark hair flying loose. She looked furious. The gentlemen had to squeeze against the corridor walls like a reluctant guard of honor, but she didn't give them a glance. Seen close-to, she was beautiful still, but looked all of her thirty or so years. Barnaby Blake walked behind her, expression anxious. She seemed to be lecturing him over her shoulder, her voice loud and carrying.

". . . hoped you'd have sold out all the boxes by now. I've no intention of dancing to half-empty houses."

"I promise you, the figures are very promising, considering," he told her.

She went on talking, taking no notice. The man with the armchair and the maid waited in the corridor as Blake held a dressing room door open for Columbine, more like a nervous host welcoming a duchess than a theater manager whose star was late. The maid and the doorkeeper followed them inside with their burdens, then the doorkeeper came out, puffing his cheeks.

"Dovey-wovey, why didn't you wait for Rodders?"

The cry came from a gentleman who'd just strolled in from outside. He was a young man so pleased with himself that he seemed to glow from inside like a fat white candle. He was probably twenty-five or so, average height and running to fat already. His head was round and slightly too large for his body, set on his shoulders without much in the way of neck intervening, his hair so fair and fine that it stood out like a halo round his head. Buckskin breeches, fine tan riding boots with pink tops that matched the tassel on his walking cane, a chestnut-colored cutaway coat over a waistcoat figured in squares of chestnut and pink completed the look of something from a child's toy box grown to life-size. The other gentlemen seemed to know him well and called out various sarcastic remarks about being late. He brushed past them and rapped with his cane on Columbine's closed door.

Barnaby Blake's voice was audible from inside, still trying to argue his case.

". . . audiences improving all the time. We'll be playing to full houses all summer with the coronation coming up. There'll be people from all over the country who've never seen anything like these shows before, fighting to get into theaters. I've had men begging me to let them invest."

It sounded as if he hoped to keep Columbine on the bill all season, which would be bad news for Daniel.

The gentleman who called himself Rodders rapped on the door again.

"Open up, dovey-wovey."

Columbine's maid opened the door a crack, said some words that I couldn't hear, and closed it in his face.

"Dovey-wovey."

The man set up a howl like a disappointed child. Barnaby Blake came out, looking annoyed at having his diplomacy interrupted, but his face changed when he saw who was causing the commotion.

"Good afternoon, Mr. Hardcastle."

"She won't let me in," the gentleman wailed. "Why won't she let me in?"

By now the sounds of the orchestra tuning up were drifting along the corridor. The chances of Columbine being ready in time for the first ballet seemed remote.

"Artistic temperament, Mr. Hardcastle. I'm sure she'll be delighted to see you at the interval," Blake soothed, as if calming a child. "My wine merchant has just delivered a case of claret and I'd appreciate your opinion. Would you join me in a glass?"

Young Mr. Hardcastle allowed himself to be led into the manager's room, with backward glances toward Columbine's door.

A smaller fuss was going on back at the dancers' dressing room. An eighth girl had arrived late and at a run, to a chorus of ironic cheers from the gentlemen and twitterings of "Where were you, Pauline?" from the girls. She was already unhooking her outdoor cloak as she ran into the room. A purple cloak and a bonnet with feathers over daffodil-colored hair; the girl I'd seen going into the church. But then, why shouldn't a dancer enter a church? Theater people are notoriously superstitious; perhaps she was praying for good luck.

"Has Madame arrived yet?" she asked the other girls, her tone suggesting that she didn't much care for Columbine. They told her that, yes, she had, so she'd better hurry up changing.

I walked toward the pit, intending to warn Daniel that curtain rise looked likely to be late. Running footsteps sounded behind me. I turned and there was Jenny in her thin costume and dancing pumps. She laid a hand on my arm, light as a falling leaf.

"Excuse me, Miss Lane . . ." She spoke in a whisper, with a Kentish accent. She was shaking with nerves or cold, but determined to say her piece. "I wanted to tell you how grateful I am. I didn't . . . didn't know anybody could be so kind."

I looked into her wide gray eyes and understood what Daniel meant about her courage, but she was fragile too. You could no more be unkind to her than to a bird fallen out of its nest. I held out my hand to her.

Instead of taking it, she suddenly threw her arms round my neck and kissed me on the cheek.

"Thank you. Thank you so much."

Then she turned and fled in a rustle of muslin, back toward the dancers' dressing room.

Chapter Four

The curtain rose half an hour late, but the audience seemed cheerful enough about it. Rodney Hardcastle and his gentlemen friends took their places in the two onstage boxes after the overture had started. Most of them were talking loudly to one another, although Hardcastle himself looked sulky. I was standing by Daniel at the piano, making myself useful sorting out music and giving myself a good view of stage boxes and stage. As the overture ended, the twin acrobats spun themselves into complicated somersaults on and off a seesaw placed in front of the curtain. They were a marvel of strong nerves and good timing, but chiefly there to give latecomers a chance to settle. When they bounded off, the orchestra went straight into the introduction to the first ballet. The curtain quivered and rose. The chorus skipped on, wafting garlands. Columbine, in green satin and gold gauze, entered en pointe as Titania, with a smile that looked as if it had been set in wax. Bursts of cheers broke out from the boxes and front row, along with a thumping of walking canes on the floor and snorts of laughter from Rodney Hardcastle's friends.

There was a joke going on among them that the rest of the audience didn't share.

I watched Columbine carefully, trying to understand why Disraeli should consider her a possible threat to the good order of society. She looked younger and more beautiful under stage lighting than close-to, but as for her dancing . . . To describe it as second-rate would have been charitable. She was the wrong shape for a dancer. Admittedly her feet were small and neat, and her ankles and calves shapely. But her breasts, only just contained by her bodice, were like a swell of downland. They were magnificent, but put her out of balance, like a schoolboy's top that can only stay upright if it keeps twirling fast. She could not twirl fast. She was insecure *en pointe*, hardly airborne in her leaps, unreliable in her pirouettes. Luckily, the ballet had been arranged so that the eight dancers were always on hand to offer discreet support. They did their work efficiently, but only Jenny danced as if there were any joy in it. Her diffidence fell away and she moved with an instinctive response to the music, sure as a fish darting through water. She belonged in some other, less tawdry, ballet. Daniel's eyes followed her every move until almost the end of the ballet.

Columbine finished triumphantly on tiptoe, the girls kneeling round her, leaning back like the petals of a flower. All that was needed was a repetition of the opening bars to get them off the stage. Daniel was already signaling with his eyes to the bassoon player to be ready for the comic fanfare that opened the burletta, so he didn't see what came next. The girls stood up and formed a line. Columbine walked past them toward the wings, curtsying to the applause at every few steps. It happened that Jenny was the last in line, standing like the rest, head up and arms extended sideways. Straightening up from her final curtsy, Columbine stretched her arm back in an arc and, quite deliberately, struck Jenny hard across the ribs. The audience probably didn't notice anything or thought Jenny was simply being clumsy when she staggered back, but from the pit I saw it quite clearly and even heard the gasp of pain that Jenny gave. She recovered almost at once, and walked off into the wings with the rest of the dancers. Then the curtain came down.

"What did she do to deserve that?"

The lead violin whispered the question to me, under cover of the bassoon blasts. He was Toby Kennedy, a big and kindly Irishman from County Cork, friend of both my father and Daniel. If Daniel assembled a group of players for anything from Haydn string quartets to the present shambles, Toby Kennedy would be there. He might have been one of the greatest violinists of his day, if it hadn't been for an easygoing temperament that made him love company and good fellowship better than his art. He must have been in his fifties but wore his age as lightly as everything else; a bear of a man with a shock of curly gray hair and a wind-tanned face from riding on the outside of coaches on his way to far-flung concert engagements.

"I don't know."

"Better not tell him. Not until afterward, anyway."

He nodded toward Daniel.

"No. He's . . . he is very fond of Jenny Jarvis, isn't he?"

He gave me a sideways look.

"Don't worry, I've seen him like this a few times before. Usually it's the soprano in whatever opera he's directing. He'll recover in time."

"I don't think it's like that," I said. "Not this time."

The violins were cued, so he couldn't answer.

Hardcastle and his friends sat through the burletta, then left noisily as the arithmetical horse began its act. They returned an hour later, even more noisily and some of them unsteady on their feet, during the instrumental prologue to the second ballet.

As far as there was a plot, it concerned the goddess Diana, out hunting with her maidens. Anything less like the chaste moon goddess than Columbine in gold-spangled muslin and a coronet sprouting blue ostrich feathers in her hair it would be hard to imagine. The high point of the dance was Columbine turning a series of pirouettes. The girls knelt down and stretched out imploring palms to their goddess, so that if she became unsteady she could take support from the one nearest. With luck, it would look like a graceful acceptance of homage rather than desperation. One pirouette safely executed, second pirouette, a hasty clutch at a nymph's hand, similarly with three. She came down flat-footed at four and a half, turned and dropped her usual curtsy to acknowledge the applause. Jenny was at the end of the line and there was no need for Columbine to touch her at all. I couldn't believe it when she straightened from the curtsy, put her hand on Jenny's outstretched palm and forced it backward with all her weight. Jenny made no sound that I could hear, but her face contorted.

Daniel positively yelled a protest that must have been audible onstage if not to the audience and, for once in his life, missed a note. Kennedy rallied the strings and the dance went on. Jenny was smiling again, the automatic smile of all the nymphs. Daniel looked at me. I signed to him to go on playing and he did, his eyes fixed on the stage.

The yellow-haired girl, Pauline, presented Diana with a wooden hunting spear. Some animal was notionally attacking them from a canvas-painted thicket. The nymphs formed a protective circle round their goddess. Columbine flourished her spear and drove the point of it straight into Jenny's shin. Jenny yelped and jumped. This time the audience couldn't have missed it. There was a hole in Jenny's stocking and blood flowing. The dancers nearest her looked horrified, while the others held their attitudes and their smiles.

For a moment it looked as if Jenny was going to take it as passively as the previous attacks; but only for a moment. Still moving with delicate grace, she kicked Columbine hard and accurately on the kneecap. Columbine's shriek was probably heard in the street outside. The gallery were ecstatic, whooping and cheering. They were too far from the stage to see the brutal reality of the thing and thought this was all part of the entertainment, much more to their taste than ballet. Most of the musicians had stopped playing by now, though Kennedy—on the principle that in theater you must keep going whatever happens—fiddled out an Irish jig that formed an oddly appropriate accompaniment.

Jenny, seeing the look on Columbine's face, tried to move for shelter behind the other dancers, but Columbine went after her, limping heavily but with more energy than she'd put into the dance. She caught Jenny by the back of the bodice, spun her round and raked her nails deeply down her cheek. By that point Daniel was climbing onto the stage. I caught his coattails.

"No—you'll only make it worse."

Jenny, with fierce stripes of red on her cheek, clutched at Columbine's hair and yanked hard. By then the rest of the audience had taken their cue from the gallery and were laughing out loud, even Hardcastle's party, who were surely in a position to see it was all too real. The laughter grew to hysteria as Jenny fell over backward on the stage, with Columbine's wig and its coronet of ostrich feathers spread across her body like the tendrils of an exotic octopus.

Columbine screeched again and clapped her hands to her head. She wasn't bald, nothing as bad as that, but her own hair was thinner than the wig, pinned close to her scalp and wet from perspiration. The combination of her small, wet head, smudged rouge and spreading circles of eye makeup above her billowing gauze was oddly clownish.

Through it all I'd been aware of the voice of Barnaby Blake shouting from the wings. He'd probably been ordering the stage-hands to bring the curtain down, because it descended so suddenly that some of the dancers who'd been watching openmouthed had to leap backward to save themselves from being knocked off their feet. Behind it, Columbine was still yelling.

Daniel ran up the steps to the stage and round the edge of the curtain. I followed. On the way he almost collided with Rodney Hardcastle, who was trying to scramble over the edge of the box, possibly with the belated idea of helping Columbine. Daniel simply pushed him aside. As I went past I glimpsed Hardcastle's round face, mouth open, expression caught between hilarity and alarm.

Onstage, the dancers and the maid Marie had clustered round Columbine and were trying to soothe her. Barnaby Blake was taking no notice of them, shouting to the stagehands to change the set.

"Suter, what are you doing here? Get back into the pit, stop that infernal jig and play the music I'm paying you for."

"Where's Jenny?" Daniel said.

"Gone to throw herself in the Thames, I hope." Blake turned to yell at a stagehand, "Just get the bed on quickly, never mind the battlements." Then, "Suter, where do you think you're going?"

Daniel went at a run past Diana's glade, into the wings and out to the dimly lit backstage corridor. He hesitated at the door to the dancers' room and noticed for the first time that I was following him.

"I'd better go in first," I said. "She may be changing."

The room was empty, the dancers still onstage.

"She couldn't have just run out in the street in her dancing clothes, could she?" Daniel said.

"I don't know. She might have been desperate to get away. She knows she's the one who'll get the blame."

We went out of the room and along the corridor to the side door. The fat man, Billy, was in the doorkeeper's room, feeding his cat by the light of a feeble gas lamp.

"Has a girl just gone out?" Daniel said.

"Someone just went rushing past. Didn't see who it was."

I followed Daniel out of the door. Late-evening crowds were pushing along Long Acre. An endless procession of carriages went by, their lamps illuminating a dense mass of pedestrians, hawkers, chestnut braziers, beggars and patrolling policemen. There was no sign of Jenny.

"I'll go to her lodgings," Daniel said.

"I'm coming with you, then."

Seven Dials, a short walk from the theater, was an area where even policemen didn't venture alone after dark.

"No. You go back to the Augustus. She might still be inside. If she is, keep her away from Columbine and tell her to wait for me."

From the tone of his voice, there was no point in arguing, so I made my way back through the crowds to the Augustus. It seemed as if I'd been away from the pit for a long time, but Othello still hadn't finished strangling Desdemona. Kennedy raised an eyebrow to ask what was going on. The audience were restive now, talking among themselves or shouting rude advice at Othello; for them, this was all an anticlimax after the scandal.

When the curtain had come down at last and the few remaining musicians had thumped out "God Save the Queen" at quickmarch speed, I told Kennedy what had happened.

"He shouldn't have gone into Seven Dials at this time of night."

"I tried to stop him," I said. "Do you know if the girl's still here?"

He didn't, so I went back along the dressing room corridor. Barnaby Blake's door was closed, but a hum of voices came from inside with Columbine's plaintive tones among them.

The door to the dancers' room was open, half-dressed girls spilling into the corridor from lack of space inside. I asked the nearest girls if they knew where Jenny might have gone.

"A good long way, if she's got any sense."

"Barney wants her guts for garters."

Pauline took no notice, staring at the rest of them with eyes like a cat on the hunt. When I repeated the question to her she turned the look on me, assessing whether I might be of any use to her, and deciding it was unlikely.

"Haven't a notion."

Only a small dark-haired dancer who looked no more than fourteen broke ranks to the extent of trying to do a kindness to Jenny.

"She's left her basket here. If you're looking for her, you could take it to her."

She darted into a corner and came out with the wicker basket.

"That's her ointments and things," one of the others said. "We should keep that for the next time one of us gets hurt."

I took the basket from the dark-haired girl and thanked her before any of them could try to grab it.

The outside door slammed and Daniel arrived breathless, as if he'd run back down the road from Seven Dials. He looked at me questioningly. I shook my head.

"Where's Columbine?"

Scared at the tone of his voice, I said nothing. But Columbine's voice, proclaiming loudly that she'd never set foot onstage again for any amount of money, sounded from behind Barnaby Blake's door. Daniel strode to the door, flung it open and went in. Columbine was standing like a tragedy queen, wrapped in her velvet and fur cloak. Barnaby had his hands spread out, appealing to her. Behind them, the maid hovered with something hot in a glass. They all turned. Daniel stopped within a few feet of Columbine.

"Get out, Suter," Blake said.

Daniel took no notice, staring at Columbine as if he wanted to hypnotize her.

"You're a wicked, talentless, selfish whore," he said. "I hope to God that somebody will treat you the way you've been treating others all your life."

Silence. Columbine stood, mouth open. Blake recovered first.

"He's gone mad. Suter, get out at once and don't come back."

"Don't concern yourself about that. I shan't set foot in any theater that woman's polluting, and neither will Jenny Jarvis."

With that, Daniel turned and strode along the corridor and out of the side door.

When somebody makes a dramatic exit, other people have to attend to the practicalities. I went back to the pit to collect Daniel's outdoor clothes and music, and to tell Toby Kennedy what had happened. We caught up with Daniel in St. Martin's Lane, still looking for Jenny and attracting attention even from the midnight beggars for his hatless and coatless state.

We took him back to his lodgings—rousing poor Izzy from her bed in the basement because Daniel had lost his key—then Kennedy insisted on seeing me home to Abel Yard. As we parted, he told me again that I shouldn't worry, that Daniel would recover; only this time he didn't sound so sure of it.

Chapter Five

The next day was Sunday. Mrs. Martley went to church while I stayed at home and tried to distract myself with guitar practice. Later, she settled at our parlor table and allowed herself one of her indulgences: catching up with her Queen Victoria album. She had a stack of magazines that in their shining youth had been delivered to ladies in the houses fronting onto the park, and went from there via the hands of ladies' maids to the kitchens, where Cook would fillet out recipes and household hints—possibly with the knife used to chop meat judging by the smears on some of the pages. They then made the sideways shift to our building because the carriage mender's wife had friends in some of the kitchens. Mrs. Martley would pore over them endlessly, looking for news of our young queen. Coming from a family of republicans, I didn't share her loyal enthusiasm but tried not to laugh at it.

"I got Mr. Suter's note," she said as she cut out an engraving of Little Vicky receiving an ambassador. "Your friend didn't come home with you last night, then?"

"No."

"Will she be coming today?"

"I don't know."

Somewhere under the gray skies, in the slums around Covent Garden, I knew that Daniel would be searching for her.

"She'll have to share your bed, I suppose."

"I suppose so, yes."

I'd worked hard at achieving my few square feet of privacy. Originally, Mrs. Martley and I had to share the attic bedroom and the double bed, each to her own side of the feather mattress with a dip in the middle. Every night Mrs. Martley, being heavier than I was, would roll down into the dip, leaving me clinging with my fingertips to the edge of the mattress to stop myself rolling on top of her. Also, she snored. Yet she claimed she couldn't get a wink of sleep all night because of my fidgeting. So I spent five shillings on a smaller bed for myself from a secondhand shop in Tottenham Court Road, and another two shillings to have it carted home. Soon afterward I acquired a long curtain which I nailed from a ceiling beam, giving us the luxury of a narrow bedroom each. I had a peg for my bonnet, a wooden chest for my clothes and an old apple box to support my candlestick.

Still concentrating on slotting her treasure onto a vacant corner of the page, Mrs. Martley said, "The landlord came round yesterday when you were out. You know Old Slippers is going?" Old Slippers was the tenant of the attic rooms above our parlor, so called because nobody had ever seen him in any other sort of footwear. "When he goes, the landlord wants to do this whole place up and let it out to a gentleman. Mr. Grindley says he wants fifty pounds for a deposit."

My heart sank even further. I'd known my hold on Abel Yard was precarious, but had hoped to keep it for a little longer. Setting up house is an expensive business, even secondhand, and with only nineteen pounds and a few shillings of my original capital left our options would be severely limited.

With thoughts of an uncertain future weighing heavily on me, Sunday was a long day; it came as a relief at half past six on Monday morning to let myself out of the small door in the double carriage gates of Abel Yard and see the red glow of Amos Legge's pipe in the dark. Cupping his hands for me to put my foot in, he threw me up to Rancie's back as if my eight stone were no more than a wisp of straw. As we crossed into the park I asked him if he'd heard of a man named Rodney Hardcastle. He laughed out loud.

"Heard of him? He owes me money."

"What!"

"Me and half London besides. Last week, his hat blew off when he was driving in the Ring and I chased it and brought it back for him. 'I owe you half a sovereign, my man,' he says, feeling in his pockets, though everybody knows they're as empty as a pauper's belly. 'I'll look forward to that, sir,' I says politely. The other grooms were laughing fit to bust. Twenty thousand, he owes, so I shan't see my half sovereign this side of Judgment Day."

"How can a man owe twenty thousand pounds?"

"Quite easy, in this town. His father's Lord Silverdale and he's rolling in money, see, so they all thought he'd pick up the son's debts. Only he says he won't, so they can all whistle for their money."

The name Silverdale was vaguely familiar. I had an idea that he'd been a government minister at one time.

"But some people get locked up in the Marshalsea for owing twenty pounds," I said.

"That's how it works, look. If you owe enough, nobody can afford to let you go down, because if you do, they sink with you."

Amos, who'd probably never owed a man sixpence in his life, explained it like a lesson in political economy.

"But it has to end somewhere, doesn't it?" I said.

"In tears, probably. They do say he's coming near the end of his rope now."

"He's friendly with a dancer called Columbine. Do you know her?"

But Amos wasn't a theatergoer and Columbine did not strike me as a woman likely to go horse riding, so her name meant nothing to him.

I wished that Mr. Disraeli would come riding up, now I had more questions to ask him. He'd wanted me to find out about Columbine's gentlemen friends, but from the way Rodney Hardcastle had been behaving, half of London already knew about his affairs, financial and otherwise. So was Hardcastle a friend of his? I was disappointed in Mr. Disraeli's taste, if that was the case. But my questions remained unanswered because Disraeli didn't appear.

When I arrived home, Mrs. Martley was even more disapproving than usual.

"You've missed poor Mr. Suter. He waited half an hour or more."

It was just past eight o'clock, hardly light yet.

"What did he want?"

"He looked as if he'd been up all night. I made him a cup of chocolate, but he only drank the half of it. That poor gentleman needs somebody to look after him."

Another dig at me. I ignored it and asked her again what Daniel had wanted.

"He left a note for you."

She produced it.

My dear Libby,

I am sorry I can't wait. I have a favor to ask. Would you very kindly attend the performance at the Augustus tonight and see if anybody there has the slightest idea where Jenny might be. As you know, Blake has forbidden me to set foot in the place. Also, I sense that the dancers might be more ready to talk to another woman than to a man. Surrey's wife (who plays Desdemona) is a decent sort of woman. I know Jenny talked to her sometimes. She might help.

*If you find out anything, please get word to me at any
time of the night or day.*
Thank you. I'm sorry to bring you into this.

Daniel

Mrs. Martley was watching me as I read.

"Bad news?"

I thought that the true answer was probably yes. Instead I told
her I'd be late back and she shouldn't wait up for me.

I had a pupil in Piccadilly who'd demanded some last-minute
coaching, having been persuaded by friends to sing "impromptu"
at an evening reception. She needed so much fussing and reas-
surance that I didn't get to the Augustus until it was almost time
for the interval. I lingered outside for a while, with the loiterers
who hoped to slip into the gallery free of charge for the second
half of the evening. A chanter was strolling up and down, singing
ballads and selling copies of the words for a penny. Chanters are
almost as good as the newspapers in their way, and often nearly
as accurate. It had always amazed me that these ballads were on
sale on the streets, sometimes only a few hours after the events
they described. Then I caught the name Columbine and stopped
to listen.

O come all you sportsmen who like a good fight
Take seats at the ballet on Saturday night
When fair Columbine is defending her crown
Against young Copper-knob, the new battler in town.

Obviously the writer of the ballad hadn't known Jenny by
name, but the detail suggested he'd been there in person.

Queen Columbine deals her a whack to the shin
But game Copper-knob swears the title she'll win.

"To spoil her coiffure, I'll my talons engage."
In the blink of an eye there are wigs on the stage.

I paid my penny and bought the word sheet. The chanter went on singing.

Says young Mr. H: "I will back Columbine
To lay out this upstart in round eight or nine . . ."

I put the ballad in my pocket, hoping Daniel hadn't heard it.

After waiting at the side door until some of the musicians came out at the start of the interval, I slipped along the corridor to the orchestra pit. Toby Kennedy had taken over from Daniel as director of the orchestra and was there with a few of the other musicians. Immediately we both asked, "Have you seen Daniel?"

"I met him in the Haymarket around seven," Kennedy said. "He's still looking for her. I told him if the poor lass has the sense she was born with, she'll have taken herself back home to the country until the fuss dies down."

"I saw him after that," a trombone player said.

He'd obviously been eavesdropping unashamedly. I supposed that a lot of the musicians were gossiping about Daniel.

"Where?" I said.

"Just outside the stage door here, when I came in. I said good evening to him, but I don't think he noticed."

Kennedy looked at me and pulled a wry face. He guessed, as I did, that although Daniel was forbidden the theater, he'd hoped against hope to see somebody who knew Jenny's whereabouts. I asked Kennedy if the ballets were being performed in Columbine's absence, wondering about my chances of talking to the other dancers.

"They're still being performed in her presence, God help us."

"But I heard her telling Blake she wouldn't set foot onstage again," I said.

"He knew the remedy for that." He mimed the passing over of money. "A hundred pounds per performance."

"What! I doubt if even Taglioni gets that much."

"No, but then, as far as I know, Taglioni has never picked a fight with another dancer onstage."

An ordinary dancer, like Jenny, might get four shillings a performance if she was lucky, with no pay for all those hours of rehearsals. I recalled Columbine's conversation with Blake; whatever her failings as a dancer, she was certainly astute when it came to business matters.

"Blake must think she's worth it, just for the buzz," Kennedy said. "He's even found another redheaded dancer in Jenny's place to keep the audience hoping."

I asked Kennedy how Columbine had performed in the first ballet.

"As badly as ever. Clumsier, if anything."

I decided to leave any attempt at questioning the dancers about Jenny until after the second ballet, because there wasn't much time left before they'd be onstage again. The players who had left during the interval were returning now and the audience were taking their seats, Rodney Hardcastle and his friends trailing in after the rest, as usual.

The head of the stagehands tapped the boards to signify to Kennedy that the scene change was complete, and the musicians launched into the introductory music. The curtain should have begun rising at the beginning of the last repeat. It stayed down and immobile, not even twitching. Accustomed to these little hitches, Kennedy signaled to play the repeat again. At the end of it, with the curtain still stubbornly down, they played the whole introduction again. By now, the gallery were getting restive. When at last Barnaby Blake, looking hot and worried, came out in front of the curtains he was greeted with catcalls and booing. He raised his hand for silence. The musicians put down their instruments.

"Ladies and gentlemen, we regret that we have had to cancel the second ballet. Madame Columbine is indisposed."

"Oh, that confounded woman," Kennedy whispered.

There was more booing. Under cover of it, Blake hissed down to the pit: "Acrobats' music. Loud."

He disappeared behind the curtain. Minutes later it rose on the Two Peas, hastily spinning themselves into an extra routine. The gallery went on shouting and booing for a while, then gradually decided it wasn't worth rioting over.

It seemed to me a useful opportunity. As the dancers were not needed for the second ballet, they should have time on their hands and be ready to talk. I slipped quietly up the stairs from the pit, into the dressing room corridor. It was blocked by a huddle of fluttering gauze and goose-pimpled flesh, as the dancers gathered to stare at something I couldn't see. A cold draft blew along the corridor. Beyond them, a woman was screaming, a continuous high-pitched sound. I touched the shoulder of the nearest dancer.

"Who's that screaming?"

"Her maid. She won't stop."

It was the small dark-haired dancer who'd remembered Jenny's basket. She was shaking from cold or fear. Over her shoulder, I saw that they were all looking at the closed door of Columbine's dressing room.

"What's happened?"

"She's dead. There's a policeman in there."

"Who's dead?"

The dark-haired girl stared at me as if I should have known.

"Columbine."

Chapter Six

The yellow-haired dancer, Pauline, was at the front of the huddle. She looked more self-possessed than the other girls and had taken time to wrap a shawl round her shoulders. When she turned to look at me there was a glint in her eyes, as if she were enjoying the excitement.

"She's been poisoned," she said.

"Who said so?"

"The doctor's in there, with the policeman. I heard him asking Mr. Blake if anybody knew what she'd been eating and drinking."

"That doesn't mean she was poisoned," one of the girls said.

"She was raving before she died," said Pauline, annoyed at being doubted. "Going on about bleeding and people not seeing."

"How do you know?" I said.

Silence, then one of the other girls said, maliciously, "Pauline was looking in at the door."

Pauline turned on her.

"Somebody had to do it, didn't they? We'd heard she'd been taken ill, so there we all were, wondering whether the ballet was on or off. Of course nobody thinks to tell us anything. So I said I'd go and ask Mr. Blake if everybody else was too scared to. But when I got to her room the door was open and Marie was crying and Mr. Blake was inside and Mr. Surrey with his face all covered in black makeup. Columbine was stretched out on her couch in her underthings. Her eyes were black, black as burnt chestnuts, and she was babbling away in this odd voice, but not making any sense."

"Did anybody say then that she'd been poisoned?" I said.

"No. I thought she'd had a fit. I asked could I do anything and Mr. Surrey said to go and get some strong coffee . . ."

"Coffee? Why?"

"I don't know. Anyway, the nearest coffee stall's half a mile away, but then the doctor came in anyway so we forgot about the coffee and the doctor said everybody was to go out except her maid. Mr. Blake told me to go back to the dressing room and tell the other girls that Madame was very ill and there'd be no ballet. So I did."

The maid Marie had stopped screaming. In the calm that followed I heard the whisper for the first time, "Jenny." It came from one of the other girls, I didn't know which, and at the sound the whole group of them went still and quiet.

"Has Jenny been here tonight?" I asked.

Only the dark-haired girl spoke.

"If she has, we didn't see her."

I asked the girls to let me through and started to walk along the corridor. Pauline asked where I was going, but I didn't answer. The door to Columbine's room opened and the actor who played Othello, Robert Surrey, came out in costume. His face was covered in black cork makeup, with lips showing pinkly through. He had an arm round Marie and she was curled up against him, her face contorted with shock and grief, as if she wanted to burrow into his padded doublet for safety. He led her past me, into another room. Almost at once, Barnaby Blake appeared from the direction of the stage, with Rodney Hardcastle walking behind him. Hardcastle seemed angry and confused.

"She was all right this afternoon. Are you sure it's not some kind of game she's playing with us?"

Blake, grim-faced, simply answered by opening Columbine's door to let Hardcastle see inside. I took a few steps forward and looked too. Columbine was lying on a couch. Somebody had covered her with a silk shawl, but it wasn't quite long enough, and her feet and ankles in their white silk stockings stuck out. Hardcastle said nothing at first, then he suddenly retched and sprayed a fountain of claret-pink vomit all over the walls and corridor so violently that it spattered my shoes. There was a nervous-looking police officer standing by the couch and a thin, gray-haired man dressed in dark clothes sitting quietly on a chair. The gray-haired man got up when he heard Hardcastle retching and came out, carrying a black bag and closing the door carefully behind him. The doctor, staying piously by the corpse of the patient he'd failed to save. Was it piety, or simply as good a place as any to wait for the arrival of a more senior police officer? He took a disapproving look at Hardcastle, now leaning on his elbow against the wall.

"Who's this?"

Blake explained to him in a whisper and the doctor looked even more disapproving.

"He'd better be taken somewhere quiet."

Blake seemed ready enough to let the doctor take charge and suggested they should all go into his office. Kennedy had arrived by now, and I could tell from the expression on his face that the news had reached the musicians.

"I'm going for a look outside," he said. "Go back and wait for me in the pit."

I knew he was going to see if Daniel might be waiting there, as he had been earlier in the evening. Instead of heading for the pit,

I followed him along the corridor. Billy the doorkeeper came in from the street, followed by two more police officers. They pushed past us and went into Columbine's room.

Kennedy and I looked up and down the street but there was no sign of Daniel or anybody but a few loiterers, wondering why the police had arrived in a hurry. We'd closed the door and turned back into the corridor when a sob sounded from inside Billy's shadowy cubicle by the door.

"Who's that?" Kennedy said.

A pale face looked up at us, then a plump boy of about ten years old got up from the floor and came out, cuddling a tabby cat and crying. I recognized the cat as Billy's but couldn't place the boy. He was clutching the cat close to his chest for comfort, tears running down onto its fur. I asked him what was the matter.

"The girls say the poison was in her syllabub," he said. "Is that true?"

"Who are you?"

"David Surrey."

That placed him: the son of Othello and Desdemona. It was a surprise that he should be grieving so much for Columbine, or perhaps it was simply shock.

"Is there anybody to look after you?"

"My mother's in our dressing room, but . . ."

I put a hand on his shoulder, and guided him to the door he indicated. It was the room where Robert Surrey had taken the maid Marie. When I knocked and opened the door I had a glimpse of Marie sitting on a chair and a woman in bodice and petticoats kneeling beside her with an arm round her shoulders. I pushed the boy gently into the room, complete with cat, but before I could close the door on him, a police officer came pounding along the corridor and shoved me aside. He went up to Marie, took her wrist and pulled her to her feet. The other woman cried out and Surrey asked what he was doing, but the policeman took no notice. He dragged Marie into the corridor and toward the outside door. Marie was too shocked to cry now, almost past walking. The door to Columbine's dressing room opened and another policeman came out, carrying a glass bowl with a silver cover. Blake followed, face grim.

"What's happening?" Kennedy asked him.

"He's arresting Marie."

"Why Marie?" I said. "What's the proof?"

Blake glanced toward the policeman with the bowl.

"They think that is."

"What is it?"

"Columbine's syllabub," he said. "Marie says it's the only thing she ate or drank all evening, and then only a spoonful or two."

"But why would Marie admit that, if she'd poisoned it?"

By now, Blake was following the police constable and Marie down the corridor. I fell in behind them.

"Cab," the leading policeman said. "Somebody call a cab."

Bow Street police office was so close that they could have walked to it in a few minutes, but the policeman was trying hard to do things properly. He clung to Marie's wrist as if scared she'd escape although she had no more energy in her than a rag doll. Billy went to the door and let out a piercing whistle, and almost at once an old cab came rattling down the street. The policeman bundled Marie into it, got in beside her and signaled to the cabdriver to close up the apron on them both. At the last minute he remembered the bowl and gestured to his colleague to hand it over.

"Bow Street," said the policeman, clutching the bowl like an invalid with a basin of gruel.

Pauline suddenly appeared beside us, in her outdoor cloak, hair tucked under her feathered bonnet. She stared at the bowl.

"What's in it? Is it arsenic?"

There was something brutal about her curiosity. Blake must have felt it too, because he snapped at her to go back inside.

"Why should you think it was arsenic?" I said.

Her cold eyes swept over me.

"Just interested."

The cabdriver swung himself back into the driving seat and they clattered away over the cobbles.

"I don't believe Marie did it," I said to Blake. "Besides, she seemed to like Columbine."

"As it happens, I agree with you. Marie was entirely devoted to Columbine."

"Then why did you let him arrest her?" I said.

"I had no choice in the matter. When a police officer is called to a murder, he can hardly leave without arresting somebody."

"Even if it's the wrong person?"

Blake sighed. He looked tired, as I suppose we all did, and possibly he'd even liked Columbine. He certainly liked the money she'd brought in.

"I don't believe Marie will spend long in the cells. The police will have to bring her before a magistrate and he'll have a higher standard of proof than an inexperienced constable."

I hoped he was right. He walked rapidly toward the stage, telling the various bystanders who were crowding the end of the corridor to get out of the way. Gradually they dispersed, with the smell of Hardcastle's vomit still poisoning the air.

The rest of the performance was canceled. Toby Kennedy insisted on escorting me home, though he'd have a long walk back from Mayfair to his lodgings in Holborn. We left the theater along with a dazed crowd of artistes, all talking nineteen to the dozen. There wasn't much grief for Columbine expressed and, now that the first shock had worn off, most of them seemed full of excitement at having firsthand knowledge of an event that would be the talk of the town.

Kennedy didn't say anything until we were clear of the rest.

"Do you think it *was* Suter that the trombone fellow saw earlier?"

"It might have been," I said. "Daniel wanted me to ask the women about Jenny. Perhaps he hoped to see some of the dancers on their way in and ask them himself."

"If Blake's right and the magistrates let the maid go, the police will have to ask more questions."

We walked in silence for a while, thinking about it.

"What is it about the syllabub?" I said. "Isn't that a strange thing to have in a dressing room?"

"Exactly to Columbine's taste, I should think: whipped cream, sugar and sherry," Kennedy said. "It was all part of her affectation. She insisted it was the only thing she could eat on rehearsal or performance days. The maid always prepared it at home and brought a big bowl of it in with her."

"And everybody at the theater knew that?"

"Of course. It was a standing joke."

Columbine had been altogether a joke, or perhaps something worse than that. But I couldn't get out of my mind the picture of those silk-stockinged feet sticking out.

"Do you know anything about her? Was she always like this?"

Kennedy had been part of London's artistic circles most of his life and had a love of gossip.

"There's usually been some scandal circulating round her. I remember when she first appeared on the London scene—must have been twenty years ago. She was about seventeen at the time and bewitchingly pretty."

"Where did she come from?"

"Nobody knew. She simply turned up on an old lord's arm at the opera one night, dressed in red satin and more diamonds than all the rest of the women put together. He put it about that she was the daughter of an Italian count, but there were rumors that she was a milkmaid from his estates in Dorset."

"Did she try to get him to marry her?"

"He had a wife already, also down in Dorset."

"Were he and Columbine together long?"

"Almost a whole season, until he killed himself."

"Killed himself?"

"Got out of his carriage and jumped off London Bridge one night. She said he was drunk and trying to show her how he used to dive off a bridge at home when he was a boy."

"Did people believe her?"

"There was no proof to the contrary, and he was always eccentric. The town said suicide but the jury brought in death by misadventure."

"Do you think she pushed him?"

"No. She had a lot to lose by his death. While he was alive he could cut down his forests to buy her more diamonds, but the estate was entailed, so once he died it went to his heir."

"What happened to her then?"

"That was when she decided to become a dancer. She was never very good, but people would always pay to look at her because of her beauty and her reputation. And of course various men became her protectors. She always had the best in houses and carriages."

We crossed Leicester Square, trying to keep clear of the worst of the mud. A chanter was still hawking the Columbine ballad by the light of a guttering tallow candle. In an attic somewhere, a man who'd dreamed in his youth of being a poet was no doubt already working on its sensational sequel.

"You said people paid to look at Columbine because of her reputation," I said. "There are plenty of scandalous women. Why was she special?"

Kennedy thought for a while before answering.

"You know the fascination cliffs or precipices have for some people? All the more if poor fools take to flinging themselves over them. It was like that with Columbine."

"The old lord wasn't the only one, then?"

"No. There was one scandal not so long ago, about a cavalry officer who turned to forgery on her account."

"How long ago?"

"About five years, I think. It's a strange thing that, now and again, even women like Columbine can fall for a man's looks instead of his money. Maybe it's a kind of a holiday for them, who can tell? Rainer, the name was. Major Charles Rainer of the Household Cavalry. He was a handsome devil, all the swagger in the world, best horseman in London, killed two or three men in duels. All the usual nonsense."

"What did he forge?"

"Bills. You know what a bill is?"

"A legal promise to pay. They're what they keep passing around to each other in the City."

"Just so. Forging them's a serious business. In theory, you could still hang for it. This man took to forging them to pay for all the presents he was giving Columbine. At least, that's what he said in the dock at the Old Bailey. He tried to get the jury's sympathy, saying he'd been tempted away from his honorable career by a wicked and ungrateful woman. It goes without saying that she'd taken up with another man by then."

"And did it get the jury's sympathy?"

"Of course not. He was found guilty and sentenced to ten years' transportation. He yelled out from the dock, cursing her."

Five years since Rainer was transported, nearly twenty years since the old lord died. It didn't seem likely that either of those scandals would be of interest to Disraeli and his friends now. We walked in silence along Piccadilly, up Berkeley Street and through Grosvenor Square. Candlelight glowed softly behind the curtains of the great houses. It was quite possible that in one of them Mr. Disraeli was sitting with the gentlemen over their port, no more than a few yards away. Well, I had some information for him, and some questions.

When Kennedy and I parted at the foot of my stairs in Abel Yard, he promised to get word to me as soon as he had news. He patted my arm and told me not to worry.

"And you—are you taking your own advice?" I said.

He didn't answer.

Chapter Seven

The next day, Tuesday, brought no word from Kennedy or anybody else. It was the dreariest of days, the gray sky seeming to press itself against the window, and the smell of sewage coming up through the building along with the damp.

It was raining on Wednesday morning when I went out and bought the *Morning Chronicle*. The report was there on page three, a column and a half.

> Police are continuing to investigate the poisoning on Monday night of the popular dancer, Madame Columbine, who died in her dressing room at the Augustus Theatre. The deceased's maid, Marie Duval, was arrested at the scene but the magistrate at Bow Street ordered her release yesterday on the grounds that there was no evidence that she was involved in the crime. She was generally believed to be devoted to her mistress.
>
> After her release, Mademoiselle Duval was among

those called on to give evidence at the inquest yesterday afternoon on Madame Columbine (whose baptis-
mal name was Margaret Priddy). Mademoiselle Duval's
distress was so evident that the coroner at one point
halted proceedings and ordered that she should be
brought a glass of brandy and water. Thus fortified,
she testified that she had been with the deceased all
day, at home and at the theater. On days when she was
performing, Madame Columbine would eat nothing but
a cream-and-sherry syllabub, personally prepared by
Mademoiselle Duval. After her arrival at the theater,
she had eaten a few spoonfuls in her dressing room.
She performed the first ballet of the evening, but was
taken ill immediately afterward. When the severity of
her symptoms made it clear that she was suffering
from more than a passing indisposition, a boy was sent
running for a doctor.

Dr. Alfred Barry, who is frequently consulted by the
police and lives nearby, was attending another patient and arrived within twenty minutes. He testified
that by then there was little to be done for Madame
Columbine, who was delirious and slipping in and out
of consciousness. He believed that her symptoms
were consistent with some form of narcotic poison
such as belladonna. Asked by the coroner whether
Madame Columbine had accused anybody of poisoning her, he replied, "No, sir. She was delirious." The
coroner asked him if he had examined, at the police
station, a bowl of syllabub brought by a police officer
from Madame Columbine's dressing room. He replied
that he had, and found in it some flecks of ground-up
black seeds. When a small sample was fed to a rat, the
animal expired.

Mr. Barnaby Blake, the manager of the Augustus Theatre, testified that he had met Madame Columbine on her arrival there and she seemed in reasonable health and spirits. He was also asked by the coroner whether, in his hearing, Madame Columbine had accused anybody of poisoning her. "No, sir," he replied. To his knowledge, did anybody in the company bear enmity against her? "No, sir." A stir among the jurors, rebuked by the coroner. Had there been an incident involving Madame Columbine and another dancer onstage on Saturday night? Mr. Blake replied that there had been some small misunderstanding in the heat of the performance. Laughter from a juror, also rebuked. When asked the name of the other dancer involved, Mr. Blake, with some reluctance, identified her as one Jenny Jarvis. On further questioning, he said he had not seen Jarvis since Saturday night and did not know her present whereabouts.

Police Constable John Morrow, of Bow Street, testified that he had called at the lodging house in Seven Dials where Jarvis resided that morning (Tuesday) but found no trace of her. Efforts to find her were continuing as the police were anxious to question her. After further evidence, the coroner instructed the jurymen on the possible verdicts they might bring in. If they decided that Margaret Priddy had been unlawfully killed they might bring in a verdict of murder. It was open to them to name the person they believed guilty of the deed but, in the absence of firm evidence and in light of the fact that police inquiries were proceeding, he would suggest that a verdict of murder by person or persons unknown was more appropriate. After some deliberation, the jurymen gave their verdict accordingly.

"Is that today's paper?" Mrs. Martley said.

"Yes."

"Mind the ink doesn't come off on my ironing. And I wish you'd take that basket of yours upstairs. It's in my way."

Her eyes went to the floor in the corner. Jenny's basket. I'd put it there on the night of the fight and hadn't given it a thought since. I snatched it up and took it upstairs to my half of the bedroom, slipped the wooden peg from its loop, and opened the lid. It was mostly filled with small glass jars and bottles and packages of folded brown paper. On top of them was a little pile of letters, tied with a green ribbon. I hesitated before undoing the ribbon, then told myself that the more I knew about Jenny, the better. The first one was a jolt to my heart, not because of the words but because it was in a hand I knew almost as well as my own.

> *Dear Miss Jarvis, I think we may snatch a little time for voice practice tomorrow, if you would care to come in half an hour before rehearsal.*

No more than that, in Daniel's handwriting, but she'd kept it. The next treasure was a piece of music manuscript, but the staves had been drawn much wider than usual and the notes were large, as if for teaching a child. Looking closer, I saw that they were in fact tiny feet in black pumps, dancing out their own tune across the paper. I followed them, humming, and it came out as a scrap of a Hungarian Gypsy tune that I knew was dear to Daniel's heart from childhood. The next letter was thicker and began *Dear Jenny* . . . A glance confirmed that it had been meant for only one pair of eyes, and those wide and gray. I tied up the bundle in the green ribbon, trying to ignore an ache in my heart. I'd known he loved her. Why should it hurt to see it written?

I turned my attention to the other contents of the basket. The jars were stoppered with cork and carefully labeled in neat schoolgirlish writing: *ointment of comfrey, ointment of cucumber, marigold lotion.* Four narrow bottles that would have held about half a pint when full, now more than half empty, were labeled in the same writing: *tincture of mallow, tincture of witch hazel, tincture of feverfew, syrup of woundwort.* Most of her stock was in dried form, either leaves or chips of root, wrapped in brown paper packets with the contents noted on the outside: *wormwood, fleabane, valerian root, sage, centaury, melissa, elecampane, pennyroyal, Solomon's seal, self-heal, woundwort.* A paper package at the bottom of the basket rustled when I poked it with my finger. It was less tidy than the rest, as if it had been opened and reclosed hurriedly. The writing on the creased paper said *thorn apple.* Inside was a flat meshed thing about the size of a teaspoon bowl, like the skeleton of a leaf, and as delicate as fine lace except for sharp thorns at the tips. Coarse black seeds spilled out from it over my bed coverlet.

While I was looking at them I heard steps coming up the stairs and the boards creaking under Mrs. Martley's feet as she entered her half of the bedroom. The curtain was drawn across and there was no reason that she should come into my side, but guilt and fear made me start sweeping the seeds back into their paper.

"If you've got those damp stockings off, I'll take them down and put them in front of the fire for you," she said.

The curtain quivered and she was on my side of it. No time to hide the basket or its contents spread out on my bed.

Always eager for something new, she pounced on it.

"I didn't know you had this. Where did it come from?"

Uninvited, she sat down on the end of my bed.

"Marigold—nothing better for clearing up ulcers. What's in the bottle? Tincture of feverfew. That's good for insect bites. I remember when my cousin's little boy got stung . . ." She was practically caressing the jars and bottles, her voice turned to a purr like somebody meeting a long-lost friend. "Valerian root's good for calming the nerves. I used to make a tea from it for my ladies when they were in labor. Pennyroyal's for clearing the blood. I'd get them to take it with a little honey as soon as they could sit up, and I never lost one of them to an infection of the blood, not one."

Since Mrs. Martley was a midwife by profession, it should have occurred to me that she'd have a good working knowledge of herbs. I watched as she opened the packets, tipped crushed leaves or shredded roots into her palm and sniffed, closing her eyes with pleasure.

"You should have told me you were taking an interest in herbs. There's so much I could tell you, and it's a thing every woman should know about. Where do these come from?"

"A friend."

"She knows what she's about. They're all last summer's gathering and nicely kept."

"They're all herbs for curing people, then?"

"Of course, what else would they be for?"

I picked up the crumpled paper with a few black seeds inside it.

"What's this good for?"

She looked at the name on it and tipped the seeds into her palm without any special concern.

"Thorn apple's good for a lot of things. It helps stop coughs if you burn the leaves and inhale them. It's good for burns and inflammations too, if you grind up the leaves and seeds and mix them with hogs' lard. I always kept some thorn apple ointment by me."

"A useful thing to have around then?"

"Oh yes, but you have to be careful with it, mind. More careful than with most of the others here."

"Why?"

She folded the seeds back in the paper and put it in the basket.

"Because if you take too much of it, leaves or seeds, it's a deadly poison. It's much the same as belladonna."

She stood up heavily.

"Now, do you want me to dry those stockings or don't you?"

Once Mrs. Martley had fussed her way out, I put the jars and packages back in the basket, much as I'd found them. After that, I sat on the bed for a long time, thinking. The conclusion was that Daniel had to know. I found a dry pair of stockings, put my damp cloak back on and told Mrs. Martley I'd return later. I kept Jenny's basket under my cloak as I walked along Piccadilly. When a police officer on his beat happened to glance at me, my heart pounded as if he could see through wool and wickerwork to the black seeds inside.

At the corner by Bond Street half a dozen people were looking at a poster tied to a railing. I was walking past when my ear caught the name Columbine. The poster looked fresh from the printer's, paper not yet ruckled up by damp, printing as black as tar. I read over the shoulder of a street urchin who was trying to puzzle out the words.

WANTED
for
MURDER
The sum of One Hundred Pounds
will be paid
to any person providing information
as to the whereabouts
of
JENNY JARVIS
who is wanted by the police for the MURDER
of Madame Columbine

It went on to describe Jenny as about twenty, of medium height and with striking red hair. A solicitor's name and address were given at the bottom of the poster for anybody with information to offer.

Between there and Bloomsbury Square I saw a dozen similar posters, each with a little group of readers. One of them was on a railing just two houses away from Daniel's lodgings, so he couldn't have missed seeing it. I knocked on his front door and waited for what seemed like a long time before it was opened by the maid, Izzy. She looked alarmed when she saw me, as if she'd been expecting somebody else.

"Is Mr. Suter in?"

For reply, she jerked her head toward the first landing. The studio door was closed and no music was coming out of it, both unusual circumstances when Daniel was at home.

"I'll see myself up," I said.

She looked as if she wanted to protest. I felt her eyes on my back as I went upstairs and knocked on the door of the studio.

"Who's there?"

Daniel's voice, sounding annoyed.

"Liberty."

"Wait a minute."

It felt like more than a minute before he opened the door. His hair was ruffled as if he'd been running his fingers through it, and there were dark circles round his eyes.

"What are you doing here?" he said.

It was hardly a hearty welcome and it looked as if he meant to keep me standing in the doorway.

"May I please come in?" I said. "We must talk about Jenny Jarvis."

He stood aside and gestured to me to take a chair. I opened my cloak and put the basket on the table, beside his piles of music.

"Hers?"

"Yes. Remember I took it home? I never had the chance to give it back to her."

It seemed as if he couldn't take his eyes off it. I sat down.

"You've seen the posters?" I said.

"Yes."

"They don't look like police posters. Who do you suppose is putting them out?"

"Rodney Hardcastle." He said the name like a curse.

"You know that for sure?"

"It's what the town's saying."

"But he hasn't got a hundred pounds. He owes tens of thousands."

"By the time anybody discovers that, it will be too late. The damage will have been done."

"You mean Jenny will have been arrested?" I said.

"It's not even true. The posters say she's wanted for Columbine's murder. The police haven't said that."

"They want to question her. That's not surprising in the circumstances, is it?"

I said it as gently as possible, afraid he'd flare up at me. Of all people, I didn't want to quarrel with Daniel.

He sighed, tore his eyes away from the basket and sat down on the piano stool.

"Was that what you wanted to talk about, the posters?"

"There's something else. I opened her basket and—"

Somebody was knocking at the front door, heavily and repeatedly. Daniel's body went stiff.

"Who is it this time?"

We heard the door open. Izzy let out a screech. Daniel jumped up.

"Libby, keep them out. I'll go and—"

Heavy feet in nailed boots were coming up the stairs. There were at least two pairs and they were in a hurry. Below them, Izzy was wailing. Daniel had his hand on the doorknob when the door burst open. A large police officer shouldered his way in, followed by another even larger. Daniel was thrown backward.

"Keep out of here," he shouted at them. "You have no right."

"We have reason to believe that you are harboring a wanted fugitive," the first policeman said. His voice was as deep and dismal as river mud. He added, as an afterthought, "Sir."

As he said it, the larger policeman was trampling heavy-footed across the room. Daniel regained his balance and moved to intercept him. The policeman simply shouldered him aside. He was making for the only possible place of concealment in the studio: a tall cupboard built into an alcove, where Daniel and his friends stored music stands and piles of scores.

"You keep out of there," Daniel said.

The policeman opened the cupboard door. At first, watching from the other side of the room, I thought there was nobody inside and breathed again. But the expression on the policeman's face told me otherwise. I moved a few steps and saw Jenny Jarvis standing upright and frozen inside the cupboard like a doll in a box. A badly used doll, though. Her face was as gray as the shawl she clutched round her, with arms crossed on her chest. Her beautiful hair was dyed a dull black, tangled like seaweed. Sheer terror had frozen her. She stared at the policeman like a rabbit with a buzzard diving down at it. He reached, grabbed her arm and pulled her out.

"Got you, missy."

She didn't attempt to resist, but the first policeman thundered across the room and grabbed her other arm. Together, they dragged her toward the door. Daniel stood in their way, arms outstretched.

"You can't—"

I let out the longest and highest screech I could manage and grabbed the metronome off the piano. The larger policeman was still wearing his top hat. I aimed the metronome at the crown of it, well above his head.

My aim was true. The hat flew off and hit the wall but the head under it was unscathed. The metronome bounced off the constable's shoulder and landed on the other constable's boot. They cursed, but kept tight hold of the unresisting Jenny.

"Arrest her too," said the larger constable to the other one.

"No," Daniel shouted. He ran to me and grabbed me by the arm. "She's nothing to do with this. She didn't know."

"They didn't either of them know." Up to then Jenny had been so passive that it was a shock to hear her talking at all. Even more surprising, her voice was firm and loud. "I got in here when Mr. Suter was out and hid myself. He didn't know till now."

"That's not—" Daniel started saying.

I screeched again and picked up a bound copy of *Messiah*.

"That one's a bloody madwoman," the larger policeman said. "Leave them. We've got the one we came for."

He moved, bumped against the table and noticed the basket.

"That yours?" he said to Jenny.

"Yes." Still in that surprisingly firm voice.

"We'll take that with us, then."

He picked it up with his free hand. They went through the door sideways, Jenny in between them, and hustled her down the stairs so fast her toes didn't touch the treads. I grabbed Daniel's jacket as he went through the door after them.

"Let them go. I swear, if you get yourself arrested, I'll make them arrest me too," I said.

He looked at my face and saw that I meant it. By the time we got downstairs they were already loading Jenny into a vehicle like a cab, though even less comfortable. One of the constables wedged himself in beside her. The driver flicked the reins, the horse lurched into a walk and the other policeman fell in step alongside as if even now fearing Jenny might escape.

Daniel stood on the curb, watching them out of sight.

"You shouldn't have stopped me, Libby."

"How in the world would it help to get yourself arrested too? You knew she was there?"

"Of course I did."

"How long have you been hiding her?"

He hesitated.

"I found her in Seven Dials yesterday."

"Just out in the street?"

"Yes."

"They could arrest you as an accomplice to murder, you know that?"

"She didn't murder the woman."

I let that pass for the while.

"At any rate, she did her best for you," I said. "As long as she sticks to the story about sneaking in without your knowledge, you should be safe."

"I don't want to be safe if she's not."

"You wouldn't be any use to her in prison, would you? Thank the gods she was thinking clearly, even if you weren't."

He glanced at me, surprised at my anger.

"But you tried to stop them arresting her."

"No. There was never any hope of that. All I was trying to do was stop you assaulting a police officer and getting arrested too."

I'd gambled that they'd be less likely to arrest an apparently hysterical woman than a man obstructing them. My throat felt rough from all that screeching.

"They'll be taking her to Bow Street, I suppose. I must go there," Daniel said.

He looked ready to set off that instant, without hat or coat.

"There's no point going anywhere until we decide what to do," I said.

I was afraid that if he arrived at a police office in his present mood he'd talk himself into a cell. He sighed but turned back toward the house. The front door was still wide open. He went inside.

"Izzy."

His call echoed round the hall. There was no answer.

"She's gone," he said.

"Yes."

The poster had done its work. A hundred pounds was more than a maid could earn in five years. I felt sad for Izzy's betrayal of him and the certainty that it had been for nothing, as she'd never get her hands on the reward.

Daniel went slowly upstairs, head bowed. We sat down in the studio.

"There's something you should know," I said.

I told him about the thorn apple seeds. After the first few words he closed his eyes as if he didn't want me to see what was going on in his mind. When I'd finished, there was a long silence.

"We don't know what poisoned Columbine," he said at last.

"No. But thorn apple's like belladonna."

"And you've managed to put that basket straight into their hands."

"Believe me, that wasn't what I wanted. But it might even be in her favor."

"How?"

"That basket's been in my possession ever since she ran out after the fight on Saturday. If she or anybody else took thorn apple out of it, it must have happened before that."

He thought about that for a while.

"Yes, come to think of it, I noticed it in the corner of your room when I was waiting for you on Monday morning."

"There's still a problem, though," I said. "It looked as if that package had been opened and closed by somebody in a hurry."

"What are you saying, Libby? She runs from the theater so distressed she doesn't even remember her basket, but she finds time to take a pocketful of poison out of it? Does that make sense?"

"No. Unless she'd taken it out earlier."

"But why? Before the fight, she'd no reason to wish any harm to the woman. No more than all the rest of us, anyway."

"We still don't know the cause of the fight. Columbine quite deliberately singled Jenny out from all the other dancers. Did Jenny give any reason?"

"I didn't want to bombard her with questions. You saw what Columbine was like. She noticed Jenny was the most vulnerable and picked on her simply out of malice."

I had my doubts, but didn't argue.

"You'd explain to the police about the basket?" he said.

"If you think it will help, yes."

"So let's go to Bow Street now."

"And remind them that she was hiding in your cupboard? Daniel, we were both of us within a few breaths of being arrested. The last thing we need is to bring ourselves to the attention of the police so soon."

"I can't just sit here while she's locked in a cell. I want to know what's happening to her."

"Very well then, I'll go to Bow Street and find out."

I hoped that I could change my manner and appearance enough to avoid being recognized as the hysterical woman. But Daniel had no intention of letting me go to Bow Street on my own. If I walked out, he'd come with me. Impasse. We sat there glaring at each other until an idea came to me.

"We'll go and get Toby Kennedy. He has a lot of lawyer friends. He'll know what to do."

Reluctantly Daniel agreed and we set out for Holborn. By now it was dusk outside, drizzling with rain. Luckily Kennedy was at home. Daniel told his story more coherently than I'd expected. I could see from Kennedy's expression that he was horrified at the legal risk his friend was running, but his advice was as practical as ever, and supported mine.

"You're not setting foot within a mile of Bow Street, Suter. Liberty and I will do anything that can be done. You will not stir from this room until we get back."

We walked quickly, under Kennedy's big black umbrella.

"Did she poison Columbine?" he asked me.

"In all honesty, I don't know." I thought of her impulsive kiss on my cheek, the way she'd summoned up enough courage to lie to the police for Daniel's sake, and added, "I hope not."

"Only 'hope'? God help poor Suter."

At the police office he suggested I should wait outside under the umbrella while he went in and inquired. I agreed, not wanting to risk meeting the two policemen again if it could be helped. I waited a long time. When he came out, his face looked grim in the light of the lamp over the door.

"They haven't wasted time. The magistrate was already sitting when they brought her in. She's been committed for trial to the Central Criminal Court, the Old Bailey."

I knew that the magistrate could hardly have done otherwise in the circumstances, but the reality of it, and what it would mean for Daniel, hit me like a punch in the stomach.

"Did you manage to see her?" I asked him.

He shook his head.

"She's with the other prisoners, waiting for the van to come and take them to Newgate."

The very name of the prison was like a stone slab falling to seal a tomb.

"You look tired out," Kennedy said. "I'll see you home and then I'll go back and tell Suter. Bad news will keep."

I was about to accept his offer, then the picture came into my mind of Jenny dancing and I thought how much worse it would be for her than women who were used to being shut in cells.

"The Augustus is just round the corner. I think I'll go there instead."

"Liberty, this is going to end badly. Stay out of it."

"How can I? Daniel helped me when I needed it."

He sighed. "I can't stop you, can I?"

I thanked him and turned away.

"For heaven's sake, girl, at least take the umbrella."

I took it.

Chapter Eight

There were new playbills plastered to the outside walls of the theater. Barnaby Blake had moved quickly in putting together a different program before interest in the Augustus could fade. A troupe of Spanish dancers—"Direct from Seville. Never seen in England before"—had taken over Columbine's star spot. Desdemona's strangling was replaced by "The bloodthirsty crimes of King Richard Crookback," presented by Mr. Robert Surrey, Mrs. Honoria Surrey and introducing their talented children, Miss Susanna and Master David Surrey. Inside, Billy the doorkeeper was mopping the corridor. His efforts seemed to be doing no more than covering trampled mud with a thin sheen of water. When I wished him good afternoon he peered at me shortsightedly over his mop, obviously with no clear idea of who I was, but made no attempt to stop me. There were still two hours to go to performance time and the dressing room corridor was deserted, the doors along it all closed. The only sound was a high voice coming from the stage.

I do not like the Tower, of any place.
Did Julius Caesar build that place, my lord?

The lines were repeated, several times over. I went into the wings and looked out on Mr. and Mrs. Surrey, the boy who'd been cuddling the cat and a pretty girl of about twelve, all still in overcoats and scarves. They were rehearsing the killing of the little princes in the Tower. As far as I could make out, the dialogue was plumped out with lines from various plays of Shakespeare, plus some that he never wrote. The boy seemed sulky and had to be prompted several times, but the girl was good and word-perfect. Her heart-shaped face and swath of fair hair seemed guaranteed to flutter handkerchiefs in the gallery. After half an hour or so, they finished their rehearsal and came into the wings, on my side.

"Excuse me, but I wonder if you could spare me a few minutes," I said. "It's about Columbine . . ."

Actors think quickly and Robert Surrey didn't hesitate.

"Yes, I've seen you with Daniel Suter, haven't I? Let's go to the dressing room. It's not so cold there."

The children had been whispering together, looking as if they were having an argument. He produced some coins from his coat pocket and gave them two pennies each.

"You two, go and find a chestnut seller. Warm your hands, and mind you bring some chestnuts back for us."

They ran off. We followed more slowly and they were out of sight by the time he opened the door next to the dancers' dressing room. It was a small and crowded room with costumes, velvet doublets and cloaks hanging from pegs, and Richard Crookback's canvas hump swung from a hook on the back of the door. A plaster bust of Shakespeare balanced precariously on the narrow windowsill.

"How can we help you, Miss . . . ?"

"Lane. Liberty Lane."

"My wife, Honoria."

She smiled at me. They were a pleasant-looking couple, he in his mid-forties, upright and broad-shouldered, she around a decade younger, with fair hair almost as bright as her daughter's and eyes that glowed even in the gray light of the dressing room. There was no affectation about them, as if acting were just like any other family business.

"It was dreadful, wasn't it?" she said. "Poor Columbine."

"They've arrested Jenny Jarvis," I said. "I want to find out more about what happened, if I can."

Robert Surrey's face went dark. Honoria Surrey moved an armful of cloaks and hoods off a chair and signed to me to sit down. The two of them settled side by side on an enormous wicker hamper, looking at me.

"You were with her, weren't you, before the doctor came?" I said to Mr. Surrey.

"Yes. I heard a commotion, Marie screaming and Blake telling somebody to run for a doctor, so I went out to see what was happening. Nobody seemed to have any notion what to do, so I had to manage the best I could. Not that it was any use. She was in a delirium by then."

"You weren't called at the inquest?"

"No. There was nothing I could tell them that the doctor couldn't tell better."

A sound came from the direction of the stage, like a distant door slamming. He frowned. "I hope the Tower of London hasn't fallen over again. That set's been doing the rounds of all the theaters since before Garrick."

"Pauline said Columbine was talking about bleeding and people not seeing."

"Yes, that's true. She was rambling about blood, but I don't know why. She wasn't bleeding or spitting blood."

"That girl Pauline has eyes everywhere," Mrs. Surrey said.

"She says you told her to get strong coffee," I said to Mr. Surrey.

"Yes, it was the only thing I could think of, to try to keep Columbine awake."

"You see, he'd had all this before, poor man." Mrs. Surrey looked up at her husband's face and put her hand over his. "Some time ago, when we were running a touring company, a poor girl poisoned herself with belladonna, so he recognized the symptoms."

He nodded.

"She was a good actress, playing Ophelia. I'm afraid she played it all too realistically, fell in love with her Hamlet, and he wanted nothing to do with her."

"There's quite often belladonna in dressing rooms," Mrs. Surrey said. "You know some girls take it to make their eyes look bigger?"

"So you thought from the start that Columbine was poisoned with belladonna?" I said.

"Yes. Either that or something very like it. After the Ophelia case, a medical student told me that she might have lived if we'd managed to keep her awake, poured strong coffee into her, made her walk and walk. I had something like that in mind this time, only it was too late."

"Can you think of any reason why somebody might have wanted to poison her?"

They looked at each other.

"Apart from Jenny?" Mrs. Surrey said.

"Yes."

"Robert and I have talked and talked about it, and we can't. It's true that she was a very irritating woman, but that's no reason to murder somebody."

I asked if they had any idea what the quarrel between Jenny and Columbine had been about. They shook their heads.

"We do try not to listen to chorus gossip," Mrs. Surrey said.

"I'm afraid dancers are mostly rather silly girls. I've had to stop Susanna from going into their dressing room. She's at the curious stage and wants to know everything."

"Five years from now, that girl will be the Viola of her generation," Surrey said. "We're not having her spoiled by the likes of Pauline."

"Or Jenny?" I said experimentally.

They looked at each other again.

"We thought Jenny was different," Mrs. Surrey said. "She seemed a shy, nicely mannered girl. She was so helpful when Robert had his sore throat."

"Brewed cup after cup of herb tea for me," he said sadly. "Melissa and sage and so on."

"Do you think she poisoned Columbine?" I said.

"We don't like to think so, but . . ."

". . . but what can we think?" She completed his sentence.

"I suppose Pauline and all the others have gone now that the Spanish dancers are here," I said.

The seven people who might know why Columbine had hated Jenny would be scattered all over London by now, if they'd been lucky enough to find work in other theaters.

"You shouldn't believe everything you read on playbills," Mr. Surrey said with a laugh. "The Spanish dancers will be mostly the same girls with mantillas and castanets. The two soloists come from as far south as Clapham."

That was good news as far as it went. I stood up and thanked the Surreys. He opened the door to let me out, setting Richard's hump swinging again. He gave it a rueful look.

"I feel as if I've been kicked by a carthorse, being bent double for an hour. Still, it's not as bad as having to black up every night. I hope you and the other man find what you were looking for."

I turned in the doorway.

"Other man?"

"Billy says there was a man around earlier this morning asking questions about Columbine. That was before we arrived. I thought he might have something to do with you."

"No. What did he look like?"

"Tall, quite gentlemanly type, with a brown face, as if he'd been in foreign parts, Billy says. Middle-aged. That's observant, by Billy's standards."

"Could he have been one of Rodney Hardcastle's circle?"

He made a face to show what he thought of Hardcastle.

"Doesn't sound like any of them I've ever seen."

Nobody was about when I stepped out into the corridor. I made my way to the door that had been Columbine's, paused and knocked softly. As I'd expected, there was no answer. I opened the door, walked in as if I had a right to be there, and closed it quietly behind me. If there was a reason beyond the impulse of the moment, it was the wish to find out more about Columbine. At first I thought the room was in the process of being cleared, because a couch was turned over and a big screen was lying flat on the floor as if ready for the removal men. It was a substantial folding screen with three panels, padded and covered in painted leather, large enough for a person to change behind. At second glance, the screen wasn't quite flat. One end of it was raised from the floor by something underneath, and a tangle of green satin and golden gauze spilled over the bare board floor. Columbine's Titania costume from the first ballet. Why hadn't somebody tidied it away before the furniture was moved? I walked over, intending to pick it up, then jumped back. There was a hand tangled in the gold gauze; a small pink hand, motionless and palm upward.

I shouted something and pulled the screen up. It was heavy and hard to move and all I could do was stand there holding it, looking down at Susanna Surrey. The child's fair hair spread out over the floor. She was still wearing her outdoor clothes and scarf. Her eyes were closed. I shouted for help again. Running steps came along the corridor and the door slammed open.

"God, what's happened to her?"

Robert Surrey was beside me, taking the weight of the screen, his wife a step behind him at first, then on her knees beside the girl.

"Susanna!"

Two blue eyes opened for a moment, screwed up against the light and closed again. The outstretched hand twitched and moved toward her mother's.

". . . pushed it over on me."

Her voice was a whisper.

"What's happening this time?"

Barnaby Blake was at the door, sounding scared and angry. When he realized what we were looking at he came in and helped Robert Surrey and me move the screen right away. By then Susanna was sitting up, curled against her mother. A rectangular red mark on her forehead showed where the wooden frame of the screen had hit her.

"I only came in for a look because David dared me. I saw her costume and went to touch it, then she pushed the screen over on me."

Her voice was stronger now. The child was an actress born and bred, and even though she was shocked and in pain she sensed that she'd never had a more attentive audience.

"Who pushed the screen over on you, darling?" Honoria said, stroking the child's hair gently away from the injury.

"She did. Her ghost did. She was angry with me for touching her costume."

"Whose ghost, darling?"

"Columbine's ghost, of course."

The adults exchanged glances over her head. Robert Surrey sighed.

"The first thing to do is get you back to our room, young lady."

"Does she need the doctor?" Blake said.

"We'll see. Arnica and a good rest may do the trick." Surrey bent down and scooped Susanna skillfully up into his arms, like King Lear carrying Cordelia. "And where's young David? I'll have some words to say to him."

It turned out that David was waiting anxiously outside the door with a paper cone of roasted chestnuts, now gone cold. His father told him in passing that it was all his fault, and the four of them disappeared into their own room, leaving Blake and me alone. He looked shaken, and I daresay I did too.

"Her ghost—that's the last straw."

"You don't believe her?" I said.

"Of course not. The child crept in here for a look round and managed to pull the screen over on herself. Imagination did the rest."

"Yes, you can hardly expect a child to be smothered in the Tower every night and not be affected by it."

"Still, it's a good thing you happened to be here," he said. "You heard the screen fall, I suppose?"

I didn't correct him as it gave me a good excuse for being in the room. Now that my heart was slowing to its normal beat, I took the opportunity to look round. A pair of point shoes lay on the floor, behind where the screen had been. Jars of makeup were scattered on a table in front of a mirror and Columbine's ordinary clothes were hanging from pegs on the opposite wall, if anything so fine could have been called ordinary: a dress of dark red velvet, a black cloak with a red lining and hood trimmed with black fur.

"I've sent a note to Marie asking her to come and clear up," Blake said. "We need this room."

A black fur muff that matched the cloak trimming had fallen on the floor. I bent to pick it up and almost dropped it again as it fell apart in my hands. It had been cut through several times over, the cuts going cleanly through the fur and the silk lining. I held it out to show Blake, my heart hammering at the savagery of the thing. He took it from me.

"Good heavens, did the girl do that?"

"Of course not. You'd need a sharp knife and quite a lot of strength. Besides, why should she?"

He put the muff on the table beside the makeup pots and moved over to the upended couch.

"And I don't suppose she did this either."

"What?"

"It wasn't like this yesterday. Somebody's turned it over."

I went to look at it and recognized the couch Columbine had been lying on when I had my glimpse of her through the half-open doorway. The couch she'd died on. It was something else that made me shiver, though. The tough upholstery canvas at the base of the couch was scored through with five or six long cuts, clean as those in the fur muff.

"What in the world has been going on?" Blake said.

"Could the police have done that?"

"Of course not. Why should they?"

"Somebody's been looking for something," I said. "I wonder if it's anything to do with the brown-faced gentleman."

"Brown-faced? Oh, I suppose Billy told you about him."

I didn't correct him, in case he was annoyed with Robert Surrey for gossiping.

"Did you see him? What sort of things was he asking?"

"Yes. He wanted to know about how she died and so on. I thought he might be trying to get up something for the newspapers, so I didn't waste much time on him."

"Did he introduce himself?"

"I didn't invite him to. He claimed to be a friend of hers, but half the world says that with people who are well-known, particularly when they're dead and can't deny it. I wish I'd taken more interest now."

We walked round the room together but found no other signs of damage.

"Whoever pushed the screen over might still be here in the theater," I said.

"Anywhere from the flies to the cellars, I suppose. We can't search the whole place, but we can look in the dressing rooms at least."

We went along the corridor, starting at Blake's office. The sparsely furnished dressing rooms would have provided few hiding places and there was no trace of a brown-faced man or anybody else.

"Probably ran for it," Blake said. "We'd better see how the girl is."

He knocked at the Surreys' dressing room and the door opened on a family tableau. Susanna was leaning back in a chair with a bandage round her head, her father kneeling beside her holding her hand, her mother putting the cork back in a bottle of arnica solution, young David sitting on the costume basket looking hangdog.

"Will she be fit to go on tonight?" Blake asked Surrey.

Susanna gave him a maiden-martyr look.

"We are always fit to go on."

Since she was obviously recovering, I risked a question.

"Did you see anybody behind the screen?"

"No."

"Or hear anything?"

"I think I might have heard somebody move, but I don't remember."

"Ghosts don't make a noise," said David sulkily.

"How do you know? You've never had one trying to kill you."

Brother and sister glared at each other. Blake and I wished her a quick recovery and let ourselves out.

"I must get on," he said. "Ten thousand chores to do before tonight. The last thing we want is a story about a vengeful ghost

going round. Heaven knows, she could be difficult enough when
she was alive."

I walked slowly back to the side door, hoping I might meet Billy
and prise more from him about the mysterious man. No sign
of him, but as I stood by his cubbyhole a woman came through
the door from the street like somebody in a hurry. Today her
cloak was red corduroy, with a matching feathered hat pinned to
her daffodil hair. For a dancer on four shillings a performance,
Pauline dressed remarkably fancy.

"Oh, you," she said. "What are you doing here?"

"You're early, aren't you?" I said.

A pair of hard brown eyes stared into mine, hostile as a cat guard-
ing a fish bone.

"I've got a right to be here. You haven't. Your man's been thrown
out."

"If you mean Mr. Suter, he's not my man."

She tried to push past me. I stayed where I was. No point in
being polite with her.

"Why did Columbine attack Jenny?" I said.

"No idea."

"Of course you know."

She shrugged.

"No odds, anyway. One of them's dead and the other soon
will be."

"You knew Jenny had been arrested, then?"

News travels fast in London, but it was surprising she'd heard
so quickly. I wondered if she'd just come from Bow Street. She
pushed her body against me and brought her face so close to mine
that I caught the briny whiff of whelks or winkles on her breath.

"It's not good for the health, being a nosey parker like you are,"
she said. "I've got friends, good friends, don't think I haven't."

She pushed past me, went into the dancers' dressing room and slammed the door loudly. She moved quickly. Quickly enough to have pushed the screen over on Susanna, left by the front entrance and come back in again? It was just possible, I thought. If so, had she been the person in Columbine's dressing room with the sharp knife? I'd have liked to follow her and ask more questions, but there was no hope of getting answers to them.

Still, my visit to the Augustus had answered one question at least. The next thing was to find Toby Kennedy and give him his reply.

Chapter Nine

"I don't believe Jenny killed her," I said.

I'd found Toby Kennedy and Daniel together in the studio at Bloomsbury Square. Daniel was sitting on the piano stool from force of habit, staring down at his hands, motionless on the keys.

"Of course she didn't."

His voice was impatient. Kennedy glanced at me over his head.

"Two hours ago you only hoped she hadn't," he said. "What's changed?"

I told them all that had happened at the Augustus.

"Whoever was looking for something in that dressing room, it wasn't Jenny," I said. "Pauline knows a lot about what's happening. She as good as threatened me."

Daniel straightened his back and looked at me.

"That man who was asking about Columbine—tell me again how Billy described him to Surrey."

I repeated the words as accurately as I could: "Middle-aged, tall, gentlemanly type, with a brown face as if he'd been in foreign parts."

Daniel's hands came to life and swept up and down the keys in arpeggios. He looked from Kennedy's face to mine and back again.

"Don't you see? Don't either of you see?"

Kennedy and I looked at each other.

"For heaven's sake, Kennedy, it was you who told me about him in the first place," Daniel said.

"What do you mean?"

From Kennedy's face, he was concerned that his friend was going mad.

"The cavalryman," Daniel said. "The one who cursed her from the dock at the Old Bailey. Rainer or whatever his name was."

"He was transported," Kennedy said, sounding exasperated. "Transported to Van Diemen's Land. It's an island off the far side of Australia, as far as a man can be transported."

"Ships must go there," Daniel said. "Even transported men must escape sometimes."

He stood up and unhooked his coat from a peg.

"Where do you think you're going?" Kennedy said.

"The *Augustus*. Somebody there must know more about this man."

Kennedy reached out a long arm and twitched the coat away from Daniel's shoulders.

"Oh no you don't, my friend. For one thing, Blake's ordered you not to set foot there."

"Blake be damned. I—"

Kennedy pushed Daniel into a chair, quite gently in the circumstances, and stood over him.

"You shouldn't be damning him. You should be blessing him."

"Are you mad? After what he said at the inquest about Jenny?"

Daniel's eyes went to a copy of the *Morning Chronicle*, scrunched up in a corner as if thrown there.

"If you'd bothered to read that properly, you'd see that he mentioned Jenny reluctantly," Kennedy said. "Even then, it was only to confirm what the dogs in the street know—that she'd had a fight with Columbine. It's what he didn't mention you should be thanking him for."

"What do you mean?"

Kennedy sighed. "Tell him, Libby."

I didn't like what I had to do, but it wasn't fair to leave everything to Kennedy.

"Blake was asked at the inquest if anybody in the company bore enmity against Columbine," I said. "He said no. He was there when you called Columbine a wicked whore and said you hoped somebody would treat her the way she treated other people."

Kennedy whistled. He must have heard something about the incident, but not the worst of it.

"My friend, are you trying to put a noose round your own neck?" He spoke sadly. "You threaten Columbine—"

"I did not threaten her."

"In court, it would sound like a threat. You then hide a woman the police want to question about Columbine's murder and obstruct police officers in their duty when they try to arrest her. You can thank Blake—and Liberty—that you're not spending the night in Newgate as well."

"I only wish I were. She's locked up there this minute with thieves, prostitutes, the dregs of London. Prison will destroy her long before they hang her, and I can't do anything about it."

The quiet despair in his voice was worse than anger. I went and knelt down on the floor beside his chair and took his hand.

"You can't help her if you're in prison too. For the moment, you mustn't do anything that will draw attention to yourself."

I tried to keep my voice calm, but was desperately scared for him.

"You can't ask me to sit at home and wait."

"No, but at least use your brain. The only way we'll help Jenny is by finding out who killed Columbine. You know the people connected with the Augustus better than I do . . ."

"And you tell me I mustn't set foot there."

". . . so there may be things you remember that are important, given time."

"We haven't got time."

"Yes, we have. It's usually weeks before people come to trial, isn't it?"

I glanced up at Kennedy, who knew these things. He nodded. We managed between us to talk Daniel into a calmer frame of mind.

"One thing you can do is walk Liberty home," Kennedy said to him. "The poor girl's been running around on your account all day and she's dropping with tiredness."

I was about to protest that I didn't need anybody to walk me home. The idea that no woman was safe on the streets of London without a protector was nonsense when you saw the numbers who went about their daily lives alone because they had no choice. Then I caught Kennedy's wink and knew his tactics were to keep Daniel occupied at any cost.

We all went together as far as halfway along Piccadilly because Kennedy was playing at an evening reception in St. James's Square. It was the time of evening when fashionable people were going out to dinner. Landaus and barouches crawled along the streets like slow barges, with their hoods up, the people inside them invisible, drivers on the boxes in their wet capes looking like things freshly dragged from the Thames, clouds of steam rising from the shoulders of the horses into the lamplight. When Kennedy left us, Daniel and I crossed the road and headed up Berkeley Street. One of the posters about Jenny, blurred and bubbled from the wet, was tied to a railing.

"I don't believe that puppet Hardcastle cared for Columbine or anyone else," Daniel said.

"He'd done something to annoy her on Saturday night," I said. "She wouldn't let him into her dressing room. And the night she was killed, he wasn't backstage. Blake had to go out front to look for him. Does that mean he still wasn't welcome in her dressing room?"

"Where's this heading, Liberty?"

"Nowhere, probably."

I didn't want to mention Disraeli again and start an argument. But the fact was, two and a half days before Columbine died, Disraeli had got up early to ask me to find out what I could about her—on behalf of friends of his. The only person I'd encountered at the Augustus who was a member of his own class was Hardcastle. Quite what Disraeli would be doing with a fool like that, I couldn't imagine, but I needed to know.

We walked in silence along the south and west sides of Berkeley Square. We were close to home now and there was a question I had to ask Daniel.

"The night she died, a trombone player said he saw you outside the Augustus. Was he right?"

Daniel took a few steps, then nodded. I tried to see his face in the light of an uncurtained window we were passing, but he kept his head down.

"What were you doing? You surely didn't expect to see Jenny there after what had happened."

"I suppose I was hoping to see somebody who knew her."

"But you'd already asked me to talk to the other dancers."

He didn't answer. We walked on.

"Did you go inside at all?" I said.

"No."

"Did you stay outside for long?"

"I don't know. What does it matter?"

"We don't know what matters, do we? Did you see anybody you didn't expect to see going in?"

"What do you mean?"

He seemed startled.

"As far as we know, somebody put poison in that syllabub between the time Columbine and Marie arrived at the theater and the first ballet," I said.

"If you're asking me whether I saw anybody go in with a bottle marked *poison*, no I didn't."

The ill-natured tone was so unlike the Daniel I knew that I might as well have been talking to a stranger.

"It's a reasonable question, isn't it? So you saw nobody except people you'd expect to see going in before a performance?"

"A man could have been hiding inside the theater all day, waiting for his chance," he said. "Why should he leave it till the last minute?"

"Are you thinking of the man Rainer?"

He answered with another question.

"Kennedy doesn't take that seriously, does he? Why not?"

I didn't tell him that I agreed with Kennedy; how could one take seriously a suspect on the far side of the world?

"Were you outside the Augustus when the boy came running out for a doctor?"

"No. Leave it, Libby. There's nothing there that will help us."

We said nothing else until we turned into Adam's Mews, walking carefully on slippery cobbles. It was almost completely dark, with the rustle of horses shifting gently in their straw behind stable doors and only a few squares of dim candlelight from the lofts above the stables, where the grooms and coach drivers lived. I asked him if he'd care to come in and drink a bowl of the soup that Mrs. Martley would certainly have waiting. He shook his head.

"Shall I come and see you tomorrow?" I said.

He stopped walking, raised his hand to touch my arm in the old, easy way, then dropped it to his side as if it had turned to lead.

"I think it would be best if we didn't see each other for a while, Liberty. This is no concern of yours."

"Of course it is."

"You almost got yourself arrested today on my account. I don't want you running any more risks for me."

"Do you think I care about that?"

"If you don't, then I should. I mean it, Libby. I'll write to you, if you like. If you want news of me, ask Kennedy."

I turned away, glad it was too dark for him to see the tears on my face. He walked with me into Abel Yard and to the foot of my staircase, raised that heavy hand in what was probably meant for a good-bye, and walked away.

When Amos and I rode out in the park early next morning, I kept a lookout for Mr. Disraeli. He owed me an explanation. There was no sign of him then, or on Friday morning. He must know about Columbine's murder. Surely curiosity, if nothing else, would provoke him to another early ride. Or was it possible that his circle knew more about it than they were prepared to admit and had closed ranks? If so, he might already be regretting that he'd approached me, however little he'd revealed.

On Monday I thought it over as I walked to Piccadilly to give a singing lesson to the self-satisfied fifteen-year-old daughter of a Conservative MP. She was one of several new pupils I'd acquired recently, after a handsome Italian music teacher had unknowingly done me a favor by eloping with one of his pupils, a twenty-year-old heiress to fifty thousand pounds. The elopement had put the mothers of Mayfair and Belgravia into such a flutter that any male music teacher younger than seventy and marginally more pleasant to look at than a Notre Dame gargoyle was considered a danger in the parlor. Daniel had lost a few pupils as a result, but managed to pass them on to me.

Today's girl was one of what I called the Vickylings. It's odd how fashion changes. Now that we had a short, round-faced queen of eighteen, with big solemn eyes and smooth brown hair, every wealthy family in London seemed to include at least one living replica of her. I wondered where they'd all come from so quickly. Was it that mothers had been hiding these girls away for years behind their taller and more interesting sisters but brought them forward now that they had become social assets? Did girls practice in front of mirrors, widening their eyes and rounding their chins? I gave the girl as much attention as she deserved, but most of my mind was composing the note that I'd decided to send to Disraeli.

I'd finished the lesson and was in the marble-floored front hall, doing up a strap of my music case, when I heard the voice of my pupil's mother on the stairs.

"Seven o'clock tomorrow evening then, Mr. Disraeli. You won't fail us, I hope."

I looked up, and there he was. He said something flattering to the MP's wife about not failing her, of all people, but spoken with a hint of mockery that suggested she shouldn't depend on it. I stepped back from the foot of the stairs, hoping not to be noticed. They went past me, still talking. A maid came forward with his cane, top hat and cloak. The cloak, I noticed, was lined in silver-gray silk to match his cravat. He took it from the maid and slung it round his shoulders in a studiedly dramatic way, half turning. As he turned, our eyes met. For a second he simply looked startled, then he smiled.

"We meet again, Miss Lane."

The eyes of the MP's wife were wide and surprised. It's one thing to let music teachers use the front door, quite another to have them recognized by guests. By now, the maid had opened the door. Disraeli stood back for me to go first and there was no choice but to accept, though I could feel the wife's disapproval like a cold draft on my back. The door closed and we stood on the step facing each other, with all the noon bustle of Piccadilly just a few yards away.

"I've been hoping to meet you," I said. "I want to talk to you about Columbine." His eyebrows rose. "You said she'd done some damage to a friend of yours. Were you talking about Rodney Hardcastle?"

He looked taken aback.

"No, I wasn't."

"But you know Rodney Hardcastle?"

"I know of him. I dine with his father, Lord Silverdale, when he's in town."

It was the first time I'd seen him uneasy. Gossiping on doorsteps was not *bon ton*. But now I had him, I'd no intention of letting him escape.

"You know somebody's been charged with murdering Columbine?" I said.

"Some dancer, yes."

"Her name's Jenny Jarvis. I suppose it's convenient for those friends of yours that Columbine's out of the way."

It was a big jump I was taking, but he'd annoyed me by not knowing Jenny's name, or pretending not to.

For an instant the look in his eyes showed I'd startled him, but the usual easy, ironic air covered it almost at once.

"Are you going toward Westminster, by any chance, Miss Lane?"

"Yes."

Wherever he was going. Politely, he took the outside of the pavement and we started walking.

"So what can you tell me about this friend of yours whom she damaged?" I said.

"Only that he is in no way relevant to her death."

"How do we know who or what is relevant?"

"My friend has been under close medical care on his country estate for the past three weeks. He tried to cut his throat. He'll live, but he'll never speak again. We all thought he'd be one of the finest parliamentarians of his generation, as his father and grandfather had been before him."

He looked solemn as a marble statue.

"And how did Columbine come into this?" I said.

"A few hours before he cut his throat, she called on him, uninvited. Nobody knows what was said."

"Was he a particular friend of hers?"

"No. That's the mystery of the thing. His family are quite sure he'd never set eyes on the woman in his life before that afternoon."

"Families don't always know everything."

"In this case, they did. If you're implying some relationship between my friend and that woman, I can assure you I know his tastes better."

"Was she blackmailing him?"

"My friend's life was entirely beyond reproach."

"The only people with entirely irreproachable lives are babies in their cradles—and I'm not even sure about some babies," I said.

"I'm certain he'd never done anything of which a gentleman might be ashamed."

He was being terribly parliamentary, as if his words were being recorded for posterity. That made me sure he was keeping something from me.

"Did you ever meet Columbine?" I said.

He shook his head like a horse shaking off a fly.

"No."

"But you know about her past?"

"No more than the world knows. She appeared out of nowhere, tried for a place in society, and failed."

"By not marrying the old lord, you mean?"

"There was never a chance of that. After he died, she took a house in Grosvenor Square and tried to set up a salon—artists, literary men and so on. Quite a few men accepted her invitation, but the ladies wouldn't tolerate her. You've probably heard the story of how Lady Shedlake dealt with her."

"No."

I hadn't even heard of Lady Shedlake.

"Invited her to a reception. Of course, La Columbine was over-joyed, thinking this was social acceptance. In she swans, all velvet and diamonds. Lady Shedlake, in front of all her guests, welcomes her like a long-lost sister. Would she care for a glass of champagne? Then, just as the footman's handing it to her, Lady Shedlake says in that very carrying voice of hers, 'Or perhaps you'd prefer a glass of milk?' "

It took a while for the malice of this to sink in. When it did, I was struck with an emotion I'd never expected: a shiver of sympathy for Columbine.

"You mean, the milkmaid story? But that was a horrible thing to do to anybody."

He shrugged.

"They say she packed up and fled to Paris the next morning. Then, when she came back, there was the business of Rainer and the forgery. She's been lying pretty low since then."

Until she accepted an engagement at the Augustus, which might have been about the same time she called on Disraeli's friend.

"I still don't understand what you wanted from me," I said.

"To be honest, Miss Lane, I don't even know myself. I believe it was an apprehension that my poor friend might not be the only one."

"You must have had a reason for thinking that."

"More of an instinct than a reason. You see, an ordinary man observes events and sees a pattern in them. If a man wishes to be extraordinary, he must see the pattern first and anticipate events."

His self-conceit was so total that I couldn't even laugh at it.

"And you observed a pattern?" I said.

"Nothing as drastic as my poor friend's case. But over the last few weeks there have been instances of men resigning from prominent positions, or withdrawing to their country estates, or generally avoiding public life in a way that puzzles me."

"And you attribute all that to Columbine?"

"I simply don't know, and I detest not knowing. I need ears and eyes everywhere."

"Tell me, was I your only pair of ears and eyes at the Augustus?" I said.

"Of course. Why do you ask?"

"One of the dancers there has been behaving strangely."

Another shrug from him implied that was only to be expected.

"You asked me to watch for her gentlemen friends. You surely knew Rodney Hardcastle was one of them, as you're acquainted with his father."

"Poor old gentleman. Rodney's his only son and their line goes back to before the Conqueror. He's virtually disowned him and says he won't be responsible for his debts."

"Debts, yes. Mr. Hardcastle's seem to be considerable."

He laughed. "Sometimes a man's debts are the most interesting thing about him. I'm sure that's true in Hardcastle's case."

He sounded much more lighthearted about that than the rest of our conversation. I remembered Amos's information that Mr. Disraeli too owed a lot of money. Because of my own money worries, the easygoing attitude rankled with me.

"You're looking disapproving, Miss Lane. Debt and credit keep the world spinning."

I didn't answer, not wanting to reveal my weakness.

"So, what do you propose to do?" he said, serious again.

"Try to prove that Jenny Jarvis didn't kill her."

"You believe you can accomplish that?"

"I don't know. But I'm not about to sit quietly by while the poor girl is hanged just so that people whose line goes back to before the Conqueror can sleep peacefully in their beds."

He stared.

"What are you implying?"

"I think you know something you're not telling me," I said.

"That isn't true. I've gone to some trouble to tell you all I know."

We stared at each other. He had fine, dark eyes that shone with sincerity. He was a politician.

"Then I shall thank you and wish you good day," I said. "I turn off here."

I'd come some distance out of my way already and I sensed that he was not going to tell me more until I found some way of unsettling that poise.

"May I call you a cab?"

"No, thank you."

"Then, if you'll permit me, I'll call one for myself. Good day, Miss Lane."

Disraeli raised his hat to me and walked away down Duke Street, signaling for a cab. One trotted to the curb beside him as promptly as if he'd had it on the end of a wire. It would, of course.

Chapter Ten

I stood on the pavement for a while, giddy at where I found myself. I'd as good as thrown down a challenge to Disraeli, and I had nothing whatsoever to back it up. After a while I found I was walking and my steps seemed to be taking me eastward toward Long Acre and the Augustus Theatre. The answer lay at the theater, I was sure of it. So far, there was no reason to doubt the maid's evidence that Columbine had eaten nothing but the syllabub. Only a person familiar with Madame's daily routine or the backstage talk in that particular production could have known about the syllabub. Narrowing the field still further, only people involved in the production could have known about Jenny's basket of herbs. Which, on the face of it, ruled out most people Disraeli was likely to know. A gentleman backstage would have been as conspicuous as a parrot among pigeons. The obvious exceptions were young Hardcastle and his coterie of clubmen. Their enthusiasm for ballet girls, if not for ballet, meant that they were often to be found backstage. The management might not approve, but customers who rented boxes by the season must not be offended.

I was prepared to bet that, with nothing much to fill their time, these gentlemen would gossip like farmwives at market. Some of the dancing girls would have gentlemen as their protectors, and perhaps the gossip from Hardcastle's circle would filter down to them. I hoped to find a dancer or two in an idle moment, prepared to talk to me.

When I went in by the side door of the theater, the clicking of castanets echoed along the deserted corridor. It came from the dancers' dressing room. I waited for a pause, knocked and went in. The only dancer there was the dark-haired girl of fourteen or so, who'd been kind about Jenny's basket. She stood in the middle of the room wrapped in an assortment of old knitted shawls against the cold, not much more than a pair of castanet-wielding arms and wide brown eyes sticking out. She looked scared when she saw me.

"I know I shouldn't be here so early, only I couldn't take the clickers back home because the people I share with 'd go off with them, and I have to practice with them, see."

She was so naïve that she even saw me as a figure of authority who might throw her out. I guessed she'd been thrown out of a lot of places in her short life, like an unwanted kitten.

"You've more right to be here than I have," I said. "Do you mind if I watch?"

Her eyes glinted. The arms stretched out, shaping sinuous curves on the air, and the castanets clattered like a miniature cavalry charge. I started humming a tune I usually played on the guitar and she began stamping and whirling, shedding shawls as she went. We went faster and faster until she collapsed laughing into a chair so rickety it almost broke apart, even under her small weight.

"Oops! Got me proper warmed up, that has, better'n brandy."

"You're very good," I said, meaning it. "What's your name?"

I felt like asking what she knew about brandy at her age, but had no right. She smiled at the compliment.

"Bel, short for Belinda. They've given me a bit of a solo, that's why I got to practice with the clickers. A bob a night more, I get for that. Pauline's sick to the guts about it, stupid cow. She thinks any solos ought to come her way. I'll have to look out or she'll be going for me the way Columbine did Jenny."

She stood up, moved to the mirror, draped a piece of black muslin round her head.

"It needs the comb thing to make it stand up. There it is."

"About Columbine and Jenny . . ."

"Do you think it makes me look Spanish?"

"Very. Do you know why Columbine was so angry with Jenny?"

Up to that point she'd been chattering away as happily as a sparrow. Now she paused, picked up a battered artificial rose and started trying to straighten its stiff gauze petals.

"Don't know."

"I think you do know." I said it as gently as possible. "I think all the girls know, but you're not telling anybody."

She'd turned her back to me, but her face was reflected in the mirror. All the sparkle had gone out of it.

"Pauline'll kill me if she knows I've been talking about it."

"About what?"

"Will it help Jenny if I tell you? I liked Jenny. She's the only one of the lot of them ever said a kind word to me."

"How can I know if it will help Jenny unless you tell me?"

She swiveled round to face me.

"It wasn't fair. She was the only one of us what hadn't done it, only Columbine didn't know that."

"Done what?"

She made an unmistakable gesture, still grasping the rose. Shock at the crudity of it, in contrast with the delicacy of her looks, must have shown on my face.

"Don't look so strange at me," she said. "You're as bad as Jenny was."

"Who with?"

"Him, of course. Rodders. Columbine wouldn't have minded otherwise, would she?"

"You mean, Columbine thought Jenny had been making love with Rodney Hardcastle?" I said.

"Yes, if that's what you call it."

"But why should she think that?"

"Because Pauline told her so."

"Why?"

"Because Columbine had got a whiff that something was going on, and if she knew it was all of us, there'd have been hell to pay. Pauline was angry with Jenny in any case, because she was the only one what wouldn't do it. So telling Columbine paid her out and got the rest of us off."

"But why should Pauline be angry?"

"She said it was because Jenny thought she was better'n the rest of us. Only some of the other girls say he'd offered Pauline a cut if he won his bet."

"Bet?"

My head was reeling, but Bel was talking as matter-of-factly as if we were discussing the price of stockings.

"His friends had bet him he couldn't get all of us to bed within a week."

"*All* the dancers?"

"Yes. He'd have done it easy, if it hadn't been for Jenny."

"You mean, you did too?"

She stared at me as if the question shouldn't need asking. Her eyes looked into mine as if into a mirror. It wasn't that they were hardened, because that would imply that they'd been soft once. Simply, this was her life and she couldn't imagine any other.

"But why?"

A stupid question. It got the answer it deserved.

"Five bob."

I heard a door slamming at the far end of the corridor, distant footsteps. Bel jumped up.

"It might be Pauline. Don't tell her I told you. She'll kill me."

She grabbed a couple of shawls and clutched them round her, as if for protection.

"This bet—did Jenny know about it?"

"Not at first, she didn't. She thought he was just asking us all out to supper. Then she got up and ran out. I told her she shouldn't of done that. It gets a girl a bad name."

The footsteps came closer, several pairs of them, and a child's voice chattering. Bel relaxed.

"It's all right, that's just the Surreys."

"You discussed all this with Jenny?" I said.

"I tried to talk to her, make her see sense. She shouldn't have come to London really. She just wanted to dance. Only, it isn't just about dancing, is it? Jenny couldn't see that. She couldn't look after herself."

At a rough estimate, Jenny must have been five or six years older than Bel, but to listen to her you'd think it was the other way round. Perhaps it was, in most ways that mattered.

"Did she know that Pauline had lied to Columbine about her?"

A nod.

"Didn't Jenny tell Columbine it wasn't true?"

"She tried. Columbine threw a perfume bottle at her, so she didn't dare try again."

I thought Bel's story explained why Columbine had been angry with Hardcastle, though Columbine hadn't known the worst of it.

"Surely Hardcastle must have realized Columbine would hear something about it," I said.

Bel shrugged.

"Don't think he cared. He was leaving her anyway."

"How do you know that?"

"Because he's getting married."

"Who to?"

"Don't know, but at the supper we went to, some of his friends were laughing at him about being the bridegroom. That's why they made the bet when they did."

"Because he was going to be married?"

"Yes. 'Last gallop round the course,' that's what they said. He didn't like it, them laughing at him. He said he didn't want to get married in any case, only he had to because of the money."

"So he's going to marry a rich wife?"

"Suppose so."

"Poor woman. Do you happen to know where Pauline lives?"

She looked scared.

"You're not going to tell her I've been talking to you, are you?"

"No, I promise I won't tell her."

"Last I heard, she was at a place called the Egyptian Palace, just up from Leicester Square."

With a name like that, I supposed it was a public house. A memory came to me of the first time I'd seen Pauline.

"Tell me, is Pauline a churchgoer?"

"Churchgoer!"

The amazement in Bel's voice gave me my answer. I wished her luck with her Spanish dance and left.

Outside, the cloud had lifted, with patches of blue sky showing, though the wind from the east was biting. With two hours or so of daylight left, I decided to head off and look for Pauline. I was so angry I wanted to shake her till her teeth rattled like Bel's clickers.

Even in fleeting sunshine, Leicester Square was its usual depressing self. A columned building that had been a theater in the past century was now a draper's warehouse. Its old name, Sans Souci, was just visible above a banner advertising three shirts for the price of two. A pile of bricks from a builder's yard had toppled over the uneven pavement. Judging by the dirt and dead leaves that had collected round them, nobody was hurrying to collect the bricks up again. The smell of drains hung over everything. In spite of all that, a building in the far corner made my heart rise with memories of childhood. It was a rotunda the shape of an upturned egg cup, several stories high. The sign said *Burford's Famous Panorama. Now exhibiting the Wonders of Old Peking.* The painted panoramas changed every so often. When Tom and I had been taken there as children, they were still featuring patriotic old favorites like *Admiral Nelson's Victories* or *The Field at Waterloo.* You paid your threepence at the door, climbed the stairs to the circular gallery inside, and walked around with the enormous oil paintings encircling you, larger than life. I was surprised to find it still in business.

But this was no occasion for childish things. I found a crossing sweeper, tipped him a penny, and asked if he knew where I'd find the Egyptian Palace. He gave me an incredulous look.

"Gyppy Palace?"

"If that's what they call it, yes."

From his reaction, I guessed it was a particularly rough place. Some of the public houses in that area were no more than thieves' kitchens.

"Up there, first on the right, halfway along."

When I crossed the street and turned to look back, he was where I'd left him, leaning on his broom and staring after me.

The first on the right was a cul-de-sac with a public house called the Red Cockade on the corner. Two rows of terraced houses in blackened brick faced each other across a muddy street, too narrow for anything except a donkey cart. The only building of any size was a more substantial house on the left, three times the width of the others. Crumbling stone columns on either side of the front door supported a triangular porch, with a sphinx lounging uncomfortably in the middle of it. The windows on the ground floor were high and broad, but curtains were drawn across, showing their yellowed cotton linings to the street. The glint of a candle shone at a gap where the curtains didn't quite meet. What sort of place drew the curtains and wasted candles by daylight? A gambling den, I supposed. Certainly the place didn't have the air of a public house.

As I waited on the far side of the street, wondering whether to simply knock and ask for Pauline, the door opened and a man came out. He looked respectable enough in terms of dress, black coat and top hat, with rounded shoulders as if he spent his working days at a clerk's stool. The door closed behind him at once. He turned up his coat collar, pulled the hat down over his forehead and scuttled down the steps as if he wanted to be away from the place. I watched him as he went at a good pace up the street, hesitating and looking round at the corner as if fearful of meeting anybody he knew.

Best to wait, I thought. Pauline would have to come out at some time to go to the theater. I had my suspicions now of what the place was, and the kind of reception I might expect if I presented myself at the front door. I moved toward the end of the cul-de-sac, where I could keep the house under observation. In the next half hour or so, one man went inside and two came out, separately, looking as furtive as the first one. By then, my suspicions had been confirmed. I wondered what Tom would say if he knew his sister was waiting outside a brothel; for the first time since he'd left, I was glad he was thousands of miles away.

I'd been waiting for perhaps an hour when Pauline came out. There was nothing furtive about her. She wore her red cloak and hat, and came swinging purposefully down the steps. I'd started toward her when a better idea came to me. She looked as if she was off to keep some appointment. I'd follow her for a while and see where she was going. She went to the corner and turned without pausing, toward Leicester Square. I hurried up the street and when I turned the corner she was still in sight. She turned left into the square, across the front of the shirt warehouse. Then she disappeared. One moment the red cloak was whisking along, the next it was gone. There was only one place she could possibly have entered—Burford's Panoramic Rotunda.

I stopped. Not for one moment did I think that Pauline had come to look at the pictures. If she'd gone inside—and she must have gone inside—then it was to meet somebody. Quite probably the same person she'd met in St. Paul's Church. A leap of logic, I admit. An even bigger leap of logic to connect it with Columbine's murder, and yet I was almost certain of it. I felt in my pocket and was relieved to find three pennies. I waited for a count of fifty for her to get past the pay booth, then went inside.

A sleepy-looking boy took my money. There was no sign of Pauline or anybody else on the spiral staircase that led to the viewing gallery, no sound of footsteps. On a winter afternoon, there weren't many customers for the Rotunda. I went up the stairs as quietly as I could. She must be in the gallery above me. No sound of voices, so perhaps the person she was meeting hadn't arrived yet. In that case, it was time for my conversation with her. If necessary, I'd stand between her and the stairs so she couldn't get past me. But the gallery was empty. There wasn't a shadow of doubt about it, and there was no place to hide. On one side was a high circular balustrade that protected customers from the stairwell, on the other the imperial palace in Peking, glowing with red and gold in the gaslight, writhing with dragons as large as ponies, peopled by moon-faced mandarins with curling fingernails and drooping mustaches. I walked all round, not believing it. Pauline *must* be in here. Then I heard the scream.

A woman's scream. It came from below and echoed round the dome. I rushed down the stairs, tripped on my skirt hem and practically fell over the no longer sleepy boy. We held each other up. He was trembling.

"Where?" I said.

Still holding on to me, he pointed to a dim corridor with ropes hanging down one side. I supposed they were used to haul the pictures into position. Since the corridor curved like the rest of the building, you couldn't see more than a yard or two along it. Shaking myself free of the boy, I walked along the corridor.

"Pauline—"

Something dark came round the curve of the corridor and cannoned into me. A man, that was all I could tell from his height and his weight. Quite tall and in dark clothes, with bad breath. Even those details, such as they were, came back to me later. All I was conscious of was being pushed back against the wall as he passed, hitting my head. By the time I could decide whether to follow him, the outside door had banged and he'd gone.

Ahead of me, somebody was whimpering. I walked on a few steps and saw Pauline on her knees in the passageway, huddled into her cloak. Her hands were at her throat.

"What happened?" I said.

She glared at me as if it were my fault, and didn't answer.

"Did he attack you?"

She struggled to get up and leaned against the wall. When she moved her hands to keep her balance, the print of fingers on her skin was visible even in the dim light. She was clearly in pain and it looked as if he'd dug his thumbs deep into her windpipe.

"He tried to strangle you?"

A nod. Her hand went back to her throat. She still looked angry with me and would have pushed past if she'd had the strength.

"Who is he?"

"Don't know."

The words came out in a painful whisper.

"Of course you know. You'd arranged to meet him here, hadn't you?"

Any inclination to be kind to her disappeared when I thought of what she'd done to Jenny. Something white rustled on the floor at her feet. I picked it up and found I was holding a newspaper.

"Is this yours?"

She shook her head.

"Were you seeing him about something to do with Columbine?"

She took a shuddering breath and tried to push past me. I grabbed her by the arm.

"He's just tried to kill you. He might have managed it if he hadn't heard me coming down the stairs. For your own sake at least, who is he?"

Running footsteps came thumping from the direction of the pay desk, then a man's gruff shout.

"What's going on?"

A squarely built man with the face of an unsuccessful boxer appeared, with the scared boy a few steps behind.

"She's hurt," I said. "Somebody just tried to strangle her."

Pauline pulled her arm away, dodged past all three of us and ran for the exit. When I tried to follow the man blocked my way, positioning himself solidly across the passage.

"If I find any more of you in here, I'm calling the police and having you put on a charge."

"I told you, somebody's tried to commit a murder in here." Speaking over his shoulder, I addressed the boy: "Did you see a man come in?"

He shook his head.

"He must have gone past you, surely. Or is there a back door?"

The man turned red with anger and shouted in my face.

"As far as the likes of you are concerned, there's not a back door, a front door or any other door. This is a respectable attraction and I'm not having you turning your tricks in here."

"You think I'm—"

"I haven't seen you before, but I know where your friend comes from. Birds of a feather. Out."

I let him walk me to the door. I was burning with anger at the injustice of it, but catching up with Pauline was more urgent than trying to save my reputation at the Rotunda. As I came outside I saw her turning the corner out of the square, walking fast. I had to credit her with animal strength, if nothing else.

I ran after her, past caring about the looks I was getting, but by the time I turned into the cul-de-sac, she was going up the steps of the house called the Egyptian Palace. The door closed quickly behind her. Inside there would certainly be people used to dealing with unwelcome intruders. I'd lost her. All I'd gained for my troubles was the knowledge that somewhere, not far away, was a man with bad breath and a willingness to kill Pauline.

After walking some way, I found I was still holding the newspaper. It was a copy of the *Morning Chronicle*, five days old. I was about to throw it away when I looked again at the date: the previous Wednesday, the edition that had carried the report of the inquest into Columbine's death. It might have been a coincidence, but I didn't think so.

Chapter Eleven

Sunrise on Tuesday brought one of those winter days when the first hint of spring is in the air. The wind was from the southwest, robins and blackbirds calling loudly from bare twigs. Amos was riding a flighty dark bay gelding. We let the horses stretch out in a gallop along the north carriage drive and jogged back toward Grosvenor Gate. On the way, I asked Amos if he'd keep his ears open for any information about Rodney Hardcastle.

"Not difficult," he said. "Anything in pertickler?"

"I've heard he's planning to get married. It would be interesting to know who to. But anything at all."

What had happened in the Rotunda the day before had opened up a new view of the case, but I was still convinced that Hardcastle's affairs had played some part in it.

"One thing I can tell you for a start," Amos said, "only he doesn't know it yet."

He gave me that sideways look that meant mischief for somebody, or "mishtiff," as he'd put it.

"What?"

"I'm not supposed to let on, but if you happened to be on the corner of Piccadilly and St. James's Street around midday, you might just see something interesting."

I could get no more out of him.

Before we left the park I did something I'd been putting off for weeks and told Amos I was ready to sell Rancie. A gentleman who rode out from the livery stables was getting married at Easter to one of the ladies with hands gentle enough to be permitted to ride Rancie. I knew her by sight. She was generally acknowledged to be one of the sweetest, kindest, prettiest young ladies in London. The gentleman wanted Rancie as his bridal present to her. I tried hard not to hate the woman.

"You sure of that?" Amos said, face grave.

"Yes."

It tore my heart to look at Rancie's finely shaped ears or the play of the muscles on her shoulder and know there wouldn't be many more rides in the park for us, but I was deceiving myself if I thought the life I was living could go on forever. The disaster that had hit Daniel was a reminder of how precarious things were for people like us, without position or money.

As luck would have it, that morning's lesson was in Bruton Street, so I found myself on the corner of Piccadilly and St. James's Street a few minutes before midday. A lot of other people just happened to be there as well, even more than might have been expected in such a fashionable part of town. Quite a few looked like coachmen or grooms in breeches and top boots, although there was no sign of Amos. There were clusters of ragged boys—the kind who offer to hold people's horses for a few pennies—some with nothing on their feet except encrusted mud from toenails to calf. Even the more respectable sort were lingering; ladies in fashionable capes and bonnets attended by boys carrying their parcels, gentlemen who at this hour would usually be calling for cards and bottles of hock in Piccadilly clubs. Carriages were drawn into the curb with men and women lounging inside them, waiting for nothing in particular.

"Is the queen coming?" I heard someone ask.

The crowd grew. It looked as if Amos's secret was known to a good part of the town. Some time after midday, one of the grooms gave a whistle.

"Here he comes."

Instantly, a dozen or so of the loitering men formed into a purposeful-looking group. Most of them were carrying coach whips or riding switches. The group split into two on either side of St. James's Street. A murmur went through the crowd and some people drew back, away from the roadway. The purposeful men were looking down St. James's Street toward Pall Mall. A two-horse traveling chariot lumbered up, with a footman in livery at the back. They let it pass. A second vehicle, a one-horse droshky with two elderly ladies on board, was allowed past too, but as soon as its wheels cleared the junction, half a dozen of the men spread out and blocked the way into Piccadilly. A third vehicle was coming up the street, a gleaming new Stanhope phaeton drawn by a dark bay cob. The driver was the only person in it, obviously a gentleman who thought highly of himself, trying to flick his whip like a professional driver, curling the lash in and throwing it back out again to one side, then the other. He was so absorbed in the game that he didn't see what was waiting at the top of the street.

"Look out, Rodders!"

The cry came from one of the club gentlemen behind me. The driver dropped his whip and looked round him, openmouthed. Heavy-booted feet thundered and people went flying on all sides as more of the purposeful men pushed in through the crowd. Rodney Hardcastle, in the driving seat of the Stanhope, saw the line across the road in front of him and wrenched at the reins, trying to turn the cob round. He got it halfway, blocking the street crossways, but by then another line of men was in position behind him, preventing his retreat, and more were arriving at a run, surrounding the phaeton with a mass of black hats and broad shoulders. The vehicle quivered as three of them jumped on board.

"What are you doing? Get orf me. Get them orf me, somebody."

Hardcastle's panic-stricken shouts rang out over the hubbub. Some people around me were laughing, others were shouting about highway robbery and calling for the police. The clubmen among the spectators almost certainly included some who had gambled and drunk with Hardcastle, but none seemed in a hurry to go to his rescue. Two of the men on the phaeton simply picked up Hardcastle and put him out over the side, fairly gently, as a market man might unload a sack of cabbages. The third man took the reins and expertly turned the phaeton round. The men who'd been blocking the way stood to the side and cheered as it went away at a spanking trot down St. James's Street.

For a few seconds, Hardcastle simply stared after it, then he started running and shouting.

"Stop them! That's my property. Stop them."

But his breath gave out before he'd run more than a few dozen yards. He collapsed on the curb as the phaeton rounded the corner into Pall Mall, the bright red varnish on its wheel spokes gleaming, the two men who'd unloaded Hardcastle making themselves comfortable on the red leather seats.

Once it was out of sight, the people in the crowd who hadn't been in on the plot stared unbelievingly at each other.

"Highwaymen in Piccadilly—I've never seen the like of it."

"We could all have been killed."

"Where were the police? That's what I want to know."

At that point, two constables did arrive and were immediately surrounded by people giving them different versions of the story.

Then, from farther back in the crowd, somebody shouted the word "repossession." The ragged boys took it up and chanted it happily, then within seconds the whole crowd was fluttering with printed leaflets. They were being distributed by half a dozen or so down-at-heel-looking men who must have been there all along, waiting for their opportunity. I grabbed a pamphlet.

Malvern and Morris

Coach builders to the gentry

Phaetons, barouches, dress chariots and the latest in broughams

built to your personal specifications. Some used vehicles also

available, restored to the highest standard.

An address on the Bayswater Road was given, about half a mile from the livery stables where Amos worked. I was certain that some of the men who had carried out the attack were his fellow workers, and was relieved that for once he'd kept out of trouble himself.

I looked up and saw that the policemen were reading the leaflet too. They seemed ill at ease. Merchants who supplied goods not paid for were entitled to apply for a warrant and repossess them, though it did not usually happen as dramatically as this. In any case, the legal niceties hardly mattered, because by then the men who'd carried out the repossession had all taken themselves off and only we curious spectators were left.

Apart, that is, from the man at the center of it all. Rodney Hard-castle hadn't gone far. He was sitting on the curb halfway down

St. James's Street with his feet tucked up to keep them out of the filth of the gutter, head in hands. A group of half a dozen or so clubmen who might have been his friends had formed a semicircle on the pavement round him, but at some distance, as if ridicule and misfortune might be contagious. Not one of them had gone close enough to put a comforting hand on his shoulder.

As I watched, he raised his head and said something to them. It looked plaintive and produced no more than a few wry looks and half-hidden grins. I moved closer to hear.

". . . told them, all they had to do was be patient for a day or two longer. I've been a good customer to them. A hundred and fifty, it cost me, and they'd have had the money within the week. Within the month, at the very outside. They just had to be patient."

The policemen went about their business, the crowd dwindled. Two of Rodney Hardcastle's semicircle broke away and strolled toward Piccadilly and, probably, the delayed first drink of the day at their club. Then the others followed, until only Hardcastle was left. I walked down the street and stood beside him. It was some time before he noticed me.

"Where are they taking it?"

His question came out as a plaintive wail. I gave him my copy of the leaflet, but it seemed to take him some time to understand it.

"I need it back," he said. "They've got to let me have it back."

"I saw you at the Augustus Theatre," I said. "I was there the night Columbine died."

He looked up, but my words hardly penetrated the cloud of misery round him. All he said was "Oh yes?"

"Why were you so anxious that Jenny Jarvis should be arrested?" I said. "They were your posters, weren't they?"

He nodded. "Because the little bitch killed Columbine."

"You and Columbine had quarreled, hadn't you? Over Jenny."

He might have told me to mind my own business, but there was no fight in him.

"That's the unfair thing. She had no cause."

"Not as far as Jenny was concerned, no. Did you manage to make up the quarrel before she died?"

"She wouldn't even talk to me. It's all so unfair."

He pushed himself to his feet and stood looking up and down the street as if he expected somebody to come and rescue him.

"If it wasn't Jenny, who else might have killed her?" I said.

"It must have been Jenny."

A disreputable-looking cab came round the corner from Piccadilly. It was bright red, the driver brown-whiskered and white-hatted. Hardcastle fumbled in his pockets.

"Seem to have come out without my money. Lend me the price of a cab fare."

"I've only tuppence in my pocket myself," I said.

It was the truth. The red cab rumbled past us, not summoned. Hardcastle gave me a look as if I were the last in a long line of betrayers, turned and began to walk toward Pall Mall. He went slowly and painfully because the soles of his boots were fashionably thin, not meant for walking. I could have caught up with him quite easily, but decided there was nothing to be gained from it.

When I got back to Abel Yard there was a note with my name on it in Daniel's writing, tucked into the doorjamb at the bottom of the stairs.

My dear Liberty,

I am continuing to inquire about Rainer or, as you probably prefer, the man with the brown face, with no success so far. Since Rainer was a Household Cavalry officer, I thought there must be somebody at the barracks who knew him. So I simply walked in and asked to see the command-

ing officer. They kept me waiting for an hour, then prac-
tically marched me, as if I were a prisoner under escort,
into the presence of a man with a lot of gold braid on his
uniform and mustaches wider than his forehead. He didn't
invite me to sit down. I asked him if he'd known a Ma-
jor Charles Rainer. He stared at me as if I were a puppy
that had made a mess on his carpet and said, "There is
no such man." I thought he'd misunderstood, so I started
explaining about the forgery trial and so on. He cut across
me and said it again, practically roared it, "There is no
such man." I suppose I must have looked as puzzled as I
felt, because he condescended to explain, after a fashion.
No Household Cavalry officer could be accused of a filthy
offense like forgery, so the minute he was charged Rainer
ceased to be a Household Cavalry officer and, from their
point of view, he didn't exist anymore. The military mind
is truly an amazing thing.

I felt hot with anger on Daniel's behalf and sorry that he should put himself in the way of such humiliation. His note went on:

It occurred to me that a cavalry officer would not have
the skills necessary to forge bonds himself and I have
been able to discover, from newspaper reports of the time,
that he indeed had an accomplice, a Fleet Street printer
named Stephen Sned. Sned was also sentenced to trans-
portation. I have begun asking round the newspapers and
print shops in the hope of finding associates of Sned, who
may know more about Rainer, so far without success.

That was even worse. Trailing round the dark alleys off Fleet Street, trying to find associates of a criminal, was almost begging to be attacked.

*I have also been back to the Augustus. Blake didn't throw
me out, in fact he was as helpful as he could be in the circumstances. I think you and Kennedy may be right, and
that he is at least trying to make things no worse for Jenny.
I told him about Rainer and tried to get a clearer description from him of the man who was asking questions at
the theater two days after Columbine was killed. Unfortunately he couldn't improve on what we know already.
He had much on his mind at the time and no particular
reason to take an interest in the man.*

I thought of the man in the Rotunda. I'd had no chance to see
the color of his complexion or even guess his age. Should I tell
Daniel about him and risk adding fuel to his obsession? It turned
out, from the end of Daniel's note, that it was a decision I'd have
to make sooner than I expected.

*One of Kennedy's friends has recommended a barrister
at the Old Bailey, Charles Phillips. We are going to see
him tomorrow morning. Kennedy thinks your observations may be helpful. He wants to know if he may call for
you at nine o'clock.*

I went upstairs, scribbled a note to Kennedy saying yes, of
course, and sent it by the boy who blew the bellows for the carriage mender's forge. My guess was that he wanted me to be present not so much for the value of my observations as for a calming
influence on Daniel. I only hoped that I could be of some use.

Chapter Twelve

Toby Kennedy called for me in a cab. Since we were visiting a barrister, I wore my best blue merino dress with darker blue bonnet and cape. On the way I told him about the man in the Rotunda. To spare my own blushes, I left out the detail of being mistaken for one of Pauline's sisterhood.

"It may have nothing to do with Columbine," he said. "Women like that always run the risk of somebody trying to strangle them."

"Then what was the newspaper doing there? And who was she meeting in St. Paul's Church the Saturday before Columbine was murdered?"

"How do you propose to find out?"

"I don't know. I'm quite sure Pauline won't tell me."

"Whatever you do, talk to me first. Don't take any more risks on your own."

I didn't promise.

"So, do we tell Daniel?"

He thought about it, then shook his head.

"Not yet."

He laughed when I told him about the repossession of Hard-castle's phaeton.

"His creditors must be at the end of their patience. After a public humiliation like yesterday, they'll all be pouncing."

I'd been thinking about debts after the discussion with Disraeli.

"Isn't it odd, though, that they're choosing to do it now?" I said. "It's usually the other way about. If a man's keeping a woman and the man dies suddenly, then her credit vanishes overnight. They swoop in and take her jewels, clothes, everything."

You couldn't be in London long without hearing of cases like that: women who'd been driven to the opera in their own carriages one season cadging gins in public houses the next.

"I wonder why Hardcastle was so insistent that he expected to come into money soon," Kennedy said. "Perhaps he thinks Columbine's left him something."

"Ye gods, do you suppose that's possible?"

"Wills are public documents. I'll see if I can find out."

The cab lurched and jangled along the Strand and Fleet Street. As we came within sight of the Old Bailey and the prison of Newgate next door to it, my spirits sank at the solidity of the walls holding Jenny and the flimsiness of hope. Daniel was waiting for us outside the Old Bailey, with a man whom Kennedy introduced to me as his friend James Harmer, a solicitor. Harmer told us that the barrister, Mr. Phillips, was appearing for the defense in three cases that day, but had been persuaded to put half an hour aside for us. We followed him through the doorway and up a staircase. It was the first time I'd been inside the Old Bailey. It wasn't a particularly old building—the courthouse had been rebuilt in my grandfather's time—but it felt as bleak as if centuries of misery were climbing out of the ground and up its walls, like damp stains.

"Charles Phillips is far and away the best barrister at the Old Bailey," Kennedy whispered to me. "He'll get her off, if anybody can."

I was only partly reassured. As a group, the Old Bailey barristers had a poor reputation and were looked down on by the rest of the legal profession. Charles Phillips came as a pleasant surprise. When we were shown into a little room that was not much more than a cubbyhole, he got up from the table where he was sitting and greeted Kennedy like an old friend. The top of his head was bald, fringed with dark curly hair and sideburns above a high white stock. His eyes were large, his voice pleasant and calming, with a strong southern Irish accent. Once the introductions had been performed, Harmer left us to go to another meeting. There were only two chairs for visitors, so Kennedy pushed some bundles of briefs aside and perched on the edge of the desk.

"Kennedy's been telling me something about it," Phillips said. "We'll do what we can, but to be frank with you, it's not the easiest of cases."

"She's innocent," Daniel said. "Shouldn't that make it easier?"

Kennedy gave him a warning glance. Phillips nodded, unoffended.

"An innocent country girl, alone and friendless in London. We'll emphasize that, of course. A fragile butterfly trapped between the grinding millstones of the law. We'll have the jury in tears, if there's a heart amongst the lot of them."

He sounded as if he meant it.

"Suppose we were able to prove that somebody else committed the murder?" Daniel said.

He managed to sound quite cool and businesslike. The barrister's forehead creased.

"Can you prove it?"

"I strongly suspect that a certain person had a hand in it."

"Are you thinking of the maid?" Phillips said.

Daniel shook his head.

"Can you prove it, or give reasonable cause for suspecting somebody else?"

Daniel didn't answer. He must have realized how unconvincing his suspicions would sound. Phillips sighed.

"There was enmity between Columbine and Miss Jarvis. There's no point in denying what the whole town knows."

"The enmity was entirely on Columbine's side," Daniel said. "Jenny had no motive to kill her."

"Are you suggesting that somebody else did have a motive?"

"Yes, I am. We can't prove it at present, but I believe we can show that somebody else had a substantial motive."

Phillips sighed again, more heavily.

"Mr. Suter, proving that somebody else is guilty is a fine and complete defense, if you can do it. Producing strong arguments that somebody else might have done it may influence a jury favorably, if you're persuasive and fortunate. But it's a risky course. If your proof isn't strong enough and you can't convince them, then the jury will hold it against you and decide, if that's the best you can do, then the accused must be guilty as charged."

Silence, apart from feet echoing on a staircase outside.

"Yes, I see," Daniel said.

"I'm sorry if I've distressed you by putting it so plainly. If you can bring me proof, I'll use it most gladly. If not, we must do the best with what we have. Could we find somebody who would give a character witness for Miss Jarvis?"

He and Daniel discussed that for a while. I could see that Phillips was surprised that Daniel knew so little about her background. Eventually they agreed that Daniel would approach Blake, who might at least say that Jenny was honest and hardworking.

There was a knock at the door and Harmer put his head round.

"Wanted in court two, Mr. Phillips."

With a brief apology, Phillips hitched up his robe, put on his wig, and went. As Harmer showed us out, Daniel asked what the

fee would be and Harmer said three guineas. It sounded quite
moderate and I think Daniel would have been comforted if it had
been higher.

Daniel, Kennedy and I lingered on the pavement outside the Old
Bailey. Daniel's eyes were on the prison next door.

"Do you want to try to see her?" I said.

He nodded. "As we're here in any case. If you two don't mind
waiting, that is."

The sight of his bowed shoulders as he went away tore at my
heart.

"Coffee," Kennedy said.

He took my arm and guided me across the road into a side
street. Halfway down it was a coffeehouse, with curved railings
round the basement and narrow leaded windows that looked as
if they hadn't changed in two hundred years. The atmosphere inside was fuggy and so charged with the smell of coffee that just to
stand there was like drinking it. The clientele all looked like lawyers or lawyers' clerks, and a row of wigs in colors ranging from
pure white to dirty straw hung from pegs along the wall. Some of
the customers looked up when we came in and seemed annoyed
to see a woman. Kennedy guided me to a table in a dark corner
and called for coffee. A waiter in a long white apron brought it
promptly. I sipped and found it was the best I'd ever tasted.

"Drink it up," Kennedy said. "You look worn out."

He wouldn't let me discuss the case at all until we'd emptied
our cups and he'd ordered two more.

"Mr. Phillips isn't very hopeful, is he?" I said.

"Between the two of us, Liberty, I doubt if he has any hope at
all. Harmer and I were talking about it earlier. Phillips will do his
eloquent best, of course—and that's pretty considerable—but it's
useless against the facts."

"There really aren't too many facts, though, are there?"

"A fight onstage, a poisoning a few days later, a suspect in possession of a poisonous substance, who runs away and hides. What more will a jury want? And another thing . . ."

He looked at me and hesitated.

"What?"

"Men and poisoning. Rightly or wrongly, they see it as a woman's crime. Your good solid juror will look at her in the dock and he won't be seeing a poor scared girl or a crushed butterfly—he'll be thinking of all the women he's ever been close to, and shivering inside."

"So any chance she has depends on proving that somebody else did it?"

"You heard what Phillips said about that."

"He doesn't believe she's innocent, does he?"

"Barristers don't let themselves think like that."

"She is, though; I'm sure of it."

He looked at me, his eyes sad.

"My dear, loyalty to Daniel is all very well, but are you sure that all this is helping him?"

I stared at him, puzzled.

"But saving Jenny's all that matters to him."

"Yes, that's the point I'm trying to make. Daniel's obsessed. You'll forgive me for speaking behind his back, but he's one of my best friends, and your father and I were friends for twenty years or more. I hope that gives me a right to be concerned for both of you."

I nodded, scared of what was coming. A flock of legal clerks had burst in, arguing in loud voices as if the whole world wanted to hear them, ranging around for a table, setting cups rattling. Kennedy had to wait until they settled.

"If she's hanged, it will almost destroy him," he said quietly. "If you'll forgive me saying so, the best thing you can do is be there to pick up the pieces at the end of it."

I felt myself getting hot and angry, but the concern in his face and voice made me hold my temper.

"You seem very sure that it will end badly."

"I can see this is the hardest thing in the world for you. It's been clear to all his friends, ever since you came back to London, that you and Daniel would marry. You're as well suited as any pair can be, and if it hadn't been for this miserable business . . ."

He trailed off. I must have let anger show on my face after all.

"You'd got us tidily married off already, had you?" I said.

"Please, Liberty, don't be offended. I don't want to be saying this, but somebody has to. It's what your father would say if he were here."

He'd picked the only weapon that would check me, and he must have known it. I turned my head away so that he shouldn't see my tears, but it was no use.

"Oh, my poor girl. I'm desperately sorry."

A clean handkerchief, his, found its way into my hand under the table. If any of the other customers were watching, they probably thought he was another legal man consoling a client.

"No, I'm sorry," I said. "You were talking about picking up the pieces."

"When this is over, Daniel is going to be in a bad state. He'll come to his senses in time and see it for the madness it was, and he'll thank his stars if you're still there waiting for him. But until that happens, it will be difficult for you. You might want to consider moving away for a while. I know somebody in Ireland who'd be only too glad of a companion like you for a month or two."

"You mean until Jenny's safely hanged," I said.

He met my eyes.

"Yes, if I'm honest, that is what I mean. I wish, for Daniel's sake, and the girl's too, that there was any chance of it going the other way, but nobody thinks it will. Another thing—since I've trespassed so far already—"

"Yes?"

"Just supposing Phillips performs a miracle and she gets off— what happens then?"

"Then Daniel will look after her—marry her, probably."

Up to then, I hadn't thought so far ahead, but my answer came without hesitation. Kennedy looked surprised.

"And you accept that?"

"Of course I do. Daniel's my best friend in the world and I owe him almost everything. What he wants, I want. Besides, we'd never so much as discussed marrying."

"I hope he knows how lucky he is in you," Kennedy said.

"It's mostly the other way about. Besides, you're forgetting one thing in all this. I meant it when I said I'm sure Jenny's innocent. I wasn't at first, but I am after what's happened."

A great sigh from Kennedy. This wasn't the way the conversation was supposed to end. He'd never know that, for a few heartbeats, the idea of running away to Ireland had seemed like a window opening, until a tenderness came over me for my life in Abel Yard, Amos and Rancie, even Mrs. Martley.

"It's a matter of being practical," I told him, although I was really telling myself. "If we can't prove that somebody else killed Columbine, we might at least show there are other suspects. Remember, Mr. Phillips said a jury could be influenced by strong arguments that somebody else might have done it."

"I'm glad Daniel didn't start talking about Rainer, at any rate," he said.

"Yes, and it's as well I haven't told Daniel about Pauline, or that filthy bet of Hardcastle's. I don't like to think what he'll do if he finds out about that."

"Yes, that's our biggest worry at present, isn't it—Daniel doing something desperate."

The seriousness in Kennedy's face and voice scared me.

"What do you mean?"

"Daniel said something odd to me that night Jenny was arrested, after he'd walked you home. He said, 'Do you know, I think Liberty half suspects I killed the woman myself.'"

"Oh."

"You don't sound as surprised as I'd expected."

"I can see why he thought it. He was outside the door of the theater the night she was poisoned. I asked him if he'd gone in. He hadn't."

"He said to me, 'Of course, I told her I hadn't gone inside.'"

"Well, that's the same thing, isn't it?"

Kennedy looked hard at me.

"You know very well it's not."

I stared down at the rings of coffee stains on the table.

"Are you saying that Daniel admitted he'd gone inside?"

"No, he didn't do that. What I'm saying is that he might have been preparing the way for saying it later, if necessary."

"But why?"

"I'm afraid he'd do anything rather than see Jenny hanged. *Anything*—you understand?"

"You mean he'd confess to the murder?"

I looked up in time to catch Kennedy's nod, so slight it was hardly a movement at all. His eyes were pleading with me not to ask the next question.

"We must go," I said.

Daniel was waiting by the thick iron-plated doors of the prison, staring at the ground, oblivious of the crowds going past. He didn't see us until Kennedy put a hand on his shoulder.

"Have you been here long?" Kennedy asked.

Daniel shook his head, but it was more of a dazed gesture than an answer.

"Did they let you see her?"

"For a while, yes, in a room with other prisoners. She's just been told: her case comes up a week on Monday. Twelve days, that's all we have. Twelve days."

Chapter Thirteen

We started walking, one on each side of Daniel, otherwise I think he'd have stayed rooted outside Newgate. He didn't speak until we were halfway along Fleet Street.

"I wonder why he asked about Marie."

"Hardly surprising," Kennedy said. "She made the syllabub. She was with Columbine every minute that the woman wasn't on-stage. It's been in my mind that the magistrates might have let her go too easily."

"But she was devoted to Columbine," I said. "That's one thing everybody agrees on."

And yet, even as I said it, I thought that a lot of things everybody agreed on turned out to be wrong. I asked Daniel and Kennedy if they knew where Columbine had lived. Kennedy remembered from having it pointed out to him as he was driving past one day, a villa opposite the barracks on the south side of Kensington Gardens, not far from some nursery gardens.

I parted from them at Chancery Lane, where Kennedy had another lawyer friend who could tell them how to find out if Columbine had left a will, and walked on alone in the thin March sunshine, past our fine new national gallery and the empty space in front of it that had been dignified with the name of Trafalgar Square, back toward Piccadilly and Hyde Park. Instead of turning up Park Lane for home, I went round the end of the Serpentine Water, then westward along Rotten Row, the road old King George had made from Westminster to his palace in Kensington, with its elegant double row of lamp standards and good surface for galloping messengers. It was midafternoon by then, so the fashionable were out in force, on horseback and in carriages. It was not a good place to travel on foot and I had to dodge and weave to save myself from being bowled over by racing phaetons or by landaus driving two abreast while the ladies in them chatted as if they were on their drawing room sofas.

Near the palace, I crossed Kensington Road and found a sign pointing to Malcolm's nursery gardens. The road it indicated was a broad and muddy track between plantations of young trees, still bare as mop handles but full of the singing of blackbirds. Less than half a mile away from Kensington Palace, it might as well have been in the country. Several villas with plenty of space between them were set back from the road in the middle of the nursery fields. They were small but well kept, with carriage houses to the side. It struck me as one of those parts of town where rich men stored their mistresses, convenient for visits, with not too many nosey neighbors.

A man was raking the gravel on one of the drives. I asked him if he knew where Columbine had lived and he pointed with his rake at the next villa down. It was built in the picturesque style with a steeply pitched slate roof, arched windows and twisted tree trunks supporting a balcony that ran all along the front, twined with bare wisteria shoots. The front door was shut, but the door to the carriage house was open, revealing emptiness inside. There were no blinds or curtains at the windows. I walked up to the front door, my feet crunching on gravel, and knocked.

After some time, a face appeared at the window nearest the door. It was a man's face, round and bright-eyed, grimacing and mouthing what was probably a request to go away. I stayed where I was, and after a minute or so the door opened halfway. The round-faced man was wearing a shirt unbuttoned at the neck, breeches and stockings, with a blanket like a shawl round his shoulders. He was thin and below average height. He wore no shoes, and grimy toes stuck out through the holes in his stockings. It looked as if I'd woken him from a nap.

"If you've come about the furniture, you can tell him he's not getting it," he said, in a voice that sounded like rattling pebbles.

"May I speak to Marie Duval?" I said.

"Who?"

"Columbine's maid."

He opened the door wider and came out on the step.

"Never heard of her. All the lady's servants were gone by the time I was put in here, along with anything they could carry. Curtains, cushions, silverware, all her clothes—just stripped the lot like caterpillars on a cabbage."

He sounded quite cheerful about it.

"You were put in here?"

"By Messrs. Hodge and Pertwee, furniture supplied to the value of three hundred and fifty-nine pounds, sixteen shillings and tuppence ha'penny."

"You're a bailiff's man?"

"That's right, miss."

"Do you think you could possibly let me in for a look round?"

He hesitated. I felt in my pocket and parted with a shilling. He grinned.

"Not much to see, there isn't."

I followed him inside. There was enough left in the downstairs rooms to show that Columbine's house must have been comfortable and luxurious: fine carved mantelpieces, patterned wallpaper, large cupboards and dining tables in walnut and mahogany. But the floors were bare, fireplaces stripped of their fenders and fire irons, no rugs, no cushions. All the soft, colorful things had been taken so that there was no trace of personality left. Columbine might have been ten years rather than nine days dead. The only souvenirs of her were a delicate coffee cup lying broken in the corner and a piece of pink ostrich feather stuck between two floorboards. A nest of scruffy blankets in the corner of the room showed where the bailiff's man slept.

"Didn't she have any family?" I said.

"None that I know of."

"Was this her own house?"

"Nah. Had it rented for her, didn't she?"

"By Mr. Hardcastle?"

"That's the one."

"And he still owes for the furniture?"

"He does. They're taking it back once they get the order from the lawyers, then I can move on somewhere warmer, thank gawd. Would you care for a dish of tea, madam?"

I thought he was joking, but he led the way into the kitchen. The shelves were empty and the cooking range cold as a stone, but he had a small fire in the hearth and a can of water warming at the sullen heart of it. He took tea leaves in a screw of blue paper from a tin on the table and whittled with a bone-handled knife at the remnant of a loaf of sugar.

"How long have you been here?" I asked him.

"I was put in a week ago today."

Just two days after Columbine died.

"Have there been any other people round asking about Columbine?"

"A wine merchant who reckons he's owed two hundred. He'll have to whistle for that, 'cos the wine's all gone."

"You haven't by chance seen anything of a middle-aged man with a brown face?"

"Nah."

He lifted the can of water from the fire with an old pair of tongs, stirred in the tea leaves.

"Or a young woman with yellow hair?"

"Strewth, lady, what do you think this is? The Argyll Rooms? We don't go in for visitors a great deal."

"And I suppose you've seen nothing of Mr. Hardcastle himself?"

"Nah, only his valley."

He poured brown liquid from the can into a tin mug and a cracked china cup and divided sugar shavings carefully between the two of them.

"Mr. Hardcastle's valet came here? When?"

He passed me the cup. The tea was thick with leaves, like a gutter in autumn.

"Two or three days after I was put in."

He took a long gulp of tea, his body quivering with the satisfaction of it. Now he didn't see me as a threat, he seemed happy enough with my presence and my questions. I suppose being a bailiff's man is a lonely job.

"What did the valet want?"

"Hardcastle's razors and hairbrushes. I'd have had to let him take those—personal effects, see—only her servants must've cleared them out along with the rest."

"So the valet had to go back to Mr. Hardcastle empty-handed?"

"He wasn't going back at all. Saved him a journey, he said."

"He was leaving his employment? Why?"

"He said he hadn't been paid for six months and all he'd got for his pains was a lady's earring."

"Earring?"

"Yes. According to him, he said he'd leave unless he got paid. Hardcastle said it wasn't convenient to give him the money at the present time and fobbed him off with this earring instead. He asked my advice on where he might find an honest pawnshop. Same place as you'd find a flying pig, I told him."

"Did he show you the earring?"

"Yes. He had it in his pocket."

"Did it look valuable?"

"Little diamonds in a circle, and a bigger one about the size of a grain of barley hanging down. I don't know about jewelry."

I knew a little about the value of jewels, having had occasion to sell some over the past year, and was doing calculations in my head.

"If they were real diamonds, that might come to more than six months' wages for a valet."

"He wasn't pleased. He reckoned Hardcastle owed him a sight more than that. Besides, what's the use of one earring?"

"So you couldn't help him about the pawnshop?"

"I mentioned a couple in Broad Court, off Drury Lane. Don't suppose they'd rook him any worse than the rest."

"Do you know where he might be now?"

"Nah."

"I don't suppose you have forwarding addresses for any of the servants here?"

"Nah."

I finished my tea and thanked him. He led the way to the front door. The bare boards of the corridor were littered with bits of dead leaf that had blown in, with a square of white among them. I bent and scooped it up. It was a note addressed to Marie Duval.

"May I take this? I'm looking for her and could give it to her if I find her."

He shrugged, so I put it in my pocket and wished him good afternoon. When I was back on the other side of Kensington Road I opened the note.

Dear Miss Duval,

You would oblige me if you could arrange to pack up and move your mistress's costumes and possessions from her

*dressing room as soon as possible since it is needed for
other artistes.*

The address at the top was the Augustus Theatre, the signature
Barnaby Blake's, and the date two days after Columbine's death.
So Marie hadn't gone back to Columbine's house.

Where was she?

"Most people, when the police let them go, they're off like dingle
bats in case they change their minds and take them in again,"
Amos said.

I was talking the problem over with him as we went for our ride
on Thursday morning.

"She could be anywhere in London, or in the country, come to
that," I said. "For all we know, she could have gone back home to
France."

"I could try and sniff something out for you. Depends whether
she went on two feet or four."

"Four?"

"If she went in a cab, carriage or cart she'd have to have someone driving her. I'll put the word around."

I thanked him, but suspected that, wherever Marie had gone,
it had most likely been on her own two feet. There was, however,
better news about Hardcastle.

"He's got rid of his groom on account of not having horses or
a carriage anymore," Amos said. "Friend of mine's finding out
where the man goes for a drink, then I'll take a drink in the same
place and see what happens."

"So he's had to part with his valet and his groom," I said. "You
could almost feel sorry for the man."

Amos shook his head.

"Sorry for that one? Don't go pouring good cream on rotten
raspberries."

* * *

When I got back, there was another note from Daniel tucked into the door, short and to the point this time.

Dear Liberty,

As far as we've been able to establish, Columbine left no will. At any rate, nothing has been filed yet. Nobody seems to know if she had any family.

I wasn't entirely surprised. Somebody as self-centered as Columbine wouldn't think about making a will because she couldn't imagine the world going on without her. As for family, she'd presumably left them behind along with her milking pail. What concerned me more was that Daniel must have come to leave the note at a time when he knew I'd be out riding, and that meant he was anxious not to see me. More than that, he didn't want me asking questions. That scared me.

Trying not to think about it too much, I came back to the question of Columbine's possessions. A woman in her position would usually have most of her assets in jewels. It was a reasonable guess that jewels were what somebody had been looking for when he (or she) slashed the muff and couch in her dressing room. A single diamond earring was a strange thing for a gentleman to give his valet. It was a strange thing for a gentleman to own in the first place. I thought about it all through Friday, between lessons, and on Saturday afternoon set off for Drury Lane and Broad Court.

There were several pawnshops in the street, which was less broad than its name, most of them with saucepans, washboards, articles of clothing and the occasional musical instrument piled haphazardly behind windows that needed cleaning. Small queues were forming, the more respectable sort coming to redeem their Sunday suits and boots for their weekly outing before returning

them on Monday, the less respectable hugging armfuls of anything that might fetch enough for a few pints of beer.

The first shop that the bailiff's man had named looked more
run-down than the rest and had just one customer, an old man in
a felt hat with his elbows on the counter as if prepared to wait all
day. The shopkeeper, a man as pale and thin as a paper cutout, was
going slowly through a pile of handkerchiefs, holding each one up
to the lamplight and staring at it. Most of them were so thin and
worn that you could have read a newspaper through them. They
both turned when I walked in.

"See to the lady first," the old man said, then fell into a fit of
coughing from the effort of speaking.

I said I was interested in a diamond earring that a young man
might have brought in recently.

"Stole from you, was it?" the ghostly man said.

"No. Have you seen it?"

He shook his head.

"Don't get much in the way of diamonds."

Looking round the shop, which was piled high with bundles of
curtains, flatirons, a dressmaker's dummy with the stuffing coming out, I could easily believe him. I wished them good afternoon
and went back into the street.

The window of the second pawnbroker looked more hopeful.
The glass was clean and somebody had taken the trouble to arrange the stock more temptingly inside. Silver teaspoons, none of
them matching, were spread out in a fan shape backed by a row
of silver-plated jugs and pewter mugs. A card covered with black
velvet had pieces of jewelry pinned to it—a charm bracelet, a few
watch chains, a garnet pendant. The sign on the door said, *Best
prices given for items of jewelry and quality silverware.* I pushed it
open, setting a sweet-toned bell tinkling, and walked in. The man
behind the counter didn't look like most people's idea of a pawnbroker. He was no more than thirty years old or so, with an ath-

letic set to his broad shoulders that contrasted with the delicacy of his long-fingered hands. He was polishing a silver watch with a chamois leather and looked up from it to smile and wish me good afternoon. I found myself smiling back.

"I'm sorry to bother you. I've come to ask about a diamond ear-ring."

"Five small stones and a pendant drop? Was it yours?"

His smile had faded.

"No. It might have belonged to . . . to a person I knew. But how did you know?"

"I'm not offered many items of that quality. I suppose you're going to tell me it was stolen?"

"No. That is to say, it might have been, but that isn't what concerns me. I was hoping I might be allowed to look at it, even sketch it, to see if it really did belong to this woman I knew."

"It was a man who brought it in," he said. "Servant type, seemed quite respectable. He said it had been given him by his employer in lieu of back wages."

"He was telling the truth about that. Do you think it would be possible for me to have a look at it?"

The wall behind him was entirely made up of pigeonholes with cloth-wrapped bundles inside them. I hoped one of them might contain the earring. If I could describe it to Bel or one of the other girls I could at least establish if Columbine had been seen wearing it.

"I haven't got it," the man said. "The person made it quite clear that he wanted to sell it, not pledge it."

"It's gone already?"

"I'm afraid so. But if it's a sketch you want, I can do you that from memory."

He put down the watch and took a pencil and paper from under the counter. As he worked, I looked at the things in the window, especially a Venetian glass mermaid hanging from a string, reflecting spangles of lamplight over bracelets and silver teaspoons when a current of air swayed her. I wondered who had owned her and in what circumstances they'd had to part with her.

"There—pretty rough, but it will give you an impression."

It was an accomplished sketch, not rough at all. If Columbine had worn such an earring, it would be enough to identify it. I thanked him and folded it away in my pocket.

"It's odd that somebody should buy a single earring so soon," I said.

He smiled and picked up the watch.

"It's not single anymore. We found its pair."

"What?"

He sounded as pleased as if he'd reunited a pair of lost lovers.

"Yes, I like diamonds. I don't see many of them here, but I have friends in Hatton Garden and on Saturdays we look at anything they've got and talk about what's come in from Amsterdam and so on. This morning, I took the earring along out of curiosity— not that it was anything very special, but just in case anybody knew where to match it up. Would you believe, somebody did!"

"Another pawnbroker?"

"The man who knew was a diamond broker, but he'd had an inquiry the day before from a man who'd bought an earring from a pawnbroker over in the Borough."

Southwark, that was, south of the river and a pretty rough area. By London standards, that was as far from the world of Columbine and Hardcastle as could be.

"I don't know the pawnbroker in question," the man went on. "I gather he runs an ordinary kind of shop and wasn't used to diamonds. He had just enough sense to consult somebody who did. The man he consulted bought the earring off him and showed it to my friend."

"Where are the earrings now?"

"On sale in Hatton Garden. I can give you the address, if you're interested."

"No, thank you. What I need is the address of the other pawn-broker."

He raised his eyebrows.

"It's not an area where ladies go much. I gather the name's Black, in Borough High Street, not far from the market."

"When was it brought in to him?"

"I'm not sure. About a week ago, I think."

That would make it about five days after Columbine's murder.

"Did you hear anything about the person who brought it in?"

"Yes. I was curious about that, wondering if it was stolen. If something valuable comes from that area, the assumption is that it was. But apparently Black swore it wasn't. He hadn't seen the woman before. She was quite respectable, nervous and soft-spoken and a foreigner. French, he thought."

"French!"

"That's what he told the man who spoke to my friend, but I shouldn't put too much weight on it if I were you. To a man like that, probably all foreigners are French."

I thanked him again and walked out into the Saturday bustle of Broad Court, mind whirling. London was full of foreigners, thousands of them French, and probably about half of those female. Of those, a fair proportion could probably be described as respectable, nervous and soft-spoken. But add the earring and there was no reasonable doubt about it.

The woman who'd walked into the Southwark pawnshop was Columbine's maid, Marie.

Chapter Fourteen

I'd intended to go straight from the pawnshop to the Augustus Theatre to see if any of the girls could identify the earring. This changed my plans. The whole case was turned upside down again and I needed time to think. I'd assumed throughout that Marie was innocent. The magistrate himself had come to that conclusion in a couple of hours. But if so, what had she been doing with Columbine's earring? One possibility was that she'd looted it after Columbine's death, but that was unlikely. First she'd been in police custody, then apparently so scared that she'd run away and hidden herself. Another was that she'd been given it by Hardcastle. It made more sense. He'd got his hands on some of Columbine's jewelry—probably by stealing it from her dressing room after her death—used one earring to pay his debt to his valet, and given the other to Marie. Why? Nobody who knew Hardcastle would believe it was a kind or sentimental gesture. If he'd given it to Marie, it would have been because he owed her a debt too. More than that, she was in a position to make him deliver payment. Payment for services rendered?

I thought about it all through a cold and rainy Sunday. The temptation was to rush to Daniel and Kennedy with what I'd found, but it would be no kindness to raise hopes only to shatter them. Also, I was still a long way from finding Marie. South of the river's another world. To anybody who's not a Londoner, that probably makes no sense at all. I could walk there in an hour—into the City, across London Bridge and I'd be there. The problem was that I had none of the mental hooks that fix you to a place. I'd spent a fair part of my life in London, but although we'd moved around a lot it had always been north of the Thames. Even notorious areas like St. Giles were familiar to me. I knew, as a cat knows her territory, which streets were safe to walk down and which weren't, and which direction to run in if threatened. Given the number of my father's friends and acquaintances, wherever I went in the whole stretch of London between Hyde Park and St. Paul's, I was likely to meet somebody I knew. South of the river, I knew nobody.

That evening Mrs. Martley and I sat at the kitchen table sharing the light of one lamp, she pasting more regal snippets into her scrapbook, I making a poor job of repairing the hem of my brown corduroy dress. It was my oldest and least liked, but, with luck, might make me inconspicuous south of the river.

I crossed our wide and new London Bridge in thick mist on Monday morning, with steam tugs whistling to one another on the Thames and a smell of sewage hanging in the air. The slums on the far side weren't so very much worse than those of St. Giles, just a bit older and even more crowded. There seemed no plan or logic to the area. Streets came to dead ends or ran into narrow passageways half choked with rubbish and leading to courtyards of crumbling houses, broken windows covered with boards or stuffed with bundles of rags. Children were everywhere, splashing barefoot in the gutters, ferreting among piles of muck and rubbish with naked backsides showing through the splits in their trousers. I saw one boy who couldn't have been much older than five chasing a smaller girl, a live rat dangling by its tail from his outstretched arm. At least nobody took much notice of me, apart from a bungled attempt to pick my pocket by a man so drunk he must have been doing it from force of habit rather than with serious hope of success. A woman alone might attract stares in Pall Mall, but here most women were on their own, carrying baskets of damp washing, bringing foul-smelling buckets out from basements, or trying to interest customers in trays of dingy-looking pies while batting thieving boys away like clouds of summer mosquitoes.

I found my way without too much trouble to Black's pawnshop. Behind the counter, a fat man wearing an old overcoat without a shirt or any other linen underneath it and smelling of stale beer, was no help.

"Excuse me, I think a woman may have come in recently to dispose of a diamond earring," I said.

"Oh yes, that will be the Empress of Russia. We get her in here all the time."

"This woman was French, name of Marie Duval, dark-haired and around thirty."

"You trying to put something on me?"

"No, I'm just trying to find the woman. Can you remember anybody of that description?"

"No."

"Or this earring?"

I gave him the sketch. He crumpled it and threw it down on the counter.

"Does it look like I deal in diamonds? Why're you asking me all this? A Peeler in girls' clothes, are you?"

"Of course not, I'm just trying—"

"Bert."

He said it loudly. A large bald man lumbered from the room at the back, like a bear from its den.

"We've got a lady 'ere asking questions about diamonds," the fat man said. "We don't want to disappoint her, do we? 'Ow about you show her your dog instead . . ."

A snarl came from behind the bald man's legs. I looked down and saw a black mastiff with piglike eyes and more teeth than I'd ever observed in a dog's mouth before. I said I was sorry for troubling them and left hastily, just remembering to retrieve the sketch.

After wasting some time walking round the streets near the pawn-shop, I decided that I was on the wrong track. I was sure Marie had used the pawnshop, in spite of the fat man's hostility, but that didn't mean she lived in the immediate area. She'd been a respectable woman, after all, and there was no reason to think she'd sunk so rapidly to the level of the slums. I walked at random, southward and then east, looking for signs of what passed for respectability in the Borough. Some comparatively new rows of terraced brick houses looked more hopeful, though the streets in between were as muddy as the builders' carts had left them, not much better than farm tracks. When I met people picking their way through the mud I wished them good morning and asked if they knew of any Frenchwomen living nearby. Most were polite, some offhand or pretending deafness, but either way the result was the same.

At length I came to a row of small shops, a baker, a cobbler and an ironmonger. My spirits rose for a moment when the ironmonger peered out from between shining columns of kettles, pans and pails dangling on strings from the ceiling and said yes, there was a Frenchwoman living at the end of the street, but on further questioning she proved to be seventy or more and had lived there for as long as he could remember.

Some time after that, throat dry and shoes clotted with mud, I put my usual question to a woman who gave the usual negative reply, but kindly and in a southern Irish accent. In what seemed like a moment of inspiration, I asked directions to the nearest Roman Catholic church. The old priest there was deaf and shortsighted but did his best to be helpful. Yes, there were some Frenchwomen in his congregation, mostly from Brittany, he believed. He didn't know the names of all of them, but could not recall a Marie Duval or any dark-haired woman in her thirties who had arrived in the area in the past few weeks. I was sure from her accent that Marie was not a Breton, so my inspiration had led me down another false trail.

The mist didn't clear properly all day, blurring outlines of buildings and making pavements slippery. I crossed back over London Bridge in the last of the light, meeting the ragpickers and the collectors of horse dung for the market gardens and dog dung for the tanneries, trundling their carts back southward with the spoils of the day. I'd gained less than they had. My day had been totally wasted and now there were only six days to go before Jenny would stand trial.

On Tuesday morning I wrote a note to Kennedy, saying I'd call at his lodgings in the afternoon. When I got there, Kennedy looked tired and, for once, as old as his years. That was a shock in a man usually as buoyant as a seagull on a wave.

"We're still a world short of anything that would convince a jury, aren't we?" he said when he'd heard me out. "We don't even know the earrings were Columbine's."

"I think I can find that out," I said. "It's just a case of—"

"And even if we can prove they belonged to Columbine, we can't prove that Hardcastle stole them. She might have given them to him as a gift."

"Why would she do that?"

"Don't think I'm attacking your theory for the sake of it. You may even be right. But it's proof we need, and we've so little time left."

"Shall you tell Daniel?"

"I can't see any harm in telling him. He'll have more chance of finding Marie than finding Rainer, I suppose. At least she's not on the other side of the world."

"No, but she might be on the other side of the Channel."

I felt disappointed and cast-down, although I knew in my heart that he was right. I asked how Daniel was, and he looked sorrowful.

"Doesn't eat, doesn't sleep. Got punched on the jaw by a man in St. Giles who stole his money and he didn't even notice the bruises."

"When shall you see him?"

"This evening at Drury Lane, I hope. They're performing *The Mountain Sylph*. I don't suppose he'll stay to hear it, but he knows he'll find me there."

It was an opera by a friend of theirs. Daniel would normally have been there, leading the orchestra. If he wouldn't even stay to hear it, things were very bad indeed.

I walked straight from Kennedy's lodgings to the Augustus, thinking there was one question I could settle at least. As I'd hoped, Bel was early; I found her with one of the other girls in the dressing room, and Pauline hadn't arrived. Bel greeted me like an old friend and wanted to know why I hadn't brought my guitar. I took her into a corner near a gaslight and showed her the sketch of the earring. She was doubtful.

"I don't think I saw her wearing anything like that. It was usually emerald or sapphire studs, to match her costumes."

"Still, she'd have lots, wouldn't she?" the other girl said, coming over to look.

I turned the conversation to Pauline. She was apparently being as disagreeable as ever and had tried to trip Bel up during her solo.

"Only I stamped on her foot, so she won't try that one again in a hurry. That's the good thing about Spanish—you can stamp."

"Have you ever seen her with a quite tall gentleman with bad breath?" I said.

"Not that I remember. But if he's been with her, bad breath won't be the only thing he's got."

"Do men leave messages for her at the theater?"

She smiled at her reflection in the mirror.

"Wouldn't be much use if they did. She couldn't read them."

"Why not?"

"'Cos the stupid cow can't read."

"You're sure of that?"

"Course I'm sure. She even has to get us to read out the playbills to her, ask anyone."

On the walk home, I ran through this new chain of events in my head. A mysterious man had come inquiring at the theater two days after Columbine's death. Five days later the man with bad breath had met Pauline in the Rotunda, obviously by appointment, and tried to strangle her. The newspaper on the floor tied it to Columbine's murder. Until then, I hadn't known which of them had brought the paper, but since Pauline couldn't read, it was almost certainly the man. Was there something in the report and his investigations at the theater that made him think Pauline was guilty? If so, why had he decided to be Columbine's avenger? Was he an old lover, a long-lost relation? We needed to find him but, without knowing his name, where he came from or even having a reliable description of him, it was even more hopeless than finding Marie. I'd loved London and its crowds all my life, but that evening I felt like howling with rage at the sheer size and complexity of it.

Then it struck me that howling was no use. I did, after all, know one thing about the man with bad breath. I knew the newspaper he read. I turned back toward the offices of the *Morning Chronicle*. The presses were thundering and the bored young clerk at the counter told me there was just time to insert an advertisement in their columns for the next day if I hurried up about it. I borrowed his pen and inkstand and wrote.

> *If the gentleman whose business was interrupted in the Rotunda on Monday last would communicate with Mr. Lane at Abel Yard, off Adams Mews, Mayfair, he might learn something to his advantage.*

I paid the fee and walked out quickly, in case caution might make me twitch it out of the clerk's hand.

Chapter Fifteen

When I rode out with Amos next morning a sharp wind from the east made our horses fidgety but the sky was clear and he had news for me. He'd discovered what public house Hardcastle's former groom favored and was in high hopes of meeting him that evening. We were back at Abel Yard and Amos had just slid off his cob to help me dismount when I saw a familiar figure approaching. He was on foot this time, soberly dressed in a black overcoat and top hat, face pinched from the cold wind. I stayed in the saddle, taking an unfair advantage I supposed.

"Good morning, Mr. Disraeli. I hope your mare's not lame."

"She's cast a shoe."

He seemed ill at ease in such unfashionable surroundings. The coach repairer's terrier sniffed at his polished boots and Mr. Colley chose that moment to come past with one of his cows—Marigold, I think—forcing us all to move aside.

"Miss Lane, there's a good friend of mine who would like to meet you. My friend believes your advice might be helpful."

"Is it anything to do with Columbine?"

For a man so ready with words, he took his time about answering. The "yes" when it came was reluctant.

"Who is she?"

"She? I didn't say so."

"No, but you went out of your way not to."

"She, then. At present, I can't say."

"So she wants my help and I'm not even to know her name?"

"My commission was to see if you'd agree to meet her. Will you?"

"You're puzzling me, Mr. Disraeli. You know my interest in all this, but I'm not entirely sure about yours. You seem to take your friends' concerns very much to heart."

"Favors to friends are a useful currency, don't you find?"

He smiled when he said it, but it wasn't a kind smile. Was he reminding me of a favor from him to me?

"Very well, I'll see your friend, but only on condition that it won't damage the interests of Jenny Jarvis. When and where?"

"I'll leave her to communicate with you directly. I take it letters will find you at this address?"

I could see his nostrils twitching at the smell of the cesspit. Our landlord was in a constant state of warfare with other house owners about whose turn it was to pay to have it emptied.

"Letters find me, yes."

He raised his hat a few inches and turned away. Amos waited until he'd gone a few steps before shouting after him.

"Mr. Disraeli."

He spun round, unused to being addressed in Amos's robust Herefordshire accent.

"What?"

"That mare's a bit on the lungeous side when they're shoeing her. If I was you, I'd get in there sharpish and knock 'em down twenty guineas."

Disraeli looked astonished, but had the grace to smile.

"Thank you. I'll think about that."

He walked away. Amos helped me dismount.

"You've just saved him twenty guineas," I said.

"Favors to friends are a useful currency, don't you find?" He said it in a fair imitation of Disraeli, then added in his own voice, "But he's not a bad sort of a chap, take him all round."

That certificate of character, more than anything else, made me decide to go on trusting Disraeli—for a while at least.

"Who's this lady you're seeing?" Amos said.

He never pretended not to have overheard. It saved a lot of time in explanations.

"I don't know, but I might have a guess."

"What?"

"Maybe it's the same lady you'll be asking the groom about tonight."

"The one Hardcastle's going to marry?"

"It's possible, isn't it? Maybe she's heard things about him she doesn't like and wants to know more."

He whistled.

"If it's that, you tell her to wait for a better horse at the next market. See you Friday morning, then."

That afternoon, two painters arrived with a handcart, slopping blobs of whitewash on the cobbles. It turned out that they'd been sent by our landlord to paint the rooms that had been Old Slippers's, ready for the gentleman tenant he hoped to find for all our rooms together. Mrs. Martley had been entrusted with the key and brought it down to the yard for them. As the men sorted out brushes and old sheets, she looked wistfully up the staircase to the empty rooms.

"Shall we?"

I nodded and followed her up two flights of bare wooden stairs. At the top of the stairs a cobweb-filmed skylight filtered the dusk of the March afternoon. On our left an open door showed a small room with an empty tea chest, a fireplace just wide enough for one shovelful of coal and a window overlooking the courtyard. I pushed open the door on the right and we stepped into a totally bare room.

"Oh, it's beautiful," I said, caught by surprise.

Mrs. Martley gave me an odd look because in any normal sense, it wasn't. The white paint on the walls had flaked off, making a scurflike margin round the floor. The ceiling was bulging down in one corner and the place already smelled of damp and mice, as if it had been uninhabited for weeks rather than just a few days. But all that was nothing compared to the good-size window looking out over a line of rooftops, steep and uneven as an Alpine mountain range, and a glimpse of treetops in the park with rooks circling. Far away to the west a gold bar of sunset edged the gray clouds.

I could live here, I thought. *I'd have my clothes trunk in the corner where the ceiling's bulging, a table beside the window with my books and writing things, and a white and blue china bowl full of apples for Rancie.*

I'd buy the glass mermaid from the pawnshop and hang her in the window, where she'd catch the sun and scatter rainbows over the white walls. On summer mornings, I'd get up and put on my riding clothes, without worrying whether I was disturbing Mrs. Martley, pick up an apple from the bowl and run down my own staircase to meet Amos Legge.

"It's a pity," Mrs. Martley said, and heaved a sigh that seemed to come up from her shoe soles. I guessed she had her own dreams, as unlikely as mine. The five shillings extra a week just might be managed if I worked hard and found more Vickylings to teach, and even the fifty-pound deposit would be possible once I'd sold Rancie. But with Rancie gone, there'd be no more morning rides with Amos Legge and the sight of the treetops in the park would be a torment rather than a pleasure.

"We were nicely settled here." Mrs. Martley sighed.

In a few weeks Jenny might be dead and Daniel driven half mad by it. I couldn't expect to lean on him anymore. The bright bar of sunset had disappeared already and the rooks had gone. I turned away from the window.

"It's the dancing girl, isn't it?" Mrs. Martley said.

The room was almost dark now. She had her back to me.

"What?"

"That's what's worrying you and Mr. Suter. I don't intrude myself where I'm not wanted, but I can't help knowing."

Her voice was low. She sounded as out of spirits as I felt.

"Yes," I said.

She came across the room and put her arm round me. I leaned my head against her shoulder, breathing in the smell of cloves and cinnamon that clung to her dress from all those apple dumplings.

"I'm sorry, Mrs. Martley."

Sorry for a lot of things I couldn't put into words—for taking her for granted, for laughing at her, for wanting to be rid of her. Now that it looked as if we were all to be scattered to the four winds, I'd have given almost anything to be back where we were before Jenny. She rocked me, murmuring soothing, wordless things as if I were a child.

We were back in our own parlor, drinking tea, when somebody knocked on the door at the bottom of the staircase into the yard. It was dark by then so I lit a candle from the fire and went down. My heart was thumping, wondering if it might be a reply to my advertisement already, but the cloaked figure on the doorstep was female, a girl shivering in the cold. As soon as I opened the door she pushed a folded piece of paper into my hand.

"If you please, ma'am, I'm to wait for a reply."

I gave her the candle to hold while I unfolded the note.

Lady Silverdale hopes it may be convenient for Miss Lane to call on her at eleven o'clock tonight. Signed Beatrice Silverdale. It took me a moment to realize that I was looking at an invitation from Rodney Hardcastle's mother. So that was Disraeli's mysterious friend. The address was less than half a mile away, on the corner of Hertford Street and Park Lane. I looked at the girl.

"Doesn't she mean eleven o'clock tomorrow morning?"

"No ma'am, tonight."

She showed neither surprise nor curiosity.

"Very well," I said. "You may tell Lady Silverdale I'll be there."

I went back upstairs and told Mrs. Martley I'd be going out late.

"You can't go traipsing all over London at night."

"It's not all over London. We're practically next door neighbors."

I showed her the note. The crested paper and the address impressed her, but she was still suspicious.

"What kind of lady wants callers at eleven o'clock?"

A lady who had something to hide, I was sure. Lady Silverdale obviously did not want her friends to see me coming and going. I changed into my red printed cotton with the pleated bodice. It was one of my most respectable garments but too light for a March night, so I wrapped my woolen cloak closely round me. Outside, the wind had risen, whipping rags of clouds across a thin crescent moon. I walked fast and arrived at the steps leading up to the Silverdales' house at five minutes to eleven. It was grand, even by Park Lane standards, with a portico at the top of the steps and two caryatids on either side like the ones on the Parthenon, illuminated by the lamplight from an uncurtained downstairs room. I tugged at the iron bell knob and before I'd even had time to let go of it the door opened. The girl who'd delivered the note was standing inside in a black dress and white cap. She stood back for me to go inside and closed the door.

The only light came from a few candles in sconces all the way

up the staircase to the top landing. The hall itself was in darkness and the doors to the ground-floor rooms closed. No sound
came from behind them. The maid and I might have been the
only people in the building. I followed her up the carpeted stairs
between the candles to the first landing, on to the second landing
and up again. The staircase was narrower now and might have
been going to a servants' attic, except there was still good deep
carpet underfoot and the candles from the smell of them were finest beeswax. The maid stopped at a white and gold painted door
and knocked.

"Miss Lane, ma'am."

She opened the door for me. It was like stepping into a cave,
with one side of it opening onto the night sky with its flying clouds
and what looked like a gigantic insect crouching in front of it. After that first step I stood, trying to get my balance as if another
move would send me over the brink. I suppose it might have been
an ordinary room once, though it was hard to tell because it was
illuminated only by patches of candlelight, closed in by shadows.
One side of it was mostly windows from knee-height to ceiling,
with only as much wall in between them as would hold the glass
in place. The head of the giant insect appeared to have eaten a hole
for itself through a wall and was sticking out on the other side.
After a moment of sheer panic I identified it as one of the largest
telescopes I had ever seen.

"So kind of you to come, Miss Lane."

The voice was low and pleasant. I looked down and saw a woman
who seemed as strange as the room. She was as small and slim as
a girl of twelve, with large eyes that glinted in the candlelight. Her
silver hair was cut short like a cap, exposing neat oval ears like sea-
shells. The hand she held out to me felt small in mine, but so full of
nervous energy I half expected sparks to rise from the contact.

"Your wig, Mama."

An urgent whisper came from the corner. A young woman was

sitting at a desk in one of the islands of candlelight, pen in hand. A thick book like a ledger and piles of paper covered the desk. Her eyes were on a table by the door, where an elaborate gray wig sat on a wooden block. Lady Silverdale laughed.

"I'm sure Miss Lane doesn't object. It saves so much time, don't you think, to be able to send one's hair to the coiffeur without one's brain having to accompany it?" Then as an afterthought, "My daughter, Anna. She helps me in my work."

The young woman gave me a neutral nod and went back to her writing. Lady Silverdale walked briskly across the room to the telescope as if she couldn't bear to be long away from it. It was so much larger than she was that a wooden platform had been built to bring her level with the eyepiece.

"One of Herschel's of course," she said, resting her hand on the brass tube much as I might rest mine on Rancie's neck. "Thirty years ago my husband-to-be said he'd give me whatever I wanted for a wedding present. I think he expected me to say emeralds, but he kept his word."

I said nothing, still trying to adjust. I'd expected Rodney Hardcastle's mother to be a fool. Her intelligence was as disconcerting as her room. She didn't seem to mind my silence and went on talking.

"It's very civil of you to call so late. I'm afraid Anna and I have become as nocturnal as owls. There's been so much cloud lately that we have great gaps in our observations and have to snatch our chances when we can."

"Observations? Are you looking for new stars?"

"Oh, they're as common as daisies in a meadow. We could have plenty of those if we wanted them." She dismissed galaxies with a wave of her small hand. "Orbits are the thing. Uranus seems to be behaving in a way that's not entirely predictable. That can't be the case of course. Everything's predictable, if only you know enough."

"Everything?"

"Oh yes. Look at Jupiter and Saturn." She spoke as if we might meet them strolling along Piccadilly. "People used to think that their orbits were unpredictable until Laplace proved otherwise. It was simply a matter of going backward and forward nine hundred years."

"That's possible?"

"Oh good heavens, yes. You can calculate backward and forward hundreds of thousands of years from observations, but you have to make sure the observations are right in the first place."

She removed her hand reluctantly from the telescope and led the way to a smaller island of candlelight on the far side of the room from where her daughter was working. Two armchairs stood on either side of a table crowded with empty coffee cups, a plate with half a sandwich, letters in a variety of handwritings. She signed to me to sit down and took the chair opposite.

"But you haven't come here to talk about astronomy, have you?"

"I've come because you wanted to speak to me," I said.

It sounded ungracious, but I was fighting an urge to like her. She didn't take offense.

"Yes. I understand you were at the theater the night the dancer died."

"That's true."

"And you believe that the other girl didn't kill her?"

"I'm convinced of it."

"May I ask you why?"

"Because of things that have happened since Jenny Jarvis was arrested. People are showing an interest in Columbine, even searching her dressing room. Why should they do that if it were such a simple case?"

"People showing an interest?"

"Yourself for instance," I said.

"Ah." Her expression of polite attention didn't change. "Then perhaps I should explain my interest to you. You know of my son, Rodney?"

"Yes."

"What do you know of him?"

"He was Columbine's lover. He has serious debts. He was at the theater on the night Columbine died."

I could see no point in tiptoeing round it and she did not strike me as the kind of woman who would want me to.

"Rodney is a worry to us," she said. Her voice was as calm as when she talked about the puzzling behavior of the planet Uranus. "I'm concerned with the effect all this is having on his father's health."

"Lord Silverdale is ill?"

I thought if the illness were serious, Hardcastle's hypothetical bride might be expecting to claim her coronet sooner rather than later.

"So far, not seriously. But he's a sensitive man and all the gossip makes things very difficult. I've persuaded him to go down to the country for a while to escape from it. You see, I am very fond of my husband."

She said it in exactly the tone of voice a person might talk of a faithful old Labrador.

"He's refused to be responsible for his son's debts, I gather."

"Of course, otherwise all these dreadful people who've brought Rodney into this state of affairs would encourage him to spend even more." She sighed and glanced over to the corner where Anna was bent low over her copying. "Daughters are so much more satisfactory, don't you think? But that's beside the point. I wanted to talk to you because you might help me spare his father further distress."

"How?"

For once, she didn't answer directly.

"I gather the case will come to trial soon."

"In five days' time."

"As soon as that? Tell me, is it likely that Rodney will be called as a witness?"

She couldn't quite keep the urgency out of her voice.

"Why do you think he might be?"

"I don't know. I know so little law. But I understand that barristers will throw in all kinds of irrelevant things to try and muddle the minds of the jury."

"It might not be entirely irrelevant," I said. "He must have known more about her than most people. He knew his way round backstage too."

I was trying to unsettle her and she guessed it. Her frown of annoyance was smoothed out almost as soon as it appeared and her voice was back under control.

"But he would be, wouldn't he? I gather that gentlemen in his set do pay calls on dancers in their dressing rooms."

"He didn't that evening. They'd quarreled. Did he tell you about that?"

She smiled. "He tells me so little, like most young men. But if he didn't go into her dressing room that night, he couldn't be a witness, could he? Whoever poisoned her must have had access to the room."

Had that been in the newspapers? At any rate she must have studied the case very carefully to know it.

"Is that generally known, that she wouldn't let him in?" she said.

"The manager Barnaby Blake knew and I daresay most of the girls in the chorus did too."

"Do the police know?"

"I don't know."

"Have they questioned you?"

"No."

She looked longingly toward the telescope and the night sky.

"Perhaps they should know. And yet, if nobody's thought of calling Rodney as a witness, we don't want to put ideas into their heads."

"Would it really be so disastrous?"

I thought Hardcastle anywhere would be a disaster, but it wouldn't help to say it. She gave me a sharp look.

"My husband has done the state some service. Do you think it's fair that he should be a public mockery because his son's standing up in the Old Bailey being questioned about associations with dancers and prostitutes?"

"What do you want me to do?" I said.

"I'm told you are a young woman of unusual judgment." (Disraeli, I supposed.) "I want you to do what you can to prevent my son from having to stand up in court. Believe me, I shall be very grateful."

It was the nearest she could come to offering me money without treating me as a tradeswoman. I suspected that she'd thought that out carefully in advance.

"You know the condition I made," I said.

"That you would do nothing against the interests of the dancer?"

"Of Jenny Jarvis."

It seemed important to me to say her name.

"Yes, but I fail to see how dragging Rodney through the mud would help her."

There was an edge of hostility in her voice now.

"There's something else," I said.

"What's that?"

"Mr. Hardcastle's valet was threatening to leave unless his wages were paid. So he gave him a single diamond earring to take to the pawnbroker. I have reason to think it belonged to Columbine."

"Have you seen this earring?"

"No, but I have a sketch of it."

I took it out of my reticule, unfolded it and handed it to her.

She held it so close to the candle flame to look that I was afraid she was going to burn it and kept my hand ready to grab it back. She laughed and returned it to me.

"I recognize that. It's mine."

"Yours?"

"Was mine, rather. I gave the pair to poor Rodney a month ago. I'm sure it's very weak of me, and of course his father's quite right not to pay his debts, but, well . . . a mother's fondness, I suppose."

"It must have been a sacrifice," I said.

"Not a great one. I hadn't worn them for years."

Her manner had changed. She wanted me to go.

"I'm glad we've had a chance to talk, Miss Lane. I should appreciate it very much if you'd keep me informed. You'll find us here at the same time any night and I'll give Jane instructions that you are to be shown up."

I looked away from her face, down at the letters on the table.

"You have a lot of correspondence."

"Oh yes." She grasped the opportunity to drop into social conversation. "This one's from Herschel's sister Caroline, nearly ninety years old and her mind's as remarkable as ever."

The closely written sheet was sprinkled with figures and mathematical symbols. I peered closely as she held it in the candlelight.

"Remarkable, yes."

She stood up and went over to the telescope. Her eagerness to get back to it was almost touching.

"There's so much to know, you see. It's quite endless."

She stared up at the sky. I stood beside her and stared down on London. Wandering stars of carriage lanterns followed their courses along Park Lane and Piccadilly. Windows near at hand blazed with lights from chandeliers or glowed, more humbly and distantly, from oil lamps. To the west was the darkness of the park, to the south a band of deeper darkness that was the Thames. Somewhere on the far side of it, Marie might be sleeping or waking. On this side, not far from the dome of St. Paul's, Jenny Jarvis would most likely be lying awake on her plank bed. Somewhere Daniel would be walking down alleyways or into dark courtyards, looking for a man with a brown face. She was right—so much to know. I envied the astronomers their almost predictable planets.

The clouds were still flying across the moon as I hurried home. My head felt as if it were spinning with the planets. She'd lied to me. It had been, in the circumstances, a quick and clever lie. When I'd pretended interest in her correspondence and pored so closely over the letter, it had given me a chance to look at her ears in the candlelight. They were, as I'd first noticed, unusually neat. They had no lobes. That wasn't so rare, but if you've no lobes, you can't have your ears pierced. The earring in the sketch the pawn-broker made for me had a hook for a pierced ear, so she couldn't have worn it, not years ago or ever. And yet, I thought she'd been telling something not far from the truth when she said she was worried about her son having to appear in the witness box.

Only it wasn't the witness box she was worried about. It was the dock.

Chapter Sixteen

There was no riding on Thursday morning because Amos had a horse to deliver to Highgate, so I was at Kennedy's lodgings soon after it got light. He'd been working late the night before and was still in his dressing gown and slippers, breakfasting on coffee and anchovy toast with a newspaper on the table in front of him. He jumped up when the servant showed me in, setting toast and paper flying.

"What's happened now?"

"Nothing bad," I said. "Progress, I think."

We sat down, he found another cup and poured coffee for me and I told him every detail of the meeting with Lady Silverdale.

"So she's nearly sure Hardcastle stole the earrings from Columbine," he said.

"It's a lot more than that. She's terrified of him facing any questions about Columbine."

"We can't prove that."

"I wish you'd stop talking like a lawyer," I snapped. "Everything I try to do, you pour cold water on."

He sighed. "Liberty, if I'm talking like a lawyer, it's because I'm having to think like one. I spent an hour or more yesterday speaking to Harmer."

It took me a moment to remember that was his solicitor friend.

"What did he say?"

"He's worried, Liberty. He says there's nothing we've found so far that Charles Phillips will be prepared to bring out in court on Monday."

"What about the earrings? What about Marie disappearing?"

"He says Phillips is too fly to try to ride wild horses in opposite directions. Either we produce one theory—and I mean one theory—with evidence to support it, or all we can rely on is Phillips's eloquence in picking holes in the case against Jenny."

"And is he hopeful?"

Kennedy shook his head.

"Have you told Daniel this?"

Another headshake.

I sank down in the chair, feeling bone weary.

"Couldn't we have the case delayed?"

"I asked that. Not much hope there either, unless we can produce a strong argument that delay would bring in fresh evidence."

"But it will. For one thing, we might find Marie."

"What good would that do? The police have already questioned her and let her go. We don't have a shred of evidence that they were wrong."

I stared down at the floor. The newspaper he'd dropped was yesterday's *Chronicle*. When I bent to pick it up from simple tidiness, my own surname leaped out at me from the advertisement columns on the front page.

If Mr. Lane has information which he wishes to impart, he may meet the gentleman referred to in his advertisement in the same locality at four o'clock on Friday afternoon.

I stood frozen with the newspaper in my hand. If there'd been a reply at all, I'd expected it to come to my home by messenger. It hadn't occurred to me that it might be by another advertisement.

"What is it, Libby?"

I showed him.

"Another wild horse, perhaps the wildest of the lot," I said. "It's the man who thinks Pauline killed Columbine."

"That's a wild leap on your wild horse. He might easily have other reasons for trying to strangle the woman. Has it occurred to you that she might be trying to blackmail him?"

"Then why did he bring the newspaper with him? There must have been something in that report that made him murderously angry with Pauline."

"If he thinks he has proof, why hasn't he taken it to the police?" Kennedy said.

"How do I know? Perhaps he wants to take his own revenge. Perhaps he's an old lover or even a long-lost brother. But it must be somebody who really cared for Columbine."

"You are not keeping this appointment."

"I most certainly am. It's the most promising development so far."

"By your own account, the man's dangerous."

"Only to Pauline, or whoever killed Columbine."

"He's expecting to meet a man. I'll go in your place."

"No, you won't. With luck it will unsettle him, meeting me. But you can come with me, if you insist."

He did insist, which suited me because I was by no means as confident about the meeting as I pretended. The Rotunda gave me the shivers, and I thought it a sinister sign that the man had chosen to meet there again. After some more arguing, we agreed to meet at Kennedy's lodgings the following afternoon.

* * *

At home, there was a message from Amos Legge waiting for me.

With ruspect, I saw our man. Something to tell you.

Realizing the effort it cost him to write, I knew the information must be important, so I put on my cloak and bonnet and walked across the park to the livery stables on the Bayswater Road. One of the grooms told me that Legge was out with some ladies, but was expected back soon. Rancie was looking out from the half door of her loose box. She made her familiar soft whickering sound when she saw me and I fed her the apple that I'd stolen from Mrs. Martley's store. The black cat, Lucy, was stretched out comfortably on Rancie's back as usual, purring loudly enough to be heard over the apple munching. Like Rancie, she'd adapted to London life and looked as sleek as a panther. Amos and his two ladies arrived back in the yard soon afterward. He was riding a dock-tailed chestnut cob, wearing his cream-colored stock, soft-topped boots and tall black hat with silver lace cockade. He gave me a wave with his riding switch as he dismounted, then concentrated on helping the two ladies down from their saddles. It seemed to take a long time and an immoderate amount of giggling. Eventually he disposed of them and the three horses and walked over to join me by the loose box door.

"I saw our man yesterday evening," Amos said. "Taylor, his name is. Queer old quist someways, but friendly enough over a glass or two. He's found a place with a livery stables out Oxford way, so I was lucky to ketch him before he flew, like."

"And you got him talking about Hardcastle?"

"Wasn't difficult. Apart from not getting his wages paid and the late nights and His Lordship's friends being sick in the phaeton and having to be cleared up after, he didn't dislike him on the whole. So I agreed that it was hard being kept up all hours with him drinking and playing cards and so on, but I didn't suppose he was bothered with too many early mornings."

I could imagine them sitting over their beer, Amos playing the country innocent to lead his man on.

"He laughed at that and said no, he couldn't recall he was ever needed before eleven o'clock in the morning, except just the once. So I said I supposed that was a long time ago. Not so long, he said, only a few weeks ago. He remembered it because it was the last long drive he took in the phaeton. He liked that phaeton, only he didn't often get much chance to drive it because in the morning Mr. Hardcastle would usually drive it himself."

"A long drive?" I couldn't resist putting in a question.

"All the way out to Hampstead at seven o'clock in the morning, and this was a month ago when it was still dark then. That's why he wanted his driver with him. He didn't care for going out in the country in the dark."

A month ago. That would make it about two weeks before Columbine died. I bit my tongue.

"'What was Mr. Hardcastle doing, going all the way to Hampstead on a dark winter morning?' I said. And he gives me a look as if he's not saying, only I can see he doesn't mean it and just wants to be persuaded. So I buy him another pint of the gnat's piss they call beer here and I say, 'It sounds as if he was up to no good.' 'Up to no good? That depends what you mean,' he says. 'Any rate, he looked like a man who was going to be hanged.'"

"Going to be hanged!"

"He looked as if he hadn't been to bed the night before, cravat all rumpled and wine-stained. Stamping around impatient because Taylor's fingers were cold and it took him a while to get the lamps lit on the phaeton. All the way out to Hampstead he kept on at him to go faster and kept taking out his watch, trying to see the time on it in the dark. Anyways, they got there just as the clocks were striking eight. There's a public house at the bottom of the hill, just before you turn to go up to Jack Straw's Castle. Mr. Hardcastle tells him to pull up there and wait for him. Says he'll be back in twenty minutes or so. Then he gets down, crosses the road and walks off."

"He doesn't like walking," I said, thinking of the occasion in Piccadilly.

"That's just what occurred to Taylor. He couldn't see, after all this fuss and bother, why he didn't just have himself driven to where he was going. So he gets curious. If the public house had been open and Taylor could have gone in for a drink, that might have been another matter, but it wasn't. Any rate, he waits a few minutes, then he drives off in the direction Mr. Hardcastle went, just for a look, like. And what do you think he comes to?"

He paused. Rancie approached the door and rubbed her nose against his sleeve. He started talking to her.

"How are we then, girl? Not been out today?"

He was being deliberately infuriating, making me wait.

"Never mind her," I said. "What did he come to?"

"Nothing much down that way at all, except a few houses with nobody about. And a church, with a closed carriage waiting out-side."

We were there at last. Amos looked sideways at me, enjoying the effect of his story.

"There were lamps lit inside the church, at that time in the morning and not a Sunday. So Taylor says to himself, 'Ho-ho, that's his game, then!' and he turns the phaeton round double quick and gets back to where he was supposed to wait. Ten minutes later, up comes Mr. Hardcastle, puffed out from walking fast. He slumps himself down in the seat and tells Taylor to get back home and look sharp about it. Doesn't say a word all the way back."

"Hardcastle was on his own?"

"He was."

"What about the closed carriage?"

"Taylor didn't see any more of it. He supposed it was still waiting outside the church."

"Could he describe it? Was there a coat of arms, for instance?"

"He didn't get that close, in case Mr. Hardcastle came out of the church and saw him. All he knows is that it was drawn by a couple of bays."

As were half the carriages in London, so that was no help. Still, what he had given me was pure gold.

"Amos Legge, you're a wonder of the world."

He nodded, taking it as no more than his due.

"Does it help, then?"

"A lot."

However secret a marriage, for it to be legal it must be entered in the church register, including the bride's maiden name. It would be a simple matter to go out to Hampstead and find the church nearest to where the phaeton had waited. One glance in the book and we would have the name of Hardcastle's rich bride.

"How soon can we ride out to Hampstead?" I said.

Amos considered.

"We could do it tomorrow, if you liked."

I was about to say yes when I remembered the meeting in the Rotunda.

"Sunday morning, then," Amos said. "We're all booked up here on Saturday."

The day before the trial, but it would have to do. Another thought came to me.

"Amos, are you doing anything at four o'clock tomorrow afternoon?"

"Nothing that can't be got out of."

"There's a gentleman I'm meeting in Leicester Square. He's tried to kill somebody."

He nodded, as if that were something quite normal.

"Just point me his way and I'll have him trussed like a Michaelmas goose soon as you can say kiss your hand."

"I don't want him trussed up. I just want to make sure he stays put long enough to answer a question or two."

"He'll stand like he's grown roots and been planted."

I said I'd meet him in Leicester Square at a quarter to four and he rode off whistling as if I'd given him good news.

I hardly slept that night. Next morning I gave music lessons to my usual Friday family, but my mind wasn't with them. I was on Kennedy's doorstep at three o'clock. He'd met Amos Legge in the past and approved my idea of adding him to the party. As we walked toward Leicester Square, Kennedy and I discussed Hardcastle's marriage. He was inclined to believe the groom's story, but pointed out that it weakened the case against Hardcastle.

"If he married two weeks or so before Columbine died, it wouldn't matter if she was trying to blackmail him or had compromising letters. He'd caught his rich bride and Columbine couldn't do anything about it."

"Why was he so concerned to keep it secret then?" I said. "As soon as the marriage register is signed, he could get his hands on his wife's money and laugh at the bailiffs. Why should he wait?"

We were still discussing it when we came to Leicester Square. Amos was waiting under a tree by the builders' yard.

"Hello, Mr. Kennedy," he said. "Still fiddling then?"

Kennedy replied politely that yes, he was still playing the violin.

I stared across at the Rotunda. A lamp over the door was lit, illuminating the signboard, but there was nobody going in or out.

"We'll wait until just after four," I said. "If our man hasn't gone in by then, we'll assume he's already inside. We'll go in together, like any normal customers. We'll let Mr. Kennedy go on ahead up the staircase, because our man is expecting to meet another man. I'll follow him. Mr. Legge, would you kindly wait at the bottom of the stairs, unless you hear one of us shouting. If a man tries to run out, hold him."

Amos just nodded. Kennedy raised objections.

"It would be safer if Mr. Legge and I went upstairs to confront him and you waited downstairs."

"It most certainly would not be safer." I had a vivid memory of the dark shape pushing past me and of Pauline slumped on the floor. "He might be downstairs. That's where he was last time. A fine thing, if he came out of the shadows to attack me and you two were up in the gallery."

Four o'clock struck, the chimes from various clocks spaced out over three minutes or more. Nobody had gone inside the Rotunda.

"He's in there already, then," I said.

We walked toward the entrance, Toby Kennedy and Amos Legge on either side of me. I hoped whoever was on duty wouldn't recognize me. In an effort to look as unlike one of the soiled-dove sisterhood as possible, I'd put on my plainest bonnet and scraped my hair back so tightly that it put a permanent frown on my forehead. A different boy, but just as bored as the first one, took our money and didn't give me a second glance. We passed the cash desk and stopped at the foot of the stairs. On either side of us, the corridor curved into shadows. I held up my hand for us to listen and wait. For a few seconds there was only the hiss and splutter of the gas lamps; then, from the gallery upstairs, the sound of footsteps. A few steps one way, pause, then a few steps the other way. Heavy but tentative, like a man waiting. Then he must have moved in front of one of the gas lamps, because a long shadow wavered over the palace of imperial Peking.

Kennedy caught my eye. I nodded, and he walked upstairs quite normally, like anybody going to see the panorama. His steps sounded firmly round the gallery above our heads, then his voice, polite but pitched loudly so that we could hear.

"Good evening, sir. May I ask if you are waiting to meet Mr. Lane?"

That was my signal. I put a warning hand on the arm of Amos, who looked inclined to follow me, then ran upstairs. Toby Kennedy was doing well, but I'd conjured up this witness and the next step belonged to me. My blood was racing. If things went well we might have our man inside a lawyer's office within the hour, telling us why he was so convinced of Pauline's guilt that he'd tried to strangle her.

In the gallery, I had my first sight of the man. He was wearing a thick black coat and carrying a top hat in his hand. He would have been tall, probably six feet or more if he'd stood upright, but his shoulders were hunched and his whole posture was that of a man run to seed. He might have been in his forties or older. He seemed to ooze a lifetime's disappointment: cheeks drooping, deep creases from his nostrils to his down-turned mouth, thin hair combed carefully across a balding head. His complexion looked more yellowish than brown, but that might have been the gaslight. He was staring at Kennedy, who had his back to me. If he'd answered Kennedy's question, his voice had been too low to carry to me.

"Good afternoon," I said. "I put the advertisement in. Do you remember me from last week?"

His eyes switched from Kennedy to me. I walked up and stood beside Kennedy, so that between us we were blocking the gallery.

"You must have loved Columbine very much," I said.

I wasn't acting on impulse; I'd thought it out carefully. That this man had loved Columbine and hoped to avenge her was the only thing that made sense. He'd see, at any rate, that it was no use pretending not to know what we wanted. I was prepared for almost anything—curses, denials, an attempt to get away. What I hadn't expected was the blank stare he was giving me. I thought that by the sheerest ill luck we'd caught some innocent stranger who'd come to pass an instructive half hour in Peking. Then he opened his mouth and, before he even said a word, I knew we had the right man. The few remaining teeth in his head were as rotten as pig-swill apples and his breath reeked like an old dog's.

"Love?" The word came out as a wavering yell, echoing round the dome. "*Love* her?"

Then, while we were still reeling from the sound, he lurched at us, head down. It was a clumsy charge, but we were caught by surprise and fell back. He blundered on toward the staircase and, at the top of it, cannoned into Amos Legge, who'd come running up, alerted by the outcry. A lesser man might have pitched backward downstairs, but Amos was immovable. He put his hands on the man's shoulders.

"Settle down now. Nobody's looking to hurt you."

He spoke gently, as if dealing with a nervous horse. The boy called up from the cash desk to ask what was happening.

"Gentleman come over a bit kecky," Amos said. "Don't you worry, boy, we're taking care of him."

There were padded benches all round the gallery, for people to study the panorama at leisure. Amos steered the man to the nearest one and sat him down. The effort of running, or perhaps the impact of Amos, had taken all the fight out of him. He leaned over wheezing, his hands dangling between his knees.

"Flask," he said. "Flask in pocket."

Kennedy gave me a glance, then felt in the man's pocket and produced a hip flask. When he uncorked it, the smell of brandy filled the air round us. The man took it, glugged several mouthfuls and coughed.

"Do you want a doctor?" I said.

I didn't want him to die on us. He shook his head and handed the flask to Kennedy for recorking.

"Quacks, all of them."

The brandy gave him enough strength to sit upright, more or less. I sat beside him. Amos moved in close to the bench.

"So you didn't love her?" I said.

From Kennedy's face, he thought I was being callous in persisting, but then he hadn't been there when this man had almost throttled a woman. The man looked me in the face. His eyes might have been his best feature once upon a time, if you liked lapdog's eyes in a man's face.

"I hated the woman you call Columbine more than anybody else in the world."

There was a kind of tawdry dignity about the way he said it, like a man making a confession of faith. My mind somersaulted.

"Good heavens, you're Major Charles Rainer," I said.

But he was giving me the blank stare again.

"Who? No. I am the Reverend Theophilus Maine."

Chapter Seventeen

Silence, then a low whistle from Kennedy.

"Maine—that was the family name of the old lord who dived off London Bridge."

"I am his son," the man said. "The younger son."

He stared into my face, as if I should have guessed his whole story from that. My mind had plumped down from its somersault and was trying to recover. I was glad when Kennedy took over the questioning.

"You hated Columbine for what she'd done to your father?"

"Her name was Priddy," he said. "We'll use that, if you please. No, it was my father's own fault. He was an unjust and lustful man. Priddy ruined my life and I'd done nothing to hurt her. Nothing."

"What did she do?" Kennedy asked.

"That's between me and my maker," said Reverend Maine.

"Oh no, it isn't," I said. "You tried to strangle a woman, just below where we're sitting now. That's between you and the magistrates."

"The woman had defrauded me."

"How?"

"She'd taken my money under false pretenses."

"What false pretenses?"

He hesitated.

"Pauline had agreed to kill Columbine for you, hadn't she?" I said.

"To kill the whore Priddy, yes."

"Tell us. Tell us everything," I said. "You've attempted murder twice over: Columbine first and then Pauline."

"They were whores, both of them."

"It's still attempted murder. Do you want to walk out of here a free man, or shall we tell the boy downstairs to call a police officer?"

He looked from me to Kennedy and then to Amos. Finding no comfort, he reached out a hand to Kennedy.

"Another drink. For my stomach."

Kennedy gave him back his flask. He drank deeply and noisily, closed his eyes for a moment, then started his story.

"I was home from my second year at Oxford. The girl Priddy was employed in the dairy. She was never satisfactory, cheeky and insubordinate. I was a young man, reading for holy orders. She made sure she caught my eye, led me on."

"How old was she?" I said.

"Fifteen, sixteen, perhaps. Who knows. Those kind of girls grow up early. There was no indiscretion, nothing that could properly be called indiscretion, on my part. I was innocent in the ways of the world. I believe now that she deliberately contrived to have us discovered."

"Discovered?"

"By my father. He was a man of hasty temper. I suppose appearances were against me, but in truth I was as innocent as Adam before Eve tempted him. My father didn't believe me. He reduced my allowance, threatened to take me away from Oxford and force me to earn my living as a tutor. The humiliation was not to be borne. I promised to see no more of the girl Priddy. She never appeared again in the dairy after that day. Naturally, I assumed that my father had dismissed her without a character."

"Instead of which, he carried her off to London and covered her in diamonds," I said.

I could see from Kennedy's expression that he thought I was being hard on the man, but the Adam and Eve story always seemed unjust to me. Maine winced.

"My father was besotted with her. He behaved altogether like a man in his second childhood. The scandal of it even reached Oxford. Can you imagine what torture that was for a proud and sensitive young man—having to listen to the jokes and speculation. Then my father dived off London Bridge and ruined my prospects forever."

"You were the younger son," said Kennedy, quite gently. "Did you have much in the way of prospects?"

"Our family is not without influence. There was a good living arranged for me, a church in Chelsea. After the scandal of my father's death, my patron withdrew the offer. He said people would be looking at me in the pulpit and thinking of my father and the milkmaid, not their own sins. Door after door closed to me. In the end, I had no choice. I signed on as a chaplain in His Majesty's navy. The longer I stayed away, the smaller my expectations were of a good living in this country. I was condemned, through no fault of my own, to the dangers and deprivations of a life at sea. Last year I returned, broken in health, with a charity pension that gives me less to live on than my father spent on his hunting dogs."

Tears were running down his cheeks, into the channels between nostrils and mouth, dripping from his chin. I was beginning to pity him. I hardened my heart, thinking of Daniel.

"So when did you decide to have Columbine killed?" I said.

"When I knew she was in London and flaunting herself on-stage. My life's almost over, in any case. The latest quack gives me six months at most. I made up my mind that, like Samson in the temple of the Philistines, I would perform one act of justice and cleansing before my death."

"How did you meet Pauline?" I said.

His eyes dropped.

"Not so much the temple of the Philistines as the Palace of the Egyptians," I suggested.

His sallow face turned red. Kennedy looked puzzled, but I think Amos Legge understood. Maine might have been telling the truth when he said he had less than the dogs to live on, but he'd somehow managed to pay Pauline's price. Perhaps, to impress a gentleman client, she'd boasted to him about being a dancer at the Augustus. To Maine's strange mind, the chance might have seemed heaven-sent.

"How much did you pay her to kill Columbine?" I said.

"Twenty pounds. Ten before and ten when it was done."

"Where did you meet her to pay the first ten?"

"St. Paul's, Covent Garden."

"Did you suggest poisoning?"

"No. It was her idea to use arsenic."

"She said arsenic?"

"Yes. When I met her afterward, she said she'd put arsenic in Priddy's bowl of syllabub."

I remembered the greed for knowledge in Pauline's face on the night of the murder, her question, "Was it arsenic?" She'd needed to know in order to collect her money. If she'd been able to read the report in the paper, she could have changed her story to fit the facts.

"Then you discovered from the newspaper that she'd lied, and you paid a visit to the theater," I said.

"How do you know that?"

"Never mind. You did, didn't you?"

"Yes. The newspaper said it was some different poison, then the police arrested the other dancer. The whore Pauline said she wanted to meet me again. I think she wanted more money. I showed her the newspaper report and taxed her with lying to me."

"A waste of time. She couldn't read."

"She laughed in my face and admitted the deception. 'Did you think I was going to risk having my neck stretched for twenty pounds when I can make that much by opening my legs a few times?' That was what she said to me."

"Was that when you tried to strangle her?"

"I never intended to kill her. I was angry."

"But you did intend her to kill Columbine?"

"To kill Priddy, yes. But the Lord provided another avenger and left me clean."

"Do you know who did kill Columbine?"

"The other dancer, I suppose."

A man's voice shouted from below, "Closing time in five minutes, ladies and gentlemen."

It sounded like the angry man I'd met last time.

"Will you let me go?"

Maine spoke quite humbly. He sounded exhausted. I looked at Kennedy.

"He is speaking the truth, I think," he said.

"About what matters, yes, I think he is."

I had no faith at all in the man's honor, but his story touched the facts as I knew them in three places: the meeting with Pauline in St. Paul's, her inquiry about arsenic, his visit backstage at the Augustus. Also, it matched exactly what I knew about Pauline's character.

"You can go, as far as we're concerned," I said.

He stood up, took a last swallow from his flask and put it away in his pocket. The three of us followed as he walked unsteadily down the stairs. This time the angry man didn't give me a second glance.

Outside it was dark, the air harsh and damp. We watched as Reverend Theophilus Maine walked across the square.

"Poor devil," Kennedy said.

I was too disappointed to pity him. I'd hoped so much that he'd point the way to our murderer, but all I'd done was waste precious time.

"He might have been telling the truth about the murder," said Amos, "but I'll give you any odds he was letting himself off lightly about the milkmaid."

"How's that?" said Kennedy.

"Reckoning the poor girl took advantage of him, and him the squire's son and five years or so older. We've heard that story before and most girls it happened to weren't as lucky as that one turned out to be."

Kennedy looked taken aback. He liked Amos but wasn't used to such free speaking from him.

"I agree," I said. "He's a mean, hypocritical man who hates women, and I don't feel in the least sorry for him."

(Though I did feel sorry, just a little.)

"So Pauline's not a murderer?" Kennedy said.

"No, the woman's everything bad you care to name, but she's not that. The one consolation is that we didn't tell Daniel about this."

"At least we know now that it wasn't Rainer at the Augustus," Kennedy said. "But then we never thought it was."

The three of us walked sadly toward Haymarket, where Kennedy had an engagement.

"I'll have the horses round about ten on Sunday morning, then," Amos said.

I thanked him. Following Hardcastle's trail seemed the only hope left now.

Sunday was a bright, cold day with clouds driven across blue sky by a wind from the east. Amos arrived leading Rancie and riding a walleyed roan cob that he said could do with the exercise. We rode at a walk toward Marylebone, then trotted around the north side of Regent's Park. Strange bellowings and roarings came from the zoological gardens.

"Some of the lads from the stables have been in there," said Amos wistfully. "They saw a hippopotamus."

We paused on Primrose Hill to rest the horses and look back over London, all the way across the river to hills far to the south. From there, we joined the main road northward and uphill toward Hampstead. It was early afternoon when we came to the village and drew rein at the foot of the steepest part of the hill.

"I reckon this is where Mr. Hardcastle told the phaeton to wait," Amos said.

"Yes, and the church is over there."

We rode toward it. The morning service was long over and evensong still some hours away, so the only people to be seen were a woman standing by a grave and a man sweeping the porch. Amos dismounted to help me down and offered to hold the horses while I went inside.

Now the time had come I felt nervous, more than half convinced I was wasting our time. I took two shillings from my pocket and slid them inside my glove, then walked toward the porch, stiff from the long ride. As I'd hoped, the man sweeping the porch was the churchwarden. On the ride, I'd thought of various ways of working up to what I wanted, but in the end it was better to come straight out with it.

"May I please see your register of marriages?"

He gave me a stare. I think my nervousness showed. It occurred to me that he might have taken me for a wronged fiancée, abandoned by a lover who'd found somebody else.

"Recent marriage, was it?"

"Oh yes, very recent. About a month ago."

He put down his broom, turned and opened the door. I followed him into the church and down a side aisle. At the end of it he took a bunch of keys from his pocket and unlocked the door to a small room. Inside were a plain table, a few upright chairs, a cupboard. The place smelled of ink and old dust. Slowly, he sorted out another key from his ring and unlocked the cupboard, revealing a stack of leather-bound books. He took the top one, opened it and put it on the table.

"These are this year's."

I thanked him and gave him the two shillings for his trouble. He stood very close to me while I looked at the book, as if scared I might rip a page out. There were about a dozen entries for the year, but one leaped out at me. *The Rt. Hon. Rodney Hardcastle.* Beside it, a sprawling signature and a second clearer signature in neat, rounded handwriting, *Margaret Priddy.* Below it, the signatures of two witnesses. One meant nothing to me. The other, in tiny handwriting, was Marie Duval. The date was early February, two weeks before Columbine was murdered.

The whole thing came as such a shock that my face probably confirmed what the churchwarden suspected about a faithless lover. It was almost the reverse. Hardcastle hadn't been as faithless as we all thought. Instead of abandoning Columbine for a rich bride, he'd married her.

Chapter Eighteen

"*I'm sorry, but I fail to see how the deceased's* alleged marriage to Mr. Hardcastle makes any difference to the case."

Monday morning, the day of Jenny's trial. Toby Kennedy and I had arrived at the doors of the Old Bailey before eight o'clock to catch our barrister on his way in. Somebody else was there before us: Daniel, in dark coat and hat, his pale face newly shaven by some unskillful barber, with cuts on the lip and cheek.

"You shouldn't be here," Kennedy had said to him.

"Do you think I'd be anywhere else?"

We might as well have argued with a statue. When Charles Phillips arrived some time later, with a train of clients and solicitors in tow, Daniel had tagged along with the rest. Now we were standing on the first-floor landing between the two courtrooms, all still in our outdoor clothes and collecting some curious looks from court officials and other barristers going up and down stairs. In less than half an hour, the judges would be taking their seats on the bench.

Mr. Phillips was a courteous man and doing his best to listen patiently, but it was clear he was less than pleased to see us.

"It's not just an alleged marriage," I said. "I've seen the entry in the register. If necessary, we can produce the coachman who drove Mr. Hardcastle to Hampstead."

"Very well, grant that the marriage took place . . ."

"Just two weeks before her death," Kennedy put in.

". . . that still does not imply any connection. You seem to be claiming that her murder was in some way a consequence of her marriage."

"Surely it casts some doubt?" Daniel said.

Phillips gave him a black look. He'd been doing his best to pretend that Daniel wasn't there. I daresay barristers are skilled at being selectively blind, but Daniel wasn't making it easy.

"Only if it gives another person a clear motive for murder," Phillips said. "Who gains by her death? Certainly not Mr. Hardcastle, if that's what you're implying."

"He'd have her money," Kennedy said.

"Was she a wealthy woman? Not that it's relevant to her murder—the money would be his whether she lived or died," Phillips said.

"As a wife, she'd have been an embarrassment to Hardcastle," Kennedy persisted, taking the line he and I had discussed on the way there. "His family would have disapproved strongly."

"So within two weeks of marrying her, he poisons her? You are intelligent people, surely you can see that to stand up in court and imply that the son of a noble and distinguished father is a murderer on no evidence but a string of perhapses is not the way to help Miss Jarvis?"

"Then what is?" Daniel burst out. "He mustn't be mentioned because his family's rich and titled and she can hang because hers isn't?"

Phillips shook his head.

"That's hardly fair. I promise you, if I knew another person to be guilty, I'd stand up and proclaim it in court were he the son of the highest in the land. As it is, we must follow the course that we've set from the start. The chain of evidence against Miss Jarvis isn't complete. Our strongest point is that no evidence has so far been produced that she was present in the theater on the night of the murder. On the other hand, our weak point is that she can be proved to be in possession of a quantity of the poison that was used."

"Not at the time that mattered," I said. "It was actually in my possession."

Kennedy had already told him that. He looked hard at me.

"Miss . . . Miss Lane, is it? I will tell you, I had thought of putting you in the witness box on that very point."

"Do it. I'll tell the court gladly."

It was in my mind all the time that, in taking the basket to Daniel's house, I'd put one of the most damaging pieces of evidence against Jenny into the hands of the police. I'd have given almost anything for a chance to put that right, but Mr. Phillips shook his head.

"If you did go in the witness box, counsel for the prosecution would have a right to cross-examine you on your evidence."

"That doesn't worry me. It's the truth."

"But is it the whole truth? Suppose I'm counsel for the other side and I ask: 'Miss Lane, were you aware of the contents of the basket?' You see? You have to hesitate. 'Did you open the packet of thorn apple seeds? When you first saw it, was the packet sealed and complete?' I can see from your face that it wasn't, and the jury would see it too. Then I'd close in with the most damning question of all . . ."

"What's that?"

"'What did you do with the basket, Miss Lane? Did you do your duty as a citizen and hand it in to the police?' You didn't, did you? You took it to the house of a certain gentleman who happened to be harboring Miss Jarvis and might even now have to face a charge on that account."

"Do you think I care about that?" Daniel said.

"It's not a question of whether you care about it or not. It's a question of whether all this would be any use in the defense of Miss Jarvis, and I assure you it would be quite otherwise. We must do the best we can with what we have and what we can do to gain the sympathy of the jury. Yes, Mr. Lewis, I'll be with your client directly."

This to a man who'd been standing on the landing for most of our conversation, trying to attract his attention. He turned back to us.

"I'm sorry, I'm engaged in court number two this morning as well. One last word—" He looked directly at Daniel for the first time in the conversation. "Once the case begins, I must impress on you that any word—even so much as a sound—from one of you in court will have the gravest consequences. It would result in your own imprisonment for contempt and inevitably turn the jury's mind against Miss Jarvis. You understand that?"

We nodded. Phillips was already making his way downstairs with his train of followers in tow.

There was a queue of people waiting to get into the spectators' gallery of court number one. There were twenty or so, mostly men but two or three women among them, chatting quietly to one another like seasoned theatergoers. I saw nobody I recognized so I guessed they were ghouls who attended murder trials from morbid interest. When the doors of the spectators' gallery opened, they had coins ready to slip into the palm of the man who showed us in and barged through, jostling one another up the stairs, eager to get good seats. We hadn't realized that we'd have to pay for the privilege of watching justice done, so by the time we'd sorted out the necessary money and climbed the stairs, only a small space on the back bench was left. We crammed ourselves into it and I had my first view of the most notorious criminal court in the land.

Opposite us was a line of windows, below them two empty rows of high-backed benches like church pews. To our right, a high curved table and three chairs for the judges dominated the room, with the royal coat of arms and a symbolic sword of justice behind them. Most of the rest of the court was taken up by a horseshoe-shaped table covered in green baize, which was piled high with thick legal books and stacks of papers tied up in pink tape. Several barristers were already in attendance, sitting on the benches alongside the table and chatting among themselves in a friendly and relaxed way, as if they were discussing the weekend's jollities rather than the legal battle that lay ahead.

Since nothing seemed to be happening in court yet, I let my mind go back to the idea that had been running around it since the ride back from Hampstead. I hadn't talked about it to anybody. Mr. Phillips had been annoyed enough by our theories as it was. If I'd as much as mentioned this idea to him, he might have parted company with us altogether. Kennedy had come closest to it when he'd said that Hardcastle's family would disapprove of the marriage, but even he wouldn't guess the rest. Naturally, any family with a position to keep up would be dismayed if their eldest son married a woman ten years or so older than he was, who had several notorious affairs to her credit, earned a living from showing her figure onstage and had started out in life squeezing the udders of cows. If the head of the family happened to be a distinguished statesman in the House of Lords, the prospect of the family coronet sitting on the milkmaid's head would be ten times worse. Still, once the marriage was made, there was nothing they could do about it. Or rather, only one thing . . .

If I'd never met Hardcastle's mother, my thinking would have stopped at that point. I'd have assumed that she was an ordinary example of her class, incapable of the ruthlessness and quickness of mind that makes a successful criminal. But I had met her, and I couldn't forget the intelligence in her eyes, or her quick thinking when she'd lied to me. I remembered her voice, too: *Everything's predictable, if only you know enough.* Perhaps a mind that found no difficulty in going backward or forward nine hundred years to hold the planets to account would scarcely have to exert itself in planning how to poison a dancer.

A stir in the courtroom below ended my reverie. The jury were filing into the pewlike benches, twelve men in dark suits with solemn faces, moving slowly as if weighted down with their own temporary importance. They looked what they probably were: moderately successful tradesmen and householders. The youngest of them was perhaps thirty, the majority middle-aged. One with silver hair and a bony forehead looked as if he might be intelligent; a pale wispy one seemed kind but ineffectual; a plump one bad-tempered and inclined to indigestion. But these were no more than passing differences; once settled in their two rows they became a collective creature, as much a part of the courtroom as the carved judges' chairs or the green baize table.

"Please be upstanding."

A shouted command from an official we couldn't see from the gallery brought lawyers and spectators to their feet as the three judges came in and took their places. Mr. Phillips arrived in the room with only seconds to spare, grabbing his wig and gown from a peg at the back of the room. Because I was looking at the judges I missed the event on the opposite side of the courtroom. Only the turning heads of the more experienced spectators in the front row gave notice that the object of all this solemnity had arrived. When I looked in that direction, Jenny was standing in the dock.

She seemed simply too small for the part that events had forced on her. Her slimness and fragility made the whole courtroom seem like an oversize stage set built by carpenters who'd misread the plan. The dock that would have held three burly ruffians side by side was a world too wide for her. She stood there expression-less, as if she'd been lowered into it like a puppet on strings. A lamp that must have been placed deliberately close to the dock so that the prisoner's face could be clearly seen emphasized the blue hollows round her eyes and the sharpness of her cheekbones. Its cruel light made the natural copper color of her hair, still streaked with black dye, look like a garish wig. Beside me, I felt Daniel's arm go as hard as stone.

We all sat down, then the barristers and clerks sprang to their feet, said a few incomprehensible words, sat down again. Another voice, from a man we couldn't see, announced *"Regina versus Jarvis,"* the charge was read and Jenny was asked to plead guilty or not guilty. She managed "Not guilty" in a firmer voice than I'd expected, but still with that blank look on her face.

Then the prosecuting barrister began to set out his case. He had an eagle's beak of a nose and was so fierce-looking that I'd expected thundering denunciations or bullying. The ordinariness of his delivery came as a surprise. At first he didn't seem to take any notice of the woman in the dock as he quietly took the judges and jury through the known facts of Columbine's death. The only hint of drama came when he described Jenny's arrest, making much of the fact that she had been hiding in a cupboard and had gone to some trouble to avoid being recognized by dyeing her hair. Throughout, he referred to her as "the prisoner." As the trial went on, I realized that this was general practice, but it seemed unfair to me. Of course she was a prisoner, but the repetition of that seemed to suggest guilt ahead of the verdict.

The first witness was the doctor called in by the police, who gave his opinion that Columbine—now referred to under her given name, Miss Priddy—had died from ingestion of a nar-cotic poison, probably *Atropa belladonna* or *Datura stramonium,* known as thorn apple. Prompted by the barrister, he told how he had been shown a sample of syllabub at the police office, with ground-up dark fragments in it which might have been from the root of *Atropa belladonna* or the seeds of *Datura stramonium*. Either would have been quite readily procurable since, in lower doses, both were used to treat inflammations or other common conditions.

Mr. Phillips rose to cross-examine the witness.

"In the case of either poison, would not the victim have had to consume some quantity to cause death?"

"No, sir. Both substances are highly poisonous. There are cases of death resulting from the ingestion of a few seeds."

"Have they a taste?"

"The taste would be bitter."

"Does it surprise you that the victim should not be conscious of the taste?"

"To some extent yes, sir. But if the syllabub were highly sugared and made with sherry, that might disguise the taste enough for a lethal quantity to be ingested."

"But it does surprise you?"

"As I said, to some extent."

Phillips sat down, looking more satisfied with that small victory than I thought he should be.

The next witness was Barnaby Blake. Somebody had to tell the story of what happened backstage at the Augustus, and the manager was the obvious person. The prosecuting barrister led him through the events of the night Columbine died, simply confirming what the court had heard already. Then we came to what we all knew would be the dangerous part.

"Mr. Blake, can you tell the court of the circumstances in which you first met the prisoner."

"Yes, sir, it was about three and a half months ago, early December. We were seeing dancers for our pantomime and Miss Jarvis presented herself and was engaged."

I liked the fact that he called her Miss Jarvis.

"Did you know anything of her background?"

"I knew she came from the country and had not danced on the London stage before, but she had some ability."

"And when the pantomime season was finished, you engaged her for other productions?"

"Yes. Her performances had been satisfactory."

He hadn't looked at Jenny, but I hoped and believed he was doing his best for her.

"Was her behavior offstage equally satisfactory?"

"Yes. She was punctual and respectful. I never heard any complaints."

"Was she helpful to the other dancers in any way?"

"What do you mean?"

"It's a simple question, isn't it? Did the prisoner perform any particular services for her fellow dancers?"

"Do you mean her ointments and lotions?"

"Answer the question, please."

"Dancers are always suffering sprains and bruises. She had some skill with herbs and would treat them."

"You are telling the court that the prisoner had knowledge of herbs?"

"That's what I said, yes."

"Did she keep a stock of herbs by her?"

"I believe so, yes."

"Did she keep a basket of herbs with her?"

"I think I may have seen her taking remedies out of a basket."

"Think you may have?"

Blake let annoyance show in his voice.

"I am the manager of a busy theater, sir. I can hardly be expected to know about every possession of every dancer."

"But you knew that she treated other dancers' injuries. I repeat, did she to your knowledge possess a basket of herbs?"

"I may have seen her with a basket. I can't be sure."

The barrister looked satisfied at having planted the basket well and truly in the minds of the jury. Beside me, Daniel stirred uneasily.

"At what point were you aware of enmity between the prisoner and Miss Priddy?"

Blake looked worried and hesitated before answering.

"I was not aware of any enmity at first."

"At first?"

"I mean, when we first engaged Miss Priddy as a soloist, in early February."

"But you became aware of enmity later?"

"Yes."

"When was that?"

"On the night that everybody knows about."

Some of the people round us laughed. The judge sitting in the middle leaned forward and spoke quite courteously.

"Mr. Blake, this court knows nothing of the circumstances except what it is told in evidence. Please answer the question."

So Blake had to go through the wretched business of the fight onstage. It seemed artificial to me. Even judges must have heard about it at the time. Blake gave his evidence as neutrally as possible, but there was no disguising the facts. I could feel the people around us settling comfortably in their seats and something like a silent sigh of satisfaction went round the gallery. This was what they'd paid their money for.

"Did you know of any reason for this enmity?" the barrister asked.

"There is quite often bad feeling and jealousy between artistes, sir."

Blake must have known much more than that. Was he trying to protect Jenny, or Columbine's memory, or Hardcastle?

"But it doesn't usually lead to murder, does it?" the barrister said.

"Objection," said Phillips, rising halfway to his feet.

The judge told the prosecuting barrister to withdraw the question. He nodded and tried another.

"Did you speak to the prisoner after the altercation onstage?"

"No, sir."

"Why not?"

"She wasn't there to speak to."

"In other words, she'd run off."

"Objection."

Again, Mr. Phillips's objection was upheld by the judge. The prosecution asked a few more questions without producing much additional information, then Mr. Phillips took his turn at cross-examining. He got to his feet, adjusted his gown, then smiled at Barnaby Blake as if they were friends who had happened to meet in the street.

"You told us, sir, that Miss Jarvis's performances were satisfactory enough for you to continue her engagement?"

"Yes indeed."

"And until the incident which you described, her performance and her general behavior were to your satisfaction?"

"Yes."

"The court has heard that she used her skills to help her fellow dancers. Would you say she got on well with them?"

Blake hesitated again. "In the main, yes."

"You have reservations?"

"She was quite shy, for a dancer. And, as I said, she came from the country while most of our girls are Londoners. I think they may sometimes have laughed at her a little."

"Did she appear to resent that?"

"No."

"In other words, she struck you as an innocent country girl, not used to the ways of the big city."

The prosecuting barrister seemed about to object to the word "innocent" but thought better of it.

"Yes, sir."

"You described the altercation onstage for us. One thing you neglected to say was which of the ladies struck the first blow."

Laughter. One of the judges glared at the gallery. Blake looked toward the middle judge, as if for rescue, and was told to answer the question.

"I was not aware of what was happening onstage until somebody called my attention to it. I didn't see the start of it."

"So you can't comment on reports that it was Miss Priddy who opened hostilities?"

"Objection."

The objection was upheld. Phillips smiled, knowing at least he'd reminded the jury of the gossip at the time, and moved on.

"Whoever began it, may I take it that Miss Jarvis would have been in serious trouble as a result of her actions?"

"Yes."

"She would have faced your anger and probable dismissal?"

"Yes."

"In the light of that, and of her admitted shyness, do you find it surprising that she should have left the theater precipitately?"

"Objection. My learned friend is asking the witness to express an opinion."

"Very well, I withdraw the question. Did you see Miss Jarvis again after that evening?"

"No."

"Did you, as manager, hear any reports from other people that she entered the theater at any time?"

"No."

"Did you see her in or near the theater on the night of Miss Priddy's death?"

"No."

Mr. Phillips smiled as if he'd made a significant point. He went on with his sympathetic questions to establish two more things that seemed to satisfy him. The first was that anybody who'd worked backstage at the Augustus while Columbine was there could have known about her habit of eating syllabub every day. The second was that, with a performance in progress, the backstage area was a crowded and busy place, with nobody keeping records of who came or went.

Finally Barnaby Blake was allowed to leave the witness box. He seemed visibly relieved as he stepped down.

"I think he did the best he could for her," Kennedy whispered to me.

The next witness for the prosecution was one of the two police constables who had arrested Jenny at Daniel's lodgings. He was a self-satisfied man and managed to make the capture of an unresisting girl sound as if he'd put life and limb at risk. When asked what color her hair had been at the time, he replied, "Black, sir, jet-black," in a tone that made it sound like a sin in itself. I looked across at the jury, hoping they'd recognize him for the pompous fool he was, and was disconcerted to see them drinking in every word. Up until then, the calmness of the proceedings had lulled me into thinking that things might be all right after all, but this sent a chill through me.

Phillips, cross-examining, asked a question which we all knew was treading on dangerous ground.

"Did Miss Jarvis attempt to resist arrest?"

"There were people throwing things and carrying on like . . ."

"We're not talking about other people, Constable. We're talking about the young woman in the dock. I ask you again: did she try to resist arrest?"

"No, sir, not as such."

"Did you seize any of her possessions when you arrested her?"

"Her basket, sir."

"Did she identify it as hers?"

"Yes."

"Was it this basket, Constable?"

The barrister nodded to a court usher, who carried a wicker basket over to the witness box. Jenny's basket, the one that had sat unregarded for four days in the corner of our parlor.

"Yes, sir."

"Did you examine its contents?"

"We did when we got it back to the station, sir."

"Did the contents include this . . . ?"

Drawing out the drama, the barrister walked slowly over to the usher, opened the lid of the basket and pulled out an untidy brown paper package.

"Was this package among them?"

"Yes, sir."

"You're sure of that?"

"Yes, sir."

"In this condition, as if somebody had opened it and done it up again hurriedly?"

"Objection!" Phillips was on his feet. "The constable is being asked to give an opinion on something he could not have witnessed."

The judge upheld the objection.

"Very well. Was the package in much the same condition as you see it now?"

"Yes, sir."

"Did you show the package to anybody?"

"To the doctor, sir."

The doctor was recalled to the witness box and testified that, on the day following the prisoner's arrest, he had been shown the basket and the package in question. The prosecution barrister asked him if he'd been able to form an opinion as to what the package contained.

"The leaves, seedpods and seed of *Datura stramonium*."

"A poison?"

"As I said, highly poisonous."

"Is it easily procurable by a layperson?"

"Reasonably so. Many chemists sell it."

"Would you be surprised to find it in the collection of a young woman who, we are told, treated bruises and sprains?"

Phillips objected. The judge overruled it.

"Somewhat surprised," the doctor said.

When it came to Phillips's turn to examine the witness, he seized on this.

"You say you were only *somewhat* surprised. Might there be any innocent reason for a person to possess it?"

"Yes. In low doses, it is effective in treatment of ulcers, inflammations and various other conditions."

"So the simple possession of it does not imply the intention of doing harm?"

"No."

Again, Phillips sat down looking as if he'd scored a great point, but I could see from the faces of the jury that they weren't impressed.

Chapter Nineteen

Soon after that, the court rose for lunch. Daniel stared at Jenny as she was taken down from the dock, willing her, I think, to look up and see him. She didn't. We held back while the other spectators filed down the stairs.

"She's a hard one, isn't she?" one of the women said. "That stare of hers sends shivers through you."

It hadn't struck me until then that Jenny's shocked blankness could be interpreted as defiance.

Outside, the smell of roast beef spread over the landing and the sound of male laughter came from behind closed doors. Judges and their officials dine well at the Old Bailey. Daniel wanted to look for Mr. Phillips and ask him about points he thought should have been made; Kennedy practically had to drag him out of the building and across the road to the coffeehouse. All the while, Daniel kept asking in various ways if we thought it was going well for Jenny.

"Surely Blake could have spoken up more for her."

"Blake did what he could," Kennedy said. "Any more and the jury would have thought he was too much on her side."

"Why didn't Phillips ask him about Columbine and Hardcastle?"

"Because it would only have been hearsay. If we wanted it in evidence, Phillips would have had to put Hardcastle in the witness box, and that wouldn't have helped Jenny."

"There must be more he can do."

"Wait for his final speech to the jury," Kennedy said. "Everybody says he's the most eloquent man at the criminal bar."

At four o'clock we filed back into the spectators' gallery. All the gas lamps had been lit, casting giant shadows of the barristers wavering round the walls. They were clearly agitated. The prosecution barrister and Phillips seemed to be arguing hotly, though in low voices. At one point Phillips slammed a book down on the green baize table with such force that everybody's eyes turned to him. Soon after that, the judges came back in and Jenny was brought back into the dock. The prosecution barrister remained on his feet as everybody else sat down.

"My lords, as you know, we are asking leave to call an additional witness."

A murmur ran round the public gallery. Everyone had assumed that the doctor had been the last witness, with only the barristers' final speeches and the judges' summing up still to come. The middle judge gave a grave nod, confirming something that had already been decided. From Phillips's furious expression it was obvious that he had been arguing to the last ditch and lost.

The usher's voice sounded faintly from the corridor outside: "Call Jane Wood."

The name meant nothing to me, but beside me Daniel said, quite loudly, "What are they doing?" Kennedy and I shushed him.

The woman who came into the box was in her early twenties, wearing a plain dress and a dark bonnet over a round, snub-nosed face. It took me a moment to recognize her as one of the dancers from the Augustus. I'd seen her onstage and in the dressing room but never heard her utter a word. There'd been nothing remarkable about her. She was sworn in, her Cockney voice nervous but clear. She didn't glance at Jenny, who stood looking down at the edge of the dock as if none of this had anything to do with her. The prosecution led Jane through the opening questions, establishing that she was employed as a dancer at the Augustus and had been present at the theater on the night of the murder.

"Do you recognize the prisoner in the dock?"

She glanced now, then quickly away again.

"Jenny Jarvis."

It was simply a statement of fact, neither liking nor enmity in her voice.

"When did you last see the prisoner?"

"That night. The night she was poisoned."

Kennedy was having to struggle to keep Daniel in his seat, bringing angry looks from the spectators around us.

"Do you mean the night Miss Priddy was poisoned?"

"Miss Priddy?"

"Columbine."

"Yes."

"Where did you see the prisoner on that night?"

"In our dressing room."

"Do you mean the dancers' dressing room at the theater?"

"That's what I said, yes."

"In what circumstances?"

"Eh?"

"What were you and she doing when you saw her?"

"I'd forgotten me garland. I had to go running back for it."

"Garland?"

She stared at the barrister as if he were slow-witted.

"Me flowers, for the ballet."

"So you went back to the dressing room for your garland. Was anybody there?"

"I told you. She was. Jenny. I said I was surprised she was showing her face there, after what happened."

"And what did she reply?"

"She said she was looking for her basket. I said somebody had taken it away."

"Did she say anything to that?"

"If she did, I didn't hear it. The music for the ballet was starting so I had to shift like a dog with a boot up its backside."

Mr. Phillips took his turn, rising heavily as if the weight of the world were on his shoulders. He tried to unsettle her on the precise time she'd seen Jenny in the dressing room, without success. She had no idea what time it was by the clock, but was adamant that it was just before the first ballet started.

"Did she say anything about Columbine?"

"No."

"Did you see her going toward Columbine's dressing room?"

"I wouldn't have, would I? She was still in our dressing room when I had to go onstage."

"Then you have no knowledge that she was anywhere but in the dancers' dressing room?"

"No."

"Why have you waited until now to give this evidence?"

"I didn't know it mattered before, did I?"

Jane Wood was allowed to leave the witness box. In the worst of circumstances, sounding both tired and disappointed, Phillips began his speech for the defense. It was a good enough speech, in its way, but he'd planned it before this last depressing evidence. In his calm Irish brogue he set out the logical arguments for the defense. It had been established that on a performance night in the theater, anybody could come and go backstage entirely unchallenged. Dozens of people were employed at the theater and all of them had friends or families with whom they would discuss events there. As a result, hundreds of people were in a position to know about Miss Priddy's habit of taking nothing but syllabub on performance days. As for a knowledge of herbs—if that were a sign of murderous guilt, then tens of thousands of respectable housewives would stand in fear of arrest. There were even a few laughs from the gallery at that.

"And so we come to the question of events onstage at the Augustus," Mr. Phillips said. "An event so widely reported and discussed naturally attracts to it all manner of embroidery and exaggeration. If in the strain and heat of a stage performance one dancer accidentally impedes another, words may be said and actions performed that are not as ladylike as we might hear or see in drawing rooms. A more experienced performer than my client—a young woman unused to the rough and tumble of the city—might have known that. Consider, gentlemen, her situation. She has flitted like a butterfly from her native countryside to perform her art on a wider stage. But she remains innocent, unblemished. She is respectful to her employer, kindly to her fellow dancers—even if they are not always appreciative enough of her kindness. Then, one evening her world is reduced to ruins. She faces anger and dismissal from her employers, ridicule on the streets of London. What should she do but seek out some dark corner to hide herself? Then, gentlemen, a worse nightmare ensues. She is dragged from her hiding place and thrust into the pitiless light of this court, accused of the very worst of crimes. All she can do, as she has done, is to declare her innocence and trust to your judgment. The case against her is flawed and circumstantial. It lies in your hands to give her justice and permit her to return to the kindly countryside that she must regret so bitterly ever having left."

He sat down, head bowed. I think he was genuinely affected by his own eloquence. But it had failed, I knew that. I'd sensed it from the fidgeting of the jurymen, the glances exchanged by a man and woman on the benches in front of us, the way one of the judges picked up a pen and pretended to make notes, though there was nothing in particular to note down. Kennedy looked at me, then quickly away again. He knew too.

The prosecuting barrister hardly raised his voice in delivering his final speech and used no eloquence to embroider the facts. He had no need. Jenny and Columbine had fought. Jenny had knowledge of the use of herbs, of Columbine's habits and the arrangements backstage at the Augustus. Jenny had hidden from the police and disguised herself. Jenny had possessed deadly thorn apple. Although there was no direct evidence that she had introduced the poison into the bowl, she'd had motive, means and opportunity, and the fact that she had not come forward when she must have known the police were looking for her spoke for itself.

The middle judge gave his directions to the jury, scrupulously fair. He summed up the established facts and told them if there were any reasonable doubt in their minds, then they should find the prisoner not guilty. I looked at their faces as they filed out and saw no sign of doubt.

Jenny was taken down from the dock, still without looking up.

"They'll be back in ten minutes," said the woman in front of us.

It took them fourteen minutes by Kennedy's watch. They came in, heads bent. Jenny had been brought back into the dock. When the foreman of the jury said the word "guilty" her mouth opened slightly and that was all. The judge, sounding as if he genuinely regretted having to do it, pronounced sentence.

"Jenny Jarvis, you are sentenced to be taken hence to the prison in which you were last confined and from there to a place of execution where you will be hanged by the neck until dead and thereafter your body buried in the precincts of the prison and may the Lord have mercy on your soul."

Jenny said and did nothing until the warder behind her put his hand on her shoulder, quite gently, to guide her back down to the cells. Then she screamed, the high, terrified scream of a child waking up and finding the monster from the nightmare is still there in the corner of the bedroom.

Her scream continued echoing in the courtroom long after she'd been taken down.

Chapter Twenty

"What will help her then? Tell me that."

We'd just come up from the cell after seeing Jenny. Daniel stood with his knuckle bleeding in drops onto the greasy pavement outside the Old Bailey, oblivious of the crowds round us. Toby Kennedy was trying to cross the road to get to us, dodging carts.

"Is it true about Jenny being inside the theater that night?" I said.

I understood now why he'd kept away from me and why he hadn't wanted to face my questions. Kennedy joined us in time to hear Daniel's answer.

"Yes, it's true."

"Then for God's sake why didn't you tell us, man?" Kennedy burst out, more angry than I'd ever known him. "Didn't you see it would make it a thousand times worse if it came out the way it did? Charles Phillips is furious, and I don't blame him."

"What could we do? It made things so black against her. And when Jane Wood didn't speak up at first, we thought she wasn't going to."

"You were outside the theater that evening," I said. "I suppose you saw Jenny coming out. Was that when you decided to take her home and hide her?"

"No, I didn't find her until the day after. She'd been hiding in the cellars of her lodgings at Seven Dials. I couldn't leave her there. She told me that she'd been in the dancers' dressing room on the night Columbine died, but I said she mustn't admit it. I knew the police would think it closed the case against her. What else could I do?"

"Be honest with your friends at least," Kennedy said. "Is there any other little detail you haven't told us, like Jenny having committed murder?"

"No!"

For a moment I thought Daniel was going to hit Kennedy. I could see Kennedy thought so too, but he stood his ground. His angry expression changed to a look of great sadness.

"Why didn't you tell us? We could have done something." He took Daniel's arm. "Look, there's a gig for hire over there. We'll go and—"

Daniel pulled his arm away and took a few steps, not toward the gig but back toward the doors of the Old Bailey. Two police constables were standing outside it. I went after him.

"Don't."

"I'm sorry, Libby."

"They won't believe you. It will only make things worse."

By then Kennedy had his arm again. The policemen looked on, mildly curious. Emotional scenes outside those doors were nothing new.

"Not another lie," I said to Daniel. "You're not good at them."

"I'm going back inside there to tell them I killed her."

Kennedy let go of his arm and stood in front of him, his voice quiet.

"My friend and brother, if you look me in the eye and tell me you killed Columbine, then I'll go in with you and support you all I can to the end."

Daniel looked at him, opened his mouth to speak, said nothing.

"Well then," Kennedy said.

He took Daniel's arm again and led him unresisting over the road to the gig.

Kennedy gave the driver the address of his own lodgings in Holborn and informed Daniel that he was coming to stay and they'd send to Bloomsbury Square for his things later.

As the driver ground his way through the traffic coming from Smithfield, Kennedy told us about the short conversation he'd managed with the barrister after the verdict.

"I asked him about an appeal. As I understand it, there can be two grounds. One is that legal mistakes were made in the course of the trial, the other is that the sentence was too harsh. Phillips needs time to cool down and consider it, but his view is that the trial was properly conducted. The chief judge, Charles Law, is considered to be the fairest and most merciful on the bench . . ."

"He's just condemned an innocent woman to death," Daniel said.

"As for sentence, once the jury found her guilty of murder, there was only one sentence possible."

"Mr. Phillips holds out no hope?" I said.

"There is the royal prerogative of mercy, but . . ."

His voice trailed off. No mercy for poisoners.

"When?" Daniel said.

The meaning was unmistakable.

"I believe that at least two Sundays have to pass," Kennedy said.

That meant that Jenny might have only thirteen mornings of life left to her before she took the short walk from the condemned cell in Newgate to the gallows outside. I didn't see how Daniel could stay sane.

"So we're in exactly the position we were," I said. "The only way to change things is by finding new evidence."

I didn't mention Lady Silverdale. As yet I had no evidence at all, only a wild idea. "God knows, we've looked hard enough," Kennedy said.

He sounded weary and I couldn't blame him.

"But we haven't, have we?" I said. "It struck me in court, we've all accepted too easily that almost anybody could have got into Columbine's dressing room. Somebody must have seen something that evening."

"Marie?" Daniel said.

At least his mind was moving.

"Yes, Marie. Everybody else backstage would have their minds on the performance. All she had to do was look after Columbine."

"I thought she'd be a witness," Kennedy said.

"Yes, so did I. Perhaps the police can't find her either. That's why they had to put Barnaby Blake in the witness box instead."

"Don't you find it odd that the girl Wood should have decided to give evidence at the last minute?" Kennedy said.

"Very. Daniel, did she have any particular enmity against Jenny?"

"No. Jenny helped her when she'd hurt her knee and it seemed Jane liked her. That's why she thought Jane wouldn't give her away."

"What changed her mind, I wonder?"

My mind went to Pauline. I couldn't see what advantage there'd be in it for her, but perhaps she'd acted out of sheer malice. I'd have to pay another visit to the Augustus.

"We could advertise in the papers for Marie and offer a reward," Daniel suggested. "And I might ask Barnaby Blake if he has any ideas. He knows his way around."

These didn't seem particularly promising lines of inquiry, given that Marie was apparently reluctant to be found, but Kennedy and I were so relieved he was suggesting something with no risk to himself for once that we encouraged him.

When we drew up at Kennedy's lodgings, the Irishman looked at me, concerned.

"You're sure you don't mind taking the gig on yourself?" he said, putting some money for the fare into my hand.

I shook my head. I understood all too well why he could not escort me to my door. He didn't dare let Daniel out of his sight.

Mrs. Martley was sitting at the table, pasting up her scrapbook by lamplight. A lamb hot pot was warming by the fire, filling the room with the smell of gravy and onions. She took one look at my face and asked what was wrong now. I told her some of it as she fussed around, stoking up the fire, sitting over me while I ate as if I were an invalid. Now and again she sighed, "That poor Mr. Suter." But mercifully she didn't put into words what was obviously in her mind: that if I'd married Daniel months ago and taken care of him like a sensible woman instead of going gallivanting around, none of this would have happened.

I scribbled a note for Amos saying that I wouldn't ride for the next two mornings, fixed it to the door downstairs and lay awake most of the night, hearing the workhouse clock striking the hours from across the graveyard.

Tuesday turned out to be one of those days that never bothered to get properly light, the sky low and drizzling, people shuffling along in waterproofs or driving in closed carriages with drivers hunched on the boxes under their capes. As I walked past Lady Silverdale's house on my way to give a lesson, I was greatly tempted to ring the bell. I could picture those clear eyes on me as I asked, *Did you know your son had married Columbine, Lady Silverdale? Did you decide to do something about it?* She wouldn't have been able to predict that. Or would she? Her powerful, unconventional mind might be capable of anything.

What if she'd found out about the secret marriage? Not an impossible supposition, given her son's lack of discretion. Lady Silverdale seemed the type to take immediate and decisive action. Having the marriage annulled was one option, but it would have made the family a laughingstock, which was exactly what she wanted to avoid. Disposing of Columbine would have been much more effective. But how would she go about it? This wasn't Renaissance Italy, where aristocrats had trained poisoners on their staff for emergencies. She'd have had to find somebody to do the deed for her. Except, wouldn't it be simpler and safer to do it herself? Her nocturnal way of life and her husband's absence in the country would make it easier for her to come and go unobserved than most ladies of her class. The obedient daughter would probably not even look up from her notes if Mother chose to absent herself for an hour. It need take no more than that. I imagined her tripping downstairs, wrapped in a cloak with a hood over her cropped head, signaling a cab. For greater safety, she might even decide to walk. At the theater, she could slip in unnoticed at the stage door and . . .

And there it collapsed. She couldn't rely on trotting in with a pocketful of thorn apple seeds and just happening to find Columbine's syllabub bowl standing ready. Somebody inside the theater would need to have helped her. Perhaps she'd had somebody spying for her at the Augustus; it might have struck her as a sensible way of keeping check on her son's activities. If so, did her spy carry out the poisoning on her orders, or simply give her the information she needed?

The questions went round and round in my head the entire time I was teaching, and I'm afraid my pupil—quite a promising harpsichord player—for once did not receive the attention she deserved.

* * *

As soon as the lesson was over I walked to the Augustus, hoping to put some flesh on my skeleton of a theory. I'd been going about things the wrong way, considering everyone at the theater as either a possible killer or a witness. That approach had got nowhere because none of them seemed to have a reason for killing her. They might not have liked her, but as their leading attraction she brought in the audiences that paid their wages. And so far, all my inquiries had failed to produce a single witness. So I'd start again. Who among the artistes or backstage staff might have been a spy for Lady Silverdale? Somebody who needed money, probably; poorly paid and with an irregular income. Unfortunately, that covered just about everybody at the Augustus.

I arrived to find Billy in his room just inside the door, rearranging brooms and buckets and trying to look busy. He gave me a nod, visibly trying to remember my name and failing. I asked him if he'd seen Mr. Hardcastle recently.

"No, not since . . ."

"Since the evening Columbine was murdered?"

"That's right."

"Did you ever see his mother in the theater?"

"His mother?"

"Lady Silverdale."

No guilty start; he wasn't even interested. I'd no great hopes of Billy because he seemed too stupid to be anybody's spy, but I hoped to find more success along the corridor, in the dancers' room. Bel was there with two other girls. There was no sign of Pauline or Jane Wood.

The girls seemed subdued. I asked them if they knew why Jane Wood had decided at the last minute to give evidence.

"We didn't know she was going to," Bel said.

"Did she show up for the performance as usual last night?"

"Yes," Bel said. "We wouldn't speak to her."

"I suppose she didn't have no choice," one of the other girls muttered.

"Do you know how the police found out about her seeing Jenny in the dressing room?"

All three of them shook their heads.

"Had she said anything to you about it?"

More headshakes.

"When are they going to hang Jenny?" Bel said, not looking at me.

"In two weeks, perhaps."

"It's wrong, making them wait like this!" Bel practically shouted it. "If the judge says people are guilty, they should take them straight out and hang them, not make them wait. Can you imagine, waking up every morning and thinking . . . ?"

Tears flooded her eyes. One of the other girls ran over and put an arm round her.

"She liked Jenny," the girl explained.

I looked around for something to dry Bel's tears and spotted what looked like a piece of clean sheet on a chair. But when I picked it up there were brown smears down the middle of it.

"That don't matter," one of the girls said. "It's only the brown stuff we put on our faces to look Spanish."

I passed the cloth to Bel and she dabbed her eyes.

"Bel—all of you—if you can think of the slightest thing that would help Jenny, please tell me."

But Bel just went on sobbing while the girl rocked her in her arms.

My next stop was the Surrey family's dressing room. Mrs. Surrey was sitting in her petticoats at the table, adding up columns of figures. I guessed she was doing the family accounts and, from her frown, they were proving problematic. The girl, Susanna, dressed in doublet, hose and a hooded cape, had arranged herself picturesquely on a pile of moth-eaten cushions, fair hair flopping over the volume of Shakespeare she was studying. Her brother, David, was trying to get the caretaker's cat to take an interest in a woolen bobble on a string, while their father carried out repairs to the strapping for Richard's hump with needle and cotton, deft as a sailor stitching a sail.

I asked Mr. and Mrs. Surrey if they knew why Jane Wood had decided to give evidence against Jenny.

"We've been wondering about that ourselves," Honoria Surrey said. "Perhaps her conscience was troubling her."

She spoke softly and I guessed that they were reluctant to discuss the matter in front of the children, though from Susanna's expression she wasn't missing a word.

"Did you ever notice anybody in the cast or backstage taking a particular interest in Columbine?" I asked them.

"Everybody, I suppose," Surrey said. "Theater people love to gossip, and she was rather a phenomenon in her way."

"Putting it bluntly, can you think of anybody who might have been taking money to spy on her?"

They looked at each other and shook their heads.

"It's not impossible," Surrey said. "But we've not noticed anything, and we spend more time here than most."

The cat, refusing to take an interest in the woolen bobble, was pawing at one of the tapes trailing from Richard's hump. Robert Surrey twitched it away from him.

"David, will you please take that cat back to Billy. I don't want it undoing all my work."

With the rueful expression of a boy who is always in the wrong, David scooped up the cat. It settled purring in his arms and I opened the door for them.

"What's all this about Columbine again?" he muttered to me as they went out.

I shut the door and followed them into the corridor, remembering how I'd seen him sobbing on the night of Columbine's death. In the unaccountable way of boys, he must have taken a liking to Columbine and might still be grieving. I was sorry for him and thought he should be allowed to talk about her if he wanted. He took a few steps along the corridor and spoke over his shoulder.

"Why are they all making so much fuss about her? She was a horrible woman. I'm glad Jenny killed her."

"What? I thought you liked her."

I was so surprised, I let the remark about Jenny pass. He spun round, a scowl on his face like his father's when about to strangle his mother onstage.

"Like her? *Like* her? I detested her."

No muttering this time. He meant it.

"Why?"

"She called my mother a nobody, just because Mother wouldn't stand aside for her in the corridor. Actors are more important than dancers, everybody knows that. My mother had a right to go first." A dowager duchess arguing the order of precedence at a state banquet couldn't have been more vehement. "She was a she-wolf, a bottled spider."

He might not become the great Shakespearean actor of his generation, but his work had given him a good line in invective. I responded in kind.

"'The tailor make thy doublet of changeable taffeta, for thy mind is a very opal.'"

"Eh?"

He obviously hadn't encountered *Twelfth Night* yet.

"I mean, you've changed your mind. You were very upset on the night she died."

I thought of him standing there with the cat clutched to his chest for comfort, much as now.

"It wasn't her I was upset about. It was Geoffrey."

"Who?"

"The cat. I thought he was going to die too."

His voice had dropped back to a normal boyish mutter. I looked down at the cat. It stared complacently back at me.

"But there was nothing wrong with the cat, was there?"

"I thought he'd be poisoned too, because he'd eaten her syllabub."

"I think we'd better go back to the start on this," I said.

I put my arm round his shoulder and the three of us went along the corridor to the caretaker's room. Luckily, there was no sign of Billy. David put the cat gently on the floor and it buried its face in the feed bowl. I sat on Billy's stool.

"I'm not going to get into trouble, am I?" David said.

"No, but this might matter very much. Did you see the cat eating from the bowl in Columbine's dressing room the night she died?"

"Not from the bowl, no. From the saucer, like he usually did."

"Usually. You mean he did it more than once?"

"Yes. Billy knew about it too. It was a joke between us, you see. But it was my idea, not Billy's."

He told the story coherently, once he got started. After the perceived insult to his mother, he'd watched Columbine closely at rehearsal and been amused by all the ceremony around her, particularly the ritual of the syllabub. He and Billy took to referring to Columbine as the cat that got the cream. Then David decided that Geoffrey should have his share of the cream as well.

"It started because Susanna dared me to go in Columbine's room."

"Why?"

"We're always giving each other dares, my sister and me. It was easy. I knew when Columbine went onstage, and Marie would be waiting in the wings with a shawl to put round her when she came off, so the dressing room was empty."

"Was this the night she died?"

"Not the first time, no. The first time was when we were re-hearsing. I thought while I was in there I'd get some of the syllabub, for Geoffrey. So I went in with a saucer and a spoon, got some of the syllabub—but not enough so that they'd notice—and gave it to Geoffrey. He liked it."

"I'm sure he did. How many times did you do that?"

"Twice when she was rehearsing, then the last night."

"Did anybody but you and Billy know about it?"

"Susanna knew."

"Nobody apart from that?"

"No."

"And on the night Columbine died?"

"Just the same. I went in and got some of the syllabub while the first ballet was on."

"Did anybody see you?"

"No. I nearly got caught, though."

"Nearly?"

"When I was in there, I could hear the audience clapping and cheering at the end of the ballet, so I knew Columbine and the maid would be back in any moment."

"Did you notice anything different about the syllabub, like black flecks in it?"

"No."

"And the cat ate it as usual?"

"Straight down."

Geoffrey looked up from the feed bowl, licking his lips.

"Was he sick at all?"

"No. I kept him with me all the time. I was so afraid he'd die any minute. Only, he didn't."

"When you went into Columbine's dressing room, was any-body else there?"

"No."

"Did you see anybody hanging around outside in the corridor?"

"No."

"David, where are you?"

His father's voice from their dressing room.

"I must go," David said.

"I'll come with you."

Before we left, he bent to stroke the cat. I'd seldom seen a healthier feline specimen.

"Are you going to tell my father and mother about this?" he asked as we went along the corridor.

"I won't, but I think you should. You didn't do anything very wrong, after all, and this may be important."

"For Jenny Jarvis?"

"Yes."

"Why?"

"I don't know yet."

I wasn't keeping anything from him. What he'd told me had turned the whole case so completely upside down that I might as well have been standing on my head, like one of the boy acrobats.

Chapter Twenty-one

A dead rat and a live cat. When the police fed a sample of syllabub to a rat, it died. The cat had feasted on a saucerful of it and flourished. The only explanation was that poison had been put into the syllabub after the boy David stole some. But he'd left the dressing room just as Columbine was on her way back to it, and from then to her death she and Marie had been alone there all the time. So only Marie would have been able to put poison in the syllabub, unless somebody had added it in the confusion after Columbine's death—but what would be the point of that? The conclusion must be that Marie was guilty, or Columbine had been poisoned by something else. But Marie insisted that she hadn't eaten or drunk anything else all evening.

It all hinged on Marie and she could be in France by now. Or dead. As I walked home, going over and over what I'd learned, it came to me that, if somebody else had paid her to poison Columbine, he or she might have made sure of her silence by having her killed too. And yet she'd lived long enough to walk into a pawnshop with the incriminating earring. Why should Hardcastle or anybody else pay her off if he'd intended to kill her?

That night I slept restlessly, plagued by dreams of searching for Marie in unlikely places, wading up to my waist in the sea or in a wood, dragged back by clinging brambles. I had to give a lesson on Wednesday morning, and on arriving home I found a note in Amos Legge's splayed handwriting: *Old Morris reckons our man is trying to steal back the Stanhope that was took off him.* My head was aching enough without another puzzle. The sun had come out, so for the sake of exercise and fresh air I decided to walk across the park to the livery stables and find out directly what he was talking about. When I suggested to Mrs. Martley that she might come with me, she jumped at the chance. The decorators were still at work in Old Slippers's rooms and the racket they made—along with a reminder that we'd soon be homeless—was having a depressing effect. Her spirits rose as we crossed the road and went through Grosvenor Gate into the park. She looked around like a woman fresh up from the country at the lambs skipping and bleating, the gentlemen on horseback, the ladies in their carriages going out on afternoon calls.

"Just look at that bonnet, and she's older than I am. No woman over sixteen should wear yellow."

I supposed she'd got that from one of the ladies' magazines that were passed on to her. As we walked, she talked happily about the queen's coronation, due in three months' time. Though many months had passed since Alexandrina Victoria had succeeded to the throne, Mrs. Martley's enthusiasm had shown no sign of waning.

"I should love to see her in her coronation dress, shouldn't you? Maybe if we got up very early and stood outside the Abbey, or perhaps Buckingham Palace would be better."

"Buckingham Palace, I think."

I said it at random, not caring. I thought there'd be some sad changes for us long before the crown was placed on Little Vicky's sleek brown head, and where to stand for the coronation was the least of our worries.

Mrs. Martley was a good walker and strode out happily, her green skirt swishing around her sensible boots, shopping basket swinging.

"I can show you Rancie," I said.

She looked doubtful.

"I haven't had much to do with horses."

"She's a lady, I promise you; much more so than I am."

But when we walked through the gateway into the yard, the door to Rancie's box was hooked open, with only the cat Lucy washing herself on the straw inside.

"Legge's out with a lady and gentleman," one of the grooms said, recognizing me. "Should be back soon, if you'd like to wait."

Mrs. Martley had never been inside a fashionable stable yard before and was fascinated by the gigs and phaetons coming and going, and the ladies in their black satin riding habits, "just like the queen's."

Then, "Oh, look at that one just coming in. Isn't she lovely?"

I knew before I turned round what I'd see, so had a chance to steel myself. The sweetest, prettiest etc. woman in London riding Rancie with easy grace, a handsome young gentleman on the chestnut hunter at her side, Amos Legge behind them on the roan cob in his hat with the cockade, the perfect groom.

"That's Rancie," I said.

"What! You ride a lovely horse like that?"

"I not only ride her, I own her."

I said it through gritted teeth. It was true for a few more weeks, at any rate.

"But how . . . ?"

She looked from me to the group that had now drawn up in the middle of the yard, then back again.

"My father sent her to me. She was his last present before he was killed."

I'm not sure if she heard or believed me. Her eyes were on Miss Sweetest, being helped down from the saddle by both Amos Legge and the handsome young gentlemen, her eyes sparkling from the excitement of the ride. She stroked Rancie's neck and watched as Amos led her away. I turned aside so that she shouldn't recognize me. Amos gave me a nod and wished me good afternoon as he and Rancie went past. I followed them to the loose box.

"The man with her, is he the fiancé who wants to buy Rancie?"

Amos nodded, bending to undo the girth buckles.

"I should talk to him. Have you told him about her feed, how she must have sliced carrot with her oats and not too much barley?"

"All in good time."

"And Lucy? He knows the cat must go with her and be well treated? They'll both be miserable otherwise. If he doesn't promise that, I'm not selling her after all."

"Don't you go fretting yourself."

Amos balanced the saddle on the half door and started unbuckling the bridle.

"I think I should talk to him, all the same. Would you mind asking him to come over, on his own."

I could face him, just, but not the woman whose hand would soon be the one resting by right on Rancie's neck, as mine was now. I thought I'd give half of the guineas I got for her straight into Daniel's hand. He'd need them. If Jenny were hanged, I didn't think he'd stay in London. A good musician can find work anywhere. He might use the money to go to Paris or perhaps Vienna, where his family came from originally. As for Amos, I supposed he'd soon be traveling home to Hereford at last. He'd been on his way there ever since I met him.

"Who's old Morris and what's this about stealing the Stanhope?" I said, watching as he slipped the bit gently from Rancie's mouth and she nuzzled him in the ribs.

"That's the man who had it took back off him, that day in St. James's."

It started to make some sense. I remembered that Morris was one of the names on the advertising bill when Hardcastle's phaeton was repossessed. Amos took Rancie's rug from the hay manger and flipped it over her back, deft as a matador with a cloak. I fastened the buckles and waited for the story.

"Day after it was took back, Hardcastle went round to Morris's yard, pleading with them to let him have it back just for the one day. Said he had to drive somewhere. Well, Morris wasn't falling for that one. Some hard words were said and Hardcastle went away. Morris thought he'd heard the last of it. He's had a few gentlemen come to look at it, thinking of buying it, only he's asking too much. Seventy guineas is over the odds for a secondhand phaeton, and red's not to everybody's taste. That's why it's still on his hands, look."

"And Hardcastle?"

"Well, it might not be Hardcastle—though old Morris swears blind it is—but the fact is while Morris has had it locked up in his coach house somebody's tried twice to break in."

"Couldn't it be just ordinary burglars?"

"Pretty daft ones, if it was. What's the point of breaking into a coach house? You've always got an apprentice or a boy sleeping overhead, and you couldn't drag even a gig out over the cobbles without waking them up. Then if you wanted to move it any distance you'd have to bring a horse along with you. Does that sound like ordinary burglars?"

"But even Hardcastle wouldn't be stupid enough to try that."

The look Amos gave me said my wits were usually sharper than this.

"Oh, I see. It's not the phaeton itself he wants, it's something hidden in the phaeton."

Amos nodded. My mind went back to Columbine's dressing room and the slits in the couch and her muff.

"In the upholstery," I said. "That's the only place you could hide something in a phaeton. Do you think he's got her jewelry tucked away in there?"

"Not impossible. What I was thinking of was his marriage lines."

That might make sense too. He might want to find the marriage certificate for one of two reasons—either to prove his right to Columbine's property or to stop anybody else finding it and spreading the news around before he was ready. Still, I preferred the jewelry theory.

"Do you think Morris would let me have a look at the phaeton?" I said.

"You could always pretend to be interested in buying it, but I don't suppose he'd let you go poking round the upholstery and spoiling it."

"No. I'll have to think of something else. Shall we ride tomorrow as usual?"

"I'll be there."

Amos picked up the saddle and bridle and opened the door for me. I walked out into the sunlit yard and saw Mrs. Martley cautiously feeding a piece of carrot to a gray Shetland pony, surrounded by a group of children and their nursemaid.

"Look, isn't this one sweet?"

True to its breed, it tried to bite her on the bottom the moment she turned away. I shoved its nose aside just in time. Miss Sweetest and her fiancé had gone by then. I pretended to myself that I was sorry to have lost the chance to talk to him about Lucy, but knew I was grateful for the reprieve. Then I thought of a reprieve that wasn't going to happen and shivered. Mrs. Martley said, "Yes, there is a cold breeze, isn't there," and we walked briskly back to our own side of the park. And with every step I was wondering how to get under the red leather upholstery of the phaeton.

The idea came to me in the early hours of the morning. I explained it to Amos when we'd reined in after our first canter.

"We'd need Morris's help. He'd have to let it be known that the springs need attention and the phaeton will be going to the workshop under us for a couple of days. We want him to move it at the busiest time of day, so word would get to Hardcastle."

"Morris isn't what you'd call an obliging sort of a man."

"We'd be helping him catch Hardcastle red-handed."

"Even so."

"How much do you think he'd want?"

Amos thought about it.

"Five pounds might do it."

It was a lot of money, and I had to keep what was left of my small store for moving to new lodgings.

"I'll see what I can do," I said. "Will you sound him out?"

He said he'd do his best and would let me know on Saturday. Though I was burning with impatience to put my idea into practice, I had to be content with that.

On Friday I kept my usual appointment with the Talbots. They were my favorite clients and paid me for the whole morning to teach piano, singing and guitar to all of them, from mother down through seven children to three-year-old toddler. The father was a Yorkshire businessman who'd made a fortune inventing new machines for spinning and weaving wool. The family had decided to try the experiment of living in London and bought a big new house in Belgrave Square. Since they knew few people in society, spoke with Yorkshire accents and always said exactly what they thought, their chances of finding a welcome in the fashionable world seemed small. At first they were snubbed whenever they ventured out, but the snubs had no effect on them. In the end, their good nature, generosity and the excellent dinners they gave opened doors to them, but they remained as unaffected as ever.

Much as I liked them, I wasn't looking forward to a morning of teaching so it was just as well the household wasn't concentrating on music. Two big wicker hampers had been carried into the drawing room and Mrs. Talbot was unpacking them, straw spread over their Turkey carpets, children, cook and most of the maids in attendance. She was on her knees by one of the hampers when I was shown in, and the face she raised to me was as happy as a child's at Christmas.

"Oh, is that the time already? Please excuse us, Miss Lane, only the hampers have arrived from Shawdale."

Shawdale was the family estate in Yorkshire. Like many families in town, the Talbots had produce sent to them regularly, but typically they did it on a generous scale. I knelt down beside her and helped as she lifted treasure after treasure from the hamper, unswathing them from snow-white napkins: pork pies ornamented with pastry cutouts of leaves and roses, and glazed so brightly they reflected the light; rich fruitcakes with their tops cracking to show insides packed with raisins and cherries; almond tarts and spiced biscuits. A few of the tarts and biscuits were broken in spite of the care in packing. The children looked pleadingly at their mother and at a nod from her swooped on them like hungry birds. Four huge hams wrapped in muslin took up the corners of the hamper. Cook took charge and passed them to the maids. As they carried them off to the kitchen, I could see their noses twitching with pleasure at the smell and hoped there'd be some good off-cuts for them.

Mrs. Talbot turned her attention to the second hamper. They must have been good at storing fruit up in Shawdale because even at this time of year there were still apples, wrinkled but sweet-smelling, and a few pears. A deep bed of straw cradled jars of jam and chutney.

"Oh, excellent—Mrs. Percy has remembered the pickled wal-
nuts. Miss Lane, you must take a jar of her marmalade home. I
promise you, there's nothing like it in London."

One of the children came over to look, biscuit crumbs round
her mouth. She whispered in her mother's ear.

"What's that, darling? The parkin? She'll surely have remembered the parkin."

Mrs. Talbot plunged into the hamper again and came up with
a ginger-smelling cube, swathed in brown paper.

"There we are, three of them. Run to the kitchen and bring
three of the big blue plates and a knife. We don't want to get our
hands sticky." She turned to me. "I always think it isn't a parkin
unless it's sticky, don't you?"

I had to confess I didn't even know what a parkin was. A
Yorkshire specialty, apparently, a kind of ginger cake. When the
plates and knife were brought we had to cut into one of the par-
kins straight away to remedy my ignorance. It was nice enough, I
thought, but not so special as to deserve the look of bliss on Mrs.
Talbot's face when she bit into her slice. Perhaps she felt embar-
rassed by it, because when she'd finished eating she remarked how
you always liked best things you ate as children. I agreed.

"I remember a tart of *myrtilles* I ate with my father and brother
on a snowy day in spring when we were crossing a pass over the
Alps," I said. "My mouth waters now even to think of it."

We talked about food for a while, then she rang the bell to have
the empty hampers carried out and we settled down to some singing; rounds and folk tunes mostly, because the children were too
full of sweet things to settle to scales. In spite of that, she insisted
on paying me, and when I left I carried with me a jar of marmalade and a generous hunk of parkin. As usual, the morning with
the Talbots had raised my spirits. I didn't realize until some time
later what else it had done for me.

* * *

On Saturday, Amos told me the result of his talk with Morris the coach builder.

"He says he'll do it Monday morning for two days. I got him down to four pounds, but he won't go no lower."

After our ride I went straight into the workshop of Mr. Grindley the coach repairer to open negotiations. He was surprised that I was simply asking him to keep the phaeton under his roof for two days without doing anything to it, but business was slack and he had space for it. I thanked him with the jar of marmalade and went upstairs to see how I could raise four pounds by Monday. With the fee from the Talbots, I had one pound, seven shillings and four-pence in cash. I burrowed in my trunk and found at the bottom of it, wrapped in an old stocking, a silver belt buckle that had been a birthday present from one of my aunts in an expansive mood. More burrowing turned up a pair of kid gloves, unworn because they were too small for me, and a blue silk shawl in good condition. I liked it and wished I'd remembered it before when there was time to wear it, but it would have to go.

I hurried to the secondhand clothing shop where I'd bought my riding habit and got twelve shillings for the shawl and gloves. The pawnshop next door offered two pounds for the silver buckle. I bargained them up to two guineas, which brought my total to four pounds, one shilling and four pence. In spite of that, I left the shop feeling as depressed as one usually does after such visits. I promised myself a treat of a cup of tea and a slice of parkin when I got home, remembering the look of pleasure on Mrs. Talbot's face when she tasted it. Then a thought came to me and I stopped dead, causing a man walking behind me to dodge and curse women who didn't know where they were going. But in that moment I knew exactly where I was going. I turned round and walked toward Soho, where a lot of French people live. I'd made few inquiries for Marie there in the past, but without conviction since I thought she was south of the river.

The area around Soho Square was busy with customers shopping for their Saturday night meals. More French than English was being spoken and a smell of good coffee filled the air so that you could easily have thought yourself in a backstreet of Paris rather than the middle of London. I joined the queue at the baker's, trying to stop my stomach rumbling at the trays of crusty bread coming from the ovens and the rows of pastries in the windows, as nicely laid out as a flower garden. When it came to my turn at the counter I parted with three pennies in exchange for a large country loaf. The baker remembered me from previous inquiries for Marie and shook his head before I'd even asked the question. No sign of her.

I tried another question instead.

"Do you know where there's a good French bakery south of the river?"

"In Calais, mademoiselle."

He smiled and shook his head as I explained I meant the Thames, not the Channel. We were speaking French and the assistant who was taking loaves out of the oven with a long wooden paddle turned and muttered something I didn't catch.

"He says there's one near St. Thomas's Hospital," the baker told me. "He has a cousin used to work there."

With an impatient queue forming behind me I got further directions. As far as I could remember, it must be quite close to the pawnshop where Marie had pawned the earring. I walked quickly home with the loaf warm under my arm, tearing off a crust to nibble when I was sure nobody was observing such unladylike manners.

"I don't know why you wasted money on that," Mrs. Martley grumbled. "We've got enough here to get through to Monday."

"It's French."

"French bread doesn't keep."

"That's because it doesn't get the chance," I said, tearing off the other crust.

Chapter Twenty-two

The phaeton arrived in Abel Yard soon after two o'clock on Monday afternoon. I was downstairs talking to the coach repairer, and the first warning we had of its arrival was a clattering of hooves and shouting from Mount Street. It turned into Adam's Mews at a lopsided gait, with one of the two bays drawing it trying to canter while the other stood on its hind legs like a circus horse. A gang of twenty or so street boys came running after it, trying to get as close to the fun as possible while keeping clear of flying hooves. The rearing horse eventually came down to earth, its front hooves striking sparks from the cobbles. With one cantering and the other trotting they turned into our yard, with no more than a hand's width to spare between the nearside wheel hub and the wall. The driver didn't shift his position by a fraction and the grin never left his face.

"Amos Legge, I didn't know you were going to deliver it yourself," I said as they pulled up.

He jumped to the ground and ran his hand down the forelegs

of the horse that had reared, checking for damage. He found none and straightened up, blue eyes sparkling.

"Guvnor's bought two young 'uns. Look well enough together, but never gone in double harness before."

"So you took them straight up Piccadilly for a training run?"

"Does no harm to get them accustomed. No great mishtiff done, apart from either or both of them on their hind legs every crossroads and a few places in between. No call for the other drivers to be cursing us the way they did."

I imagined a furious logjam of carriages from Mayfair to Whitehall. Amos never did things by halves. By now everybody living and breathing in West London would know that the red-upholstered phaeton, formerly the property of Rt. Hon. Rodney Hardcastle, had transferred to Abel Yard.

The carriage repairer and his apprentice had come out of the workshop at the first sound of hooves and were examining the phaeton with appreciative eyes. They helped Amos unharness the horses and maneuver the phaeton into the space left vacant for it in the workshop.

"I'll take these two and see them bedded down, then I'll be back here after it's dark," Amos said.

"Very well. Have supper with us."

Amos went over to the horses and did complicated things with the buckles of their double harness. When he'd finished he vaulted onto the bare back of the one that had reared, holding the other by the driving reins.

"You're not going across the park like that, are you?" I said.

"Why not? A good gallop will get the devilment out of them."

I reached up and slid Morris's four pounds into his pocket. He turned to wave as the horses clattered across the cobbles and out of the gateway, more sedately than they'd arrived.

He returned at six o'clock, on foot for once, wearing a new

brown corduroy jacket and mustard-colored stock. When he took off his cap, his hair looked damp from the washing I guessed it had gone through under the stable yard pump. Mrs. Martley had seen him in the livery yard but seemed wonderstruck to have a man of his height and good looks in our parlor, beaming his blue-eyed smile at her. He took up so much room that we had to dodge round him to put food on the table. Mrs. Martley had flown into a panic when I told her we'd have a guest for supper and sent me running to Mr. Colley for a jug of cream from the Guernseys and as many eggs as he could spare, then downstairs to the forge with one of her special treacle tarts and strict instructions to stand by and see it didn't burn, then out again with a quart jug to the nearest beerhouse. All this had been annoying because I had my own preparations to make for the evening, but I'd managed so that, by the time Amos arrived, everything was in place.

"I do like to see a man enjoying his food," Mrs. Martley said as Amos started on his second plateful of ham and eggs.

I waited until she'd gone to the sink downstairs with a bowl of washing up, then told Amos my plan.

"If he comes tonight, I don't think it will be until late," I said. "If we're in the workshop from ten o'clock, that should be enough."

"The other times he tried, it was well after midnight," Amos said.

"There's a big old-fashioned traveling chariot in the workshop, waiting to have new springs fitted. I've taken some cushions and blankets down there. We'll be quite comfortable while we're waiting. I've put in a candle lantern, and a flint lighter. If we hear him unbolting the door of the workshop, we must wait before lighting it to give him time to do whatever he's going to do in the phaeton. He'll have to bring a lamp to work by, but he'll have no reason to look inside the traveling chariot. While he's in the phaeton, I'll get down quietly from the chariot, creep round and bolt the workshop door on the inside . . ."

"I'll do that," Amos said.

"It makes more sense for me to do it. I'm lighter and can move more quietly. I oiled the inside bolt this afternoon, so it should move without making a noise. I practiced getting out of the chariot and over to the door, and it takes twenty seconds by daylight. Double that, because it will be dark apart from his lamp in the phaeton, and give it a count of forty before you light your lamp and get out, making as much noise as you like. Then we close in on him, catching him red-handed."

"What happens if he hears or sees you going for the door?" Amos said.

"In that case, he'll shout out and you make your move at once, without waiting to light the lantern."

I knew that was the weakest part of my plan. It would take luck to slide the bolt before the person in the phaeton realized what was happening. I'd wear a dark dress and my lightest shoes, meant for dancing quadrilles, and hope for the best.

"He'll have a knife, perhaps a pistol," Amos said, sounding unworried.

"Hardcastle's no fighter."

"Anything will fight when it's cornered," Amos said. "But don't you worry, I'll settle him if he does."

"Settle who?" Mrs. Martley said, coming back into the room.

She must have heard Amos from the stairs. Expecting opposition, I broke the news to her that Mr. Legge and I would be spending the night in the carriage repair shop, waiting for an intruder.

"But there's nothing to worry about," I said. "We'll be quite safe."

"Your reputation's not worth worrying about? Sitting in the dark with a gentleman all night's nothing to worry about?"

"I'm sorry, Mrs. Martley, but this is nothing to be ashamed of and I'm going to do it whether you like it or not."

"Then I'm sitting up along with you," she said.

Amos and I looked at each other in silence.

"Well, a three-horse team it is then," Amos said.

The three hours in the coach shop were some of the oddest I'd ever spent. We sat there in the dark, on the cracked leather seats of the traveling chariot that smelled of old hay and musty wine, like three people being drawn by invisible horses along a flat and endless road. We'd arranged ourselves exactly as we might for a real journey, Mrs. Martley and I on one seat with our faces toward the nonexistent horses, Amos opposite, all of us tucked up in our blankets because the night was cold, and we had the door on my side partly open so that we could hear everything.

At first there was a dim glow from the last of the fire in the forge showing the phaeton in silhouette, but that soon died down so the blackness was complete. The chariot rocked and creaked on its old springs when one of us moved, making far more noise in the stillness than I'd noticed by day. That was worrying, but there was nothing to be done about it. The scuttlings of mice or rats and something larger that might have been a cat hunting broke the silence now and then. After a while Mrs. Martley wadded up her pillow and fell asleep with her head against the window, snoring gently. Amos had the countryman's ability to sit entirely still. I did my best to imitate him but was so strung up that the slightest sound had me looking in the direction of the outer door, as if I could see through the darkness.

Eleven o'clock, then twelve sounded from the workhouse clock and a tawny owl screamed, flying over the graveyard. Beside me, Mrs. Martley stirred.

"Is something happening?"

"Not yet, no."

He might not come tonight. We might have to go through all this another night. In his place, though, I shouldn't wait. He had no way of knowing how long the phaeton would be here. Mrs.

Martley went back to sleep. I rubbed my hands together, to keep them supple for working the bolt. The small rasping sound the palms made sounded like footsteps in dry leaves. Then suddenly there were footsteps, real footsteps, outside, coming cautiously across the cobbles of the yard. The movement I made when I heard them set the chariot creaking, drowning them out.

"Him," I whispered.

We all froze. The creaking died away. A grinding of metal on metal came from the direction of the door. When I'd oiled the inside bolt I'd deliberately left the outer one as it was, so that the noise would be our alarm. The person there was working it backward and forward, trying to move it. It slid at last with a screech, then the latch clicked up and the wooden door grated on the cobbles. Whoever was there opened it just enough to let himself in, but the dim starlight coming from the yard seemed so bright in comparison with the dark inside the coach house that I was afraid he'd see us sitting there in the chariot. Foolish, of course. Coming into total darkness, he'd be blind as a mole. For a moment I saw a silhouette against the starlight. Then the door ground shut, the latch clicked again and he was inside with us.

All we could see of him at first was a line of yellow light as thin as a piece of straw, moving uncertainly away from the door. Then it stopped moving and became a pool of light, but still unsteady, dodging from floor to walls and back again. He was carrying one of those candle lanterns with a shutter that can be turned to hide the light—a burglar's lantern. He was nervous. We could hear his harsh, quick breaths. The dodging light found the phaeton and came to rest. He followed it across the floor. When he turned toward us the light fell on his face for a moment. No doubt about that round, pale face like a pantomime moon against the darkness. Hardcastle. We had our man.

Moving less cautiously now, he hauled himself into the phaeton and put the lamp down on the seat beside him. It was on the side farthest from us so his body blocked most of the light. I craned forward, but all I could see was his silhouette, hunched over. Then he slid down and seemed to be kneeling on the narrow space of the phaeton's floor, facing the seat. Almost time to move. My nerves were twitching to go at once, go now and make sure of him, but I forced myself to sit tight. All we had so far was evidence that Hardcastle wanted his phaeton. There had to be more than that.

It seemed an age until anything else happened, then a sawing sound came from the phaeton, like a knife hacking through tough meat, and a few muffled curses to show he was finding it heavy going. Time to move.

I pushed the chariot door wide open and swung my legs round, moving carefully to try to stop the springs creaking. For all my care, they squeaked as I slid out, but I hoped he wouldn't hear it over the noise he was making. I stood for a moment, hand on the side of the chariot, getting my bearings. The light from his lantern came nowhere near the chariot, so I was still in darkness, but it was throwing some light on the workshop door on the far side of the phaeton. I'd have to cross this half-lit area to get to the bolt, something I hadn't allowed for in my plan. Still, no time to work out another one now. I took a few steps, trying to remember the sequence I'd worked out by day. Four steps toward the far wall, then turn left toward the doors and be careful not to bump into the forge. Although the fire had died, heat was still radiating from the bricks, telling me I was on the right path. I went past it, aware of the swishing of my footsteps and my heartbeat feeling loud enough to fill the coach house. The hacking and cursing from the phaeton went on. I was on the edge of the pool of lamplight now. It looked terribly bright but the bolt was only two or three steps away. No time for caution now. I dived for it.

"Hey, what's that? What's going on?"

Hardcastle's alarmed voice from the phaeton. Simultaneously, the chariot doors banged back, Mrs. Martley shouted something and Amos's feet came thundering across the floor. I reached the bolt, shot it across and braced myself with my back to the door. Hardcastle stood upright in the chariot, mouth open, a knife in his right hand. For a moment he stared at me, then vaulted clumsily over the side of the phaeton and ran toward me. His vault must have toppled the lantern over because it went out and we were suddenly in complete darkness.

"Get away from her," Amos yelled.

"Don't touch her," Mrs. Martley shouted.

From the sound of it, she was on her feet too. A hand pawed at my waist.

"Please, please . . ."

Hardcastle's gasping voice. It was coming from below, as if he was kneeling on the floor. Ridiculously, it sounded as if he were pleading with me to let him stab me because through the fabric of my skirt I felt something sharp pressing against my knee. I tried to kick out, but he was clinging to me like a sloth to a branch, pulling himself upright on my legs. Blasts of wine-soaked breath hit my nostrils.

"Please, oh please . . ." He was almost sobbing.

"Let go of her."

Amos's voice, from a few steps away. Then, from the same direction, the muffled crash of two bodies colliding and a shriek from Mrs. Martley. My two rescuers had run into each other, giving Hardcastle his chance. He got himself almost upright and managed somehow to hit me under the chin with the top of his head. It was probably more by luck than any skill of his, but my head snapped back and I staggered sideways. I could hear him rattling the door, groping for the bolt. Then he found it, opened the door and starlight came in.

"Miss Lane, are you all right?"

Amos's arms were round me.

"Yes, for goodness' sake, go after him."

Something rushed past us, flapping like a windblown umbrella into the yard. There was a clanking sound, a whoosh of water, a man's yell and a bad smell. Then Mrs. Martley's voice, harsh and loud as we'd never heard it before.

"And don't you dare come back."

Amos and I rushed out of the coach shop just as the latch clicked on the door from the yard into the mews. It swung open and Hardcastle went running through it. I ran, shouting to Amos to follow, trying to keep my balance as my shoes skidded on slimy stuff on the cobbles. I ran out into Adam's Mews just in time to see him turning into the passageway to Mount Street. Amos overtook me and I ran after him along Mount Street. As I rounded the corner into South Audley Street, Hardcastle was still in sight.

"Only a couple of furlongs in it," Amos said over his shoulder, not even sounding puffed. "He's not a stayer."

"He doesn't need to be," I panted. "He's near the finishing post already."

I'd realized where we were, just a few houses away from the Silverdale family's London residence. Even as I said it, Hardcastle disappeared.

"Gone to ground," Amos said. "He'll be hiding in one of the basements. We'll dig him out, don't you worry."

"Quite the reverse of basement, I'm afraid."

We were outside the Silverdales' house now. I came to a halt, hand on the stitch in my side. Most of the house was in darkness, but a window on the top floor glowed with soft candlelight. I imagined Lady Silverdale and her daughter at this moment having their studies interrupted by the family heir, stinking from the contents of the waste bucket.

"Where's he gone then?" Amos said.

"Just where any boy in trouble goes: home to Mother."

Chapter Twenty-three

Back at Abel Yard, Amos and I lit the lantern and had a look at the phaeton. The red leather of the driving seat had been gashed and pulled away from the nails that had been holding it, stuffing gaping out.

"Like her dressing room," I said, thinking of the knife slits in her couch and muff. I held the lamp while Amos knelt down on the floor of the phaeton and looked at the gash.

"The nails had been taken out from this bit of the seat, then put back quite clumsy like," he said. "He hid something here, right enough."

"And this time he was in too much of a hurry to bother with taking the nails out again," I said. "Is there anything there?"

Amos put his hand into the gash and rummaged around.

"Nothing there. Whatever it was, he got away with it."

"I didn't notice him carrying anything, did you?"

"If it was jewelry, he could have slipped it in his pocket."

Lamplight glinted on something lying on the floor near my

foot. I hoped it might be a piece of jewelry, but it turned out to be a knife that Hardcastle must have dropped when he ran away.

"Wait a moment," Amos said. "What's this?"

He'd been kneeling on it, on the floor of the phaeton. A plain brown leather portfolio, tied with black tapes. I moved the lamp as he untied it, showing a thick pile of papers inside.

"We'll take it upstairs and look at it in better light," I said.

We found Mrs. Martley with tea already brewed.

"Did he get away, then?"

She'd become as eager as a huntress. From the smell of soap clinging to her, she'd been scrubbing her hands to take away the smell of the waste bucket. I spread out the contents of the portfolio near the oil lamp on the table and we all crowded round.

"Lawyers' things, by the look of them," Amos said.

The papers on top of the bundle were written on parchment-like paper in legal language. It took me a while to realize that they were property deeds, nine of them altogether, registering the sale of various London properties to Columbine under her real name of Priddy. The dates covered the past ten years and the properties themselves ranged from a shop in Bond Street through various houses in Kensington and Knightsbridge to a villa in Maida Vale. The earlier the date, the less expensive the property, suggesting that she'd plowed the profits from rents into new investments. Next came an orderly pile of share certificates. As far as I could make out, she owned a quarter share in a hotel of dubious reputation near the Haymarket: twenty percent of an omnibus company, of all things; and thirty percent of the Augustus Theatre.

"No wonder they had to tolerate her whims, and no wonder she was nagging poor Blake about ticket sales," I said. "There must be tens of thousands of pounds here altogether. She was a wealthy woman."

And a clever one. Any diamonds she'd collected in her career had been turned into property in fast-growing London. While she lived in houses paid for by her lovers, the value of her investments grew year by year.

Amos, no great hand at reading or writing, seized on a document he could recognize.

"I said there'd be her marriage lines."

He was holding the certificate of the marriage of Margaret Priddy and Rodney Hardcastle. Another paper was attached to it by a small pearl-headed pin: a family tree of the Silverdale family for many generations back, neatly copied in a round, schoolgirlish hand that I recognized from Columbine's signature in the church register. So when she'd decided to make what turned out to be her final investment and buy a title for herself by marrying Hardcastle, she'd done her research methodically, like the good businesswoman she was. I felt the stirrings of admiration for her. True, she'd exploited her looks for all they were worth, but there must have been a bedrock of common sense that told her looks didn't last and the day would come when gentlemen weren't clamoring to pay her rent and buy carriages for her. She faced that day indebted to no one, a woman of property who'd added a husband in society and the prospect of "Your Ladyship" to the luxuries she'd arranged for herself. I raised my teacup in a silent toast to her.

The other papers in the portfolio looked less impressive; there were several dozen of them in various shapes, sizes and handwritings. They ranged from fine-quality writing paper with the addresses of gentlemen's clubs at the top, through hastily written scraps that might have been torn out of notebooks, to the back of a tavern bill. I was bundling them back into the portfolio, sure we'd already seen the documents that mattered, when I noticed the sums of money recorded on them. They were sprinkled with pound signs and figures with a formidable number of naughts behind them. The smallest were for several hundred pounds, the larger ones for sums that made my head reel. I glimpsed "compound sum of £15,000" in black slashing writing on lined paper; "to a total of £20,000" on torn yellow paper in ink so rusty that it might as well have been blood.

"They're IOUs," I said, fanning out a disorderly handful of them.

"All people who owed her money?" Mrs. Martley said.

"I suppose . . . no."

I put them down on the table and started studying them more closely. Columbine's or Margaret Priddy's name didn't appear on any of them. The sums owed were to various people and at various dates. As for the debtors who had signed the IOUs, they were even more amazing than the sums involved. Most of them were people I'd heard of. They included five politicians, two Whigs and three Tories, several members of the House of Lords, a famous actor and a minor member of the royal family.

"What in the world was Columbine doing with a bundle of IOUs?" I said.

"Looks as if she's been buying up paper," Amos said cheerfully.

"What do you mean?"

"Gentleman gets into debt and gives his note of hand to somebody for so many thousand. Then the gentleman the money's due to gets tired of waiting for his money, or maybe needs some himself in a hurry, so he sells the bit of paper on to somebody else, for less than what's on the face of it, and the first gentleman owes the person who's bought it for the same amount he did in the first place to the other gentleman."

I stared at him, trying to keep pace. I'd forgotten he'd become such an expert on the economics of fashionable debt.

"So if Columbine had let it be known that she was prepared to buy up IOUs, she could have all these people owing her money?"

"That's the size of it, yes."

"Would the people who'd written the IOUs in the first place know that the debts were now owing to her?"

"Not of necessity. Probably not until she told them to brass up."

"And they hadn't paid up, otherwise she wouldn't still have the IOUs."

"That's right. When the gentleman brasses up, he gets his bit of paper back in his hand."

"What would be the point of having them if she wasn't getting any money for them?" Mrs. Martley said.

"Revenge," I said.

Fashionable society had laughed at the milkmaid and thought she could do nothing about it. It had taken time, patience and some skillful investments, but Columbine had put herself in a position where she could do society damage—within reach of a title that went back to the Conqueror and in possession of enough IOUs to embarrass a lot of important people. So far there'd been one attempted suicide and, if she'd been dropping hints, a lot of people must have been very nervous about who she might choose to visit next. Mrs. Martley looked at me, puzzled, but it was too much to explain.

"What are you going to do with all this?" Amos said, looking at the papers covering the table.

"Take them to a lawyer."

Amos seemed content with that and said he'd better go. He had to be on stable duty at five in the morning, less than three hours away. We agreed to do without our ride in the park, but he said he'd bring a steady cob in the morning to take back the phaeton and try and calm Morris about the ripped seat. As we parted at the entrance to the mews I asked him to give my love to Rancie. I'd thought of several other things that he must tell the new owner about taking care of her, but from excitement and tiredness they'd slipped my mind.

Mrs. Martley had gone to bed by the time I got back upstairs. I sat at the table, read through all the documents, then placed them in the portfolio and tied the tapes in a bow. After a moment's thought, I untied it again and took out two pieces of paper. For the remaining few hours of darkness I kept the portfolio and the knife within reach beside my bed. When I carried them to Toby Kennedy's house as soon as it was light, the two pieces of paper stayed where I'd hidden them, at the bottom of my clothes chest.

I had to wait in the cubbyhole that passed for Kennedy's study until he was out of bed and dressed. He came down, sleepy-eyed, but the sleepiness vanished when he looked at the top papers in the portfolio.

"And Hardcastle inherits all this?"

"As her husband, I suppose he does. But look at the rest."

His eyes widened as he leafed through the IOUs.

"Ye gods, she was a dangerous woman. She could have done more damage to society with these than a mob with axes and fire-brands."

"I think that's what she probably intended. But if people owe that much money, wouldn't they be in danger anyway, whoever had the IOUs?"

He shook his head.

"Not in the same wholesale way. People who lend money have an interest in keeping the roundabout going. Now and again the moneylenders may let a man go bankrupt as an example, but it's in their interest to keep most people spinning and spending. They know that, sooner or later, fathers will die and estates get sold, so they'll have their money and interest. But if serious debts come into the hands of somebody who wants to do damage, it would be like thrusting an iron bar into the workings of the roundabout."

"From what you're saying, it would be in the interests of any-body in that portfolio to have Columbine killed."

"Yes. And that's dozens, including some very highly placed people."

"And a little dancer from the country is the one they're going to hang for it. You must show this to Mr. Phillips."

"Yes, I shall, this very morning."

"And you'll tell him about Hardcastle trying to steal it from the phaeton? I have two witnesses, if necessary."

"Is that his knife?"

I'd put it down beside the portfolio. Kennedy picked it up and tried the edge with his thumb.

"It's not very sharp, is it?" he said.

"No. That's the only thing that's worrying me. The person who was looking for something in her dressing room must have had a knife as sharp as a razor. You could tell from the way he'd sliced into the muff and the couch. Why should a man who'd used a sharp one suddenly choose a blunt one?"

"Perhaps he'd lost it."

"In that case, why not buy another sharp one?"

But it seemed to worry me more than it did Kennedy. He was staring at the papers, obviously thinking hard.

"We should tell Daniel about this."

"Perhaps after you've seen Mr. Phillips. We don't want to raise false hopes. Where is Daniel?"

"Asleep upstairs. He was pacing about into the early hours. Normally I'd agree with you, but as things stand, if there's even the slightest glimmer of hope, we should let him know as soon as possible."

"Why? Has something else happened?"

Kennedy looked at me as if wondering whether to tell me or not.

"He's seen Jenny again."

"To speak to?"

"No. There's a chapel inside Newgate. They let visitors in on Sunday—for a fee, of course. The visitors sit in the gallery looking down at the prisoners. The prisoners have to be there, they have no choice. According to Daniel, they're marched into the pews and sit there staring down at the floor, knowing the people in the gallery are gawping at them."

"That's barbaric."

"The condemned murderers have a pew of their own, a kind of cattle pen with seats, right in the middle of the chapel, so that people in the gallery can look down and know who's going to be hanged in a few days."

"Poor Daniel. How did Jenny look?"

"Like a mouse, when the cat's got it between her paws, he says. It just sits there, looking quite calm, only it's not calm at all, it's just accepted everything's all over."

"Did she know he was there?"

"He doesn't think so. A warder told him they should be grateful it isn't worse. Until a few years ago there was a black-painted coffin in the middle of their pen, so they all had to sit round looking at the empty coffin and be prayed over."

"It must have driven him nearly mad."

"It did. I was up all Sunday night with him, trying to persuade him not to . . ."

His voice trailed away.

"Not to do what he was going to do at the Old Bailey?" I said. "Go to the police and say he killed her?"

Kennedy nodded.

"So you can see why I want to give him some sort of hope. He'll do it if he has to, you know. He won't let her hang."

I tied up the portfolio, impatient now for him to take it upstairs and show Daniel.

I listened to his footsteps going upstairs, his voice on the landing saying Daniel's name, softly. Then more steps. I imagined him putting the portfolio on the bed, perhaps touching Daniel's shoulder to wake him with the first news for weeks that—if not good yet—had at least some hope in it. But something was wrong. Kennedy called Daniel's name again, this time more sharply, then his footsteps went quickly into another room.

"Daniel, are you in there?"

By the time Kennedy came back downstairs, my heart was thumping.

"He's not there," Kennedy said. "He must have gone out while I was asleep. Oh God, I thought I'd talked him out of it."

"How can we find out if he . . . ?"

"We can't go to the police," Kennedy said. "If he hasn't been to them yet, we don't want to put the idea in their heads."

"How, then?"

"If he has, Phillips will have heard by now. I'll go round to the Old Bailey."

"I'll come with you."

"No, Libby. We need one of us to wait here, just in case Daniel comes back."

There was sense in that, so I helped Kennedy on with his overcoat and reminded him to take the portfolio to show Mr. Phillips.

Kennedy was away for nearly three hours. As he walked through the door he said, "At least he hasn't done it yet, Libby. Not as far as I can make out."

"Then where is he?"

"I've no idea. I've been hoping against hope that I'd find him back here."

"What about his own lodgings?"

"I tried there on my way back. They haven't seen him for days."

I'm sure he was imagining, as I was, Daniel walking the pavements, nerving himself to walk into a police office.

"Is it worth trying some of the theaters?" I said.

"As well that as anything else, I suppose. But he hasn't worked since her trial."

We did the rounds of Covent Garden, Drury Lane, the Augustus. Nobody had seen him.

We stood for some time opposite Bow Street police station, hoping against hope that he wasn't already inside, talking his life away.

"Did you show Mr. Phillips Columbine's portfolio?" I said.

"Yes, he's keeping it for the while. He said it was interesting."

"Interesting! No more than that?"

"He admitted that, if it had come to light before the trial, he'd have been strongly tempted to put it in evidence. But once the verdict's been given, the standard of proof rises. He has to be able to argue that if the jury at the trial had known about it, they couldn't reasonably have reached the verdict they did."

"Surely that's the case?"

"No. He admits it proves that quite a number of people, including Hardcastle, might have had a motive for killing her. But that's a country mile from proving that any of them did."

We started walking aimlessly. It was early afternoon by now, the streets crowded. I suppose we were both clinging to the hope that we'd suddenly see Daniel coming toward us.

"I suppose it's just possible that he's had an accident of some kind," Kennedy said.

"How could we find out? We daren't risk asking the police."

"We could check the hospitals."

The nearest we could think of was the Middlesex Infirmary, just to the west of Tottenham Court Road. We went there and were directed to an admissions clerk in a small room. He ran his finger down a ledger.

"Five emergency admissions since eleven o'clock last night: a woman in childbirth, an elderly gentleman run over by a carriage, two inebriated tinkers who'd been fighting, and a boy with suspected appendicitis."

Kennedy asked if he might be allowed a look at the tinkers, just to make sure. The clerk raised his eyebrows.

"If my friend had been attacked or had had an accident, he might look like a drunken tinker," Kennedy explained.

The clerk opened the door for him and their steps receded along the corridor. They were back in a few minutes, with Kennedy shaking his head.

"If a person happened to be attacked around Fleet Street, what hospital would he be taken to?" I said.

"Probably the new Charing Cross Hospital in Villiers Street," the clerk said.

We thanked him for his help and left, crossing back over Tottenham Court Road.

"Why did you ask about Fleet Street?" Kennedy said.

"He spent a lot of time there when he was looking for Rainer."

"I think he's given that up now. I told him about the wretched Maine, so he knows it wasn't Rainer at the theater. It was mostly Marie he was looking for."

A harassed-looking doctor at Charing Cross Hospital had been on duty since ten o'clock the night before and couldn't remember a man of Daniel's description being admitted. He added that he was so tired that his patients were pretty much a blur, so called an orderly to make sure. The result was the same. When we asked what other hospital we might try, they suggested the Westminster, opposite Westminster Abbey. Again, it was quicker to walk. We hardly talked to each other on the way. I guessed that Kennedy was as fearful as I was by then and didn't want me to know it.

At the Westminster, there was a brief flare of hope when a doctor said a dark-haired gentleman with a broken leg had been admitted around midnight. Kennedy was taken to look, but again came back shaking his head.

We crossed the road and stood outside the Abbey, with a sharp wind blowing wisps of straw and paper round our feet. When a cab came in sight, Kennedy raised his arm and signaled to it.

"Where are we going now?" I said.

"Back to my lodgings. With luck, he'll have come home by now."

He hadn't. Kennedy called to the maid to make tea.

"I don't want tea," I said.

"Yes you do." He walked me over to a chair and made me sit down. I sat gazing at the unlit fire in the grate, thinking it was all my fault. If I hadn't been so greedily intent on keeping my freedom and Rancie, I might have saved Daniel from all this.

"I suppose we'll have to check the mortuary," I said.

"It hasn't come to that yet. There are still some more hospitals. If anything had happened to him south of the river, he'd be at St. Thomas's."

"And there's St. Bartholomew's, by Smithfield market," I said.

It was the nearest one to Newgate and the Old Bailey. We decided to go there first, then cross the river.

The cab journey seemed to go on forever. Near Smithfield, all the traffic had come to a tangled and bad-tempered halt because the roads were crammed with beasts being driven to market. In the end, we paid the cab off some way from the hospital and went on foot, picking our way along thoroughfares slimed with cattle droppings.

St. Bartholomew's has been looking after London's casualties for five hundred years or more, and with a special ward set aside for emergencies brought in from the streets. We stood in a cubbyhole of an office near the entrance to the ward while another clerk ran through another long list of admissions for the previous night, murmuring to himself and running his pen down the entries.

"Woman, too young, too old, workshop accident."

His pen stopped suddenly.

"Man. Admitted half past one in the morning, found by passersby outside St. Sepulchre's in Snow Hill, unconscious, with head injuries. Brought in on porter's cart. Respectable appearance, thirties."

St. Sepulchre's was just across the road from the Old Bailey. Kennedy asked to see the man. The clerk rang a bell and an orderly came to take him to the ward. The clerk offered me a seat and went on checking his ledger. Kennedy was back within minutes, accompanied by a young doctor with a wooden stethoscope tube sticking out of his top pocket.

"It's him, Libby. We've found him!"

Chapter Twenty-four

I felt like jumping up and hugging Kennedy, but he looked more worried than triumphant.

"He's badly hurt, conscious, but doesn't seem to recognize me. The doctor says he's been giving them trouble."

"What kind of trouble?"

The doctor perched on the edge of the clerk's desk.

"He's received a serious blow to the head and there's certainly evidence of concussion. There's some damage to his right arm too, but that's only bruising. Please excuse me for asking this, but has your friend any history of mental disturbance?"

"He's as sane as anybody," Kennedy said.

"It's the effect of the blow, then. He's tried several times to get out of bed, and keeps asking for his clothes. He says he has urgent business to attend to. Then he keeps calling for liberty. Is he politically inclined?"

"It's my name," I said. "Can I go to him?"

Kennedy shook his head.

"The doctor and I were discussing whether he should be taken home."

"I shouldn't normally recommend it so soon," the doctor said. He had a pleasant voice with a West Country burr. I could sense he was doing his best for us. "But the essential for recovery in these cases is that the patient should be kept as calm as possible, and these outbursts aren't helping him. If he can be cared for at home . . ."

"He can come to me," I said. "Mrs. Martley can help nurse him."

". . . and you have access to a competent physician . . ."

"I'll see to that," said Kennedy.

". . . then it might be the best course. I'll go and write a note to your doctor and Brown here will see about transport."

There was no question of jolting Daniel home in a cab. The clerk offered to summon a two-horse ambulance for us, but we'd have to pay for it ourselves. Kennedy and I had six shillings between us, which the clerk thought would be enough. We waited half an hour while the clock ticked and the clerk's pen scratched. Eventually an orderly put his head round the door and said the ambulance was outside and they were just carrying the gentleman into it.

There was room for the two of us to ride inside, on pull-down seats. As he helped me in, Kennedy warned me not to be shocked by Daniel's appearance. It was late afternoon by then with the light going, and the inside of the ambulance was dim. The first thing I could make out was a blanket-wrapped bundle on a broad shelf, a white bandage, and then Daniel's face under it, almost as white, eyes closed.

Kennedy took the seat next to me and the driver closed the door and got up on the box. The ambulance cart was so well sprung that it was more like being in a boat than a vehicle, and its windows were small and high up, so we couldn't see out. This added to the unreality of our journey back across London. For most of the time, Daniel didn't move or open his eyes. Only, when I thought we must be somewhere near home, I looked up and saw him staring at me.

"Liberty?"

His voice sounded surprisingly normal.

"Yes."

"There's something I'm trying to remember. It's important."

"Don't worry. Don't think about it now. We're taking you to my house."

"Phillips. Take me to Phillips."

"My dear fellow, don't worry about that now," Kennedy said. "We'll do whatever's necessary."

Daniel looked at us, eyes feverishly bright in the dimness, then gave a sigh and closed them.

He was still unconscious when we reached home, and Kennedy and the ambulance driver carried him upstairs. I ran ahead to warn Mrs. Martley. As soon as he was laid down on the couch in our parlor and the ambulance man had gone, she took charge. While she made him comfortable, I was set to work making up the fire, putting the kettle on to boil, fetching pillows from our beds. Once he was settled, Kennedy looked at his watch and said he must go to his orchestra.

"I'll look in on my doctor friend on the way and send him round. Then I'll be back as soon as the performance is over to see how he's doing."

The doctor came an hour later and confirmed what his colleague in St. Bart's had said: concussion, rest, calm. He was worried that Daniel might be feverish and recommended sponging his face below the bandage with cold water, persuading him to take some gruel or well-diluted beef tea when he woke. I sponged his face while Mrs. Martley made gruel, working by firelight in case lamplight disturbed him.

At some point between the doctor's visit and Kennedy's return he woke up enough to be propped on pillows and swallow some spoonfuls of gruel. He looked puzzled, as if he didn't know where he was or who we were. Afterward he went to sleep again. Mrs. Martley asked me in a whisper what had happened.

"I wish I knew."

When Kennedy came back he insisted on sleeping in an armchair beside Daniel for the night and sent Mrs. Martley and me upstairs for some rest.

The next two days were a blur. With the curtains drawn, we were hardly conscious of light or dark. I saw daylight—mostly damp and raining—when Mrs. Martley sent me on errands: to the butcher's for steak to make beef tea, to the grocer's for barley water, to the chemist for valerian root and melissa that she brewed into soothing teas for Daniel. It was a relief in its way to be given orders. Kennedy came and went several times a day. The doctor visited three times, took Daniel's pulse, looked into his eyes and continued to warn about fever. He never asked for a fee, either then or later, so either he was doing it from friendship or Kennedy was paying him.

Sometimes, unpredictably, Daniel would call out my name, whether I was sitting by him or in the bedroom upstairs. It was always the same thing. He was trying to remember something. I must go to Phillips and tell him. But when I asked gently what Phillips must be told, he couldn't remember.

Around daylight on what must have been Thursday morning, the bellows boy came running upstairs from the courtyard to say there was a man with two horses waiting for me. Until then, I'd forgotten all about Amos. I ran downstairs to where he was waiting on the chestnut hunter, holding Rancie by the reins, and explained what had happened. He was full of concern and muttered about what he'd like to do to the robbers if he got hold of them.

"If I can help, you send for me, promise me that."

I promised and allowed myself just one long stroke down Rancie's sleek neck before they went away. Back upstairs, Mrs. Martley shouted to me to wait outside the door while she finished seeing to Mr. Suter. She did everything for Daniel, sponging his body with warm water, bringing him bedpans. I offered to help, but she said that wouldn't be right for an unmarried woman. My share of the task was to carry the bedpans downstairs and empty them.

"And you'd better be getting the stains out of his good shirt," she said, on one of my reappearances upstairs. "If it goes to the laundry woman like that, she'll be charging us extra."

In between the nursing, she'd taken it upon herself to sort out Daniel's clothes, brushing and hanging up the jacket and sponging the waistcoat. It was her flag of hope: Daniel would be up and about one day, needing them again. I wished I could be as hopeful. The shirt she bundled into my arms was a good linen one, stained all down the front and round the cuffs with his blood. She couldn't have known how terribly it brought back the time less than a year ago when I'd stood by my father's body and held his shirt, similarly stained.

I filled a bowl with cold water, following her instructions to soak the stains, then dab them with oil of eucalyptus. It made them paler but didn't obliterate them altogether. Only one long smear on the cuff and right sleeve reacted differently. It was much the same rusty brown color, but cold water and eucalyptus oil made no difference to it. On the other hand, it turned paler when I rubbed it with a soapy rag, which had made no difference to the bloodstains. I puzzled about it in the idle way you think about things that don't matter as a relief from things that do.

Sometime on Thursday evening, when the light was going, Daniel called to me again.

"Liberty?"

I was sitting on the rug beside the fire, rolling up strips of sheet for bandages.

"I'm here."

His eyes focused on me. They were different, not puzzled anymore. He started speaking, quickly but coherently.

"I've remembered. You must tell Phillips at once. I've remembered what happened."

I went over and knelt down by the couch.

"I had a message about Rainer," he said.

"Rainer? But—"

I thought he was rambling, back to his old obsession. He went on, speaking urgently.

"The message had been delivered to my lodgings. Somebody sent it on to me at Kennedy's place. It said if I waited outside St. Sepulchre's after midnight, a man with some information about Rainer would meet me."

"Was it signed?"

"No. There was no name or address."

"Why didn't you tell Kennedy?"

"The note said I wasn't to tell anybody or bring anybody with me."

"So you went. That was begging to be attacked."

"It doesn't matter. I waited there, quite a long time after midnight. Then, when there was nobody else about, a man came walking down the street toward me. He was walking like a military man, upright and confident, nothing like the porters or vagrants you get around Smithfield at night. When he came into the lamplight, I saw his face. It was brown and creased, as if he'd spent a long time in the sun, with a mustache like the cavalrymen wear. I knew then. I might have said to him, 'You're Rainer,' or perhaps he said he was, but I'm not sure of that."

"Then he hit you?" I said.

"No, while I was looking at him, somebody must have come

up from behind. I fell against Rainer. I think he must have held me up while the other man hit me again. The next thing I knew, I was falling and there was shouting and feet running. That's all. I don't remember anything else until I woke up in a hospital bed and nobody would listen to me. What day is this?"

"Thursday."

He looked scared, as if he couldn't trust time anymore, tried to get up and fell back on the couch, eyes closed. Mrs. Martley came in, angry with me.

"What have you been doing? Didn't I tell you not to let him get excited?"

He was hardly conscious by then. She put an arm round his shoulders and made him sip one of her brews. When Kennedy arrived, much later, he was asleep again. I took Kennedy to a corner of the room and explained in a low voice what had happened.

"I thought even Daniel had stopped believing in Rainer. Why did he suddenly spring to life again?"

I'd been doing a lot of hard thinking while I waited for Kennedy.

"Whoever sent that note must have known he'd been looking for Rainer," I said.

"You believe there really was a note?"

"Yes."

"Half London must have known he was looking for the man," Kennedy said.

"Yes. It would have been the easiest way of decoying him anywhere."

"But why? He'd already had his pockets picked several times over. Even the underworld must have known he'd nothing left worth taking."

"There's something else," I said.

I walked softly across the room so as not to disturb Daniel and picked out his shirt from the basket waiting to go to the laundry-woman. The bloodstains were much paler after my work with the oil of eucalyptus, but the brown smear on the sleeve and cuff showed clearly.

"He says he fell against the man," I said. "He probably put his arm up. This is theatrical makeup."

"Ye gods. You're sure?"

"I saw the girls using something very like it at the Augustus."

"But why in the world would anybody pretend to be a figment of Daniel's imagination?"

"To make him stand still long enough for somebody to come up behind and cosh him."

"But why? If this was a sham Rainer . . ."

"It was."

"Then Daniel couldn't possibly be a threat to a convict who's breaking rocks on the other side of the world."

"No. I think he's a threat to somebody because he's looking for Marie. Rainer was simply the bait to catch him."

Kennedy put his hands to his forehead.

"So what do we do?"

"What we've been trying to do since the trial. Find Marie."

Chapter Twenty-five

Next morning I went out before sunrise, leaving Daniel sleeping and Mrs. Martley watching over him. Kennedy hadn't wanted me to go alone, but there was a rehearsal he couldn't afford to miss. He'd asked me to wait, but I'd refused. For one thing, I didn't want to lose any more time. For another, my plan seemed so unlikely to succeed that I didn't want anybody to witness its collapse. By the time I crossed London Bridge it was a bright but cold day, with the sun glinting on the river, sailing barges coming up on the rising tide and steam paddleboats threshing their way against it out to sea. On the south side, I went along the Borough toward St. Thomas's Hospital. The directions from the baker in Soho hadn't been precise, so I had to walk along the High Street on one side of the hospital, Joiner Street on the other and all the small streets in between looking for the shop. The first baker I found reacted as if I'd accused him of high treason.

"The frog place is the other side, further down."

I found it, not far from the place where I'd started my unsuccessful search for Marie, a thin slice of shop squeezed between a greengrocer's, with nothing in the window except cabbages and a few dried-out oranges, and an ironmonger's. Its window was mostly filled with pound loaves and meat pies, apart from a defiant corner where a glazed apple flan and some tartlets clustered round a small French flag. The man behind the counter was elderly and had a defeated look, but his eyes lit up when I spoke to him in French. Where had I learned it? he wanted to know. Ah yes, the good nuns. He'd even heard of the convent school in Normandy where my father had left me for a year when I was eleven and too young to join him on his travels. The baker came from Caen himself, but his sister-in-law had a cousin who'd been a nun there. Had I known her? Well, a pity, but it was a good place, good to talk about it.

I asked the baker if he had many French customers.

"Quite a few, yes. Especially on Sunday mornings."

"Why Sunday mornings?"

"On Sunday mornings, I bake brioche. I should like to do it every day of the week, but there's so much work to it and good butter is so expensive, it wouldn't pay. Believe me, mademoiselle, I have a queue of people outside. I have to take on an extra boy for Sunday mornings only. We can't take them out of the oven fast enough. People come from as far away as Bermondsey."

"You recognize all your customers?"

"Of course."

"And you notice when there are new ones?"

"Yes, there isn't much time to talk, but I like to ask them where they come from in France."

"There's a woman I'm trying to find. She'd have moved here quite recently. Her name is Marie Duval."

I described her as well as I could. Before I finished he was smiling.

"You mean my little Mademoiselle Triste?"

"Sad? Why?"

"That's what I called her. Sunday before last, she arrived too late, came running up after we'd finished baking. Nearly crying, she was. So I promised her, if she came the next Sunday, I'd keep some aside for her."

"Did she come?"

"Oh yes."

"So that's two Sundays you've seen her?"

"Yes."

"Do you know where she lives?"

"No, but it can't be far from here. That first Sunday it was a cold morning, and she came running up without a cloak or overcoat, only her indoor clothes and her bonnet. She said she'd smelled the brioche."

So Marie was within sniffing distance of where we were standing. How far would that brioche smell travel, on a cold Sunday morning? Probably a long way to a French exile. It was helpful, but not helpful enough.

"Do you know anything else about her?" I said.

"Only that she trims bonnets for a living. Last Sunday, she dropped her change. She said her fingers were sore from all the bonnets."

I thanked him, saying truthfully that one Sunday I hoped to return and taste his brioche. So as not to waste his time, I bought some almond biscuits and stood eating one, looking round. It didn't seem like an area for milliners. On an impulse, before my luck could go cold, I walked up to a young woman who looked more brightly dressed than most of the people of the Borough, in a bonnet trimmed with unseasonable roses.

"Do you know anywhere near here that trims bonnets?"

She took it as a compliment to her taste.

"Sweatshop just over there in Back Pig Yard. They ain't no good, though. I can tell you where to get one like mine, if you want."

I let her tell me and thanked her. She'd pointed to a narrow opening between two buildings across the street.

I walked down it, squeezing between piles of rubbish. It opened onto a mean courtyard surrounded by buildings of soot-darkened brick in various states of disrepair. A reef of broken tiles took up one side of the yard, under bare and sagging roof timbers. The building opposite seemed in better repair than the rest, though the windows were cracked and the paintwork faded. Several new packing cases stood outside it. The gleaming yellow straw around them was the brightest thing in the yard.

I went through a narrow doorway and up a wooden staircase. Women's voices sounded from a half-open door on the first landing. I knocked. There was no answer and the conversation inside went on, uninterrupted. I pushed the door and walked in.

At first I thought there was sunshine coming into the room, it seemed so bright. The brightness came not from sunlight but dozens and dozens of summer bonnets, the cheap ones in varnished yellow straw that looked like unhealthy confectionary. They were piled on trestle tables, stacked against the walls, lined up on the windowsill. Three large rolls of ribbon—red, yellow and blue—hung from a stand by the window. A glue pot stood on a trestle over a spirit lamp in the corner, filling the room with the smell of rancid meat. Two women were working at the tables; a third was standing at the roll of yellow ribbon, cutting off a length, measuring it with her arm from fingertip to elbow. The two at the table stared at me. I'd never seen them before. The third had her back to me.

"Marie?" I said.

She turned, the ribbon looped between finger and thumb. Her mouth fell open. She'd recognized me.

"It's all right," I said. "I'd just like to talk to you, please."

She glanced toward the door. I think it was in her mind to run.

"Marie, don't try to get away. I've found you this time and I'd find you again if necessary. We've been looking for you so long, and you can help us."

I might be speaking to a murderer, or a murderer's accomplice, but nothing was to be gained by outright accusation at this stage. Besides, the poverty of Marie's surroundings suggested she hadn't received a fee for services rendered, either from Lady Silverdale or from anybody else.

The other two women were looking at us curiously, without pausing in their work, their fingers folding red and blue ribbon into rosettes. Marie glanced toward them and back at me.

"Can we go somewhere to talk?" I said.

"I have no time to talk."

"Just for a minute or two, please. You could save somebody's life."

"Jenny's life, you mean?"

She walked over to her table, trailing the ribbon.

"Yes. You knew she'd been sentenced?"

"It was in the newspaper. My uncle told me."

"She didn't kill Columbine," I said. "Don't you want to help her?"

She shrugged. "That's no concern of mine."

I moved close to her so that our arms were almost touching and spoke in a low voice.

"Has it occurred to you that you might be in danger too?"

She opened her mouth to say something, then closed it, picked up a pair of scissors and started cutting the ribbon into lengths.

"I know now why Columbine was killed," I said. "I know a lot of other things as well. I know she married Mr. Hardcastle and you were a witness."

The scissors halted in mid-snip.

"You didn't tell the police about that, did you?" I said.

She mumbled, "They didn't ask."

"I don't suppose you told them about stealing her earring, either."

"I didn't steal it."

The indignation in her voice brought looks from the other two women. She began snipping at the ribbon again.

"You pawned it."

"I had a right to. She'd have wanted me to. She always paid me my wages, every month. It was a month nearly when she died. She'd have wanted me to have my wages. She was good to me."

"If she was good to you, surely you must want the person who killed her to be punished."

She bit her lip and said nothing. I hate bullying, but there was no other way.

"A friend of mine was nearly killed, just for trying to find you," I said. "Until whoever killed Columbine is arrested, you're in danger."

She shook her head. It looked more like a gesture of distress than denial.

"Did you poison her?" I said.

She stared at me, scissors open in mid-snip.

"No. Why should I? We were like sisters, her and me. Even the police could see that."

"Did she eat any of the syllabub, after the first ballet?"

"No. She wasn't well enough. It was true what I told the police. She took only a spoonful or two, just before the ballet, to keep her strength up. She had no appetite."

"The poison wasn't in the syllabub before the first ballet," I said.

"I know that. I told the police, but they wouldn't believe me. I told them, 'Madame would notice if there was the slightest lump in her syllabub, the tiniest speck of dust on it. Are you saying to me that she would eat syllabub with black seeds in it and not notice? I assure you, she would have thrown the whole bowlful on the floor.'"

The anger in her voice convinced me. The other women were grinning at each other, not understanding English but sure we were having an argument. They probably thought it was about some man.

"Then somebody put it in there after she died to confuse the police," I said. "Was it you?"

"No. Why would I do that?"

"Do you know who did?"

"No."

"Who came into the room after she was taken ill?"

"The whole world. Everybody."

I remembered that she'd been genuinely hysterical, in no condition to see who came and went.

"So we know it wasn't the syllabub that poisoned her. But something did. What?"

She picked up a length of ribbon and started pleating it into a rosette. I repeated the question.

"How should I know? I can't stop. I have to do twenty an hour."

"You told the police that she ate and drank nothing all evening except water and the syllabub."

"That was true."

"And the water?"

"From the tap. We all drank it. I drank it."

One of the other women went over to the glue pot in the corner and poured some of it into a dish. The smell was sickening, but none of the three seemed to notice.

"You see, it doesn't make sense," I said.

Marie whipped out a needle from the bodice of her dress, secured the rosette with two quick stitches, stuck the needle back and started pleating the next.

"That's not my fault. It's the truth I'm telling you."

"I believe you," I said. "But the fact is, Columbine was poisoned. And from what you say, nothing she ate or drank can account for that."

A shrug. The woman with the dish of glue was sticking red

rosettes onto her pile of straw bonnets, punching them in place with precise hatred.

"She can do twenty-four an hour," Marie said. "I can only do twenty."

"How much do you get paid for them?" I said.

"Penny for twenty."

So working for twelve hours a day without a break would bring her a shilling. No wonder she wouldn't stop.

"That evening, before she was taken ill, did you see anybody backstage who hadn't been there before?" I said.

"No."

"You're sure? Not an elderly woman?"

"No."

"Did Pauline come into Columbine's dressing room?"

"Of course not. Do you think I'd let her come prying round?"

"What about Mr. Hardcastle?"

"No."

"They'd quarreled, hadn't they? About Jenny?"

She nodded.

"Only it wasn't Jenny's fault," I said. "Hardcastle and his friends talked about a 'last gallop round the course.' I suppose he meant a last fling as a supposed bachelor before his marriage became public. Columbine must have been hurt and angry."

"She knew what he was like. I told her there were other men, better men."

She was more animated now.

"What did she say to that?"

"She laughed. She said there might be better men, but he was the best she could afford."

"She knew he was marrying her for her money?"

"Yes."

"And she was marrying him for his title?"

"Why else?"

"Was she angry with you for criticizing her?"

"No. I told you, she laughed. She said, 'I've come a long way from the cows' udders, haven't I?' We laughed about it together. I came from a farm too, in Normandy. Only I'm not doing as well as she did."

My unexpected sympathy with Columbine flared again. This woman had genuinely liked her.

"So Mr. Hardcastle married her for her money," I said. "Do you think he killed her for it?"

"I don't know."

Her fingers had slowed down and there was sadness in her voice.

"Did he steal from her?"

"He stole the earring. I saw him pick it up from the floor of her dressing room one day and put it in his pocket. I asked him for it, but he pretended he hadn't got it. That was why I sold the matching one after she died, because he'd have it otherwise. They only gave me two pounds for it, in any case."

"How long had you worked for Columbine?"

"Ten years. I'd just come over from France and I was a needle-woman, working on some of her costumes. She asked me if I'd like to be her maid."

"You were with her when she knew Rainer?" I said.

She bit her lip and nodded.

"And you know about him making threats against her from the dock?"

"He was a wicked man. He told lies about her."

She stabbed so savagely with her needle at a rosette that the point broke through and pierced her finger. She sucked it, looking at me as if it were my fault.

"What kind of lies?"

"He pretended she knew about what he'd been doing. She had no idea in the world."

"About forging bonds, you mean?"

Another nod. Privately, I thought it quite likely that Columbine had been willing to profit from forgery, particularly if somebody else took the risk of ending up in the dock.

"Was she glad when he was transported?"

"Of course."

"Did she ever speak of him coming back again?"

"She said she hoped he'd die in Van Diemen's Land. A lot of people do."

"Has he come back?"

She stared at me.

"How could he? He was sent away for ten years."

"Did she say anything about him escaping and being back in London?"

"No."

"Did she seem scared of anything in those last few weeks of her life?"

"No. She was never scared."

She walked across to the table with the spools of ribbon. I followed and held out my arms so that she could wind the ribbon round them. Back at the table, she unwound it—without thanking me—and cut it into longer lengths than before.

"You really liked Columbine?" I said.

I'd almost given up hope of getting anything useful from her. Simply, I was interested in the new picture of Columbine I'd been building up in the last few days.

"She was kind to me. I was only a silly girl when I came to her. She taught me a lot."

"Would you have stayed with her once she and Mr. Hardcastle set up house together?"

"Of course. She said she needed somebody to laugh at him with her. Also, when she was in society, she'd have many beautiful new dresses and I'd help her look after them. That was my métier, after all."

She picked up a bonnet in her left hand and a knife in her right. I thought she intended to destroy it for its tawdriness, but all she did was make precise slits in each side. Methodically, she did the same to the next one.

"What will you do now?" I said. "Shall you go back to France?"

"How can I? I don't have the money for the fare."

"Why don't you get work with another lady as a maid?"

"How? With her dead, and not able to give me a character. The police making out I killed her. Who would employ me?"

The knife flashed in and out, and the varnished straw made pucking sounds as it was pierced.

"Why did you come all the way across the river to find work?"

"My uncle owns this place. He said he'd give me a roof over my head until I made enough money for my fare home."

I saw through her eyes the thousands upon thousands of glazed straw bonnets separating her from Normandy, with only a Sunday-morning brioche for pleasure. She'd gained nothing by Columbine's death.

"I didn't know Columbine very well," I said, "but it struck me that she had a temper." She nodded, using the point of the knife to poke the end of a ribbon through the slits she'd made in the bonnets. "Did she ever lose it with you?"

"Sometimes, but I understood. It wasn't her fault. She had much suffering in her life."

"Suffering?"

"She was not in good health. Sometimes it was a martyrdom for her to dance, to smile, but she did it always."

"Was that why she had to have her chair and cushion in the wings and so forth?"

"Yes."

I was still skeptical. Most dancers have to pirouette and smile through their injuries, but few have a lady's maid waiting in the wings.

"I suppose it was her feet that hurt her," I said, thinking of her *en pointe*.

Marie was indignant.

"Never. Madame had beautiful strong feet, the finest feet in London. A gentleman wrote a poem about them."

"What was her trouble, then?"

She folded the ends of two ribbons in half and cut swallowtails, moving slowly for once. I had to strain to hear as she uttered two words in French under her breath.

"*Les hémorroïdes.*"

It wasn't a term familiar to me until one of the other women, who must have been listening with ears flapping for any word she could understand, gave a bellow of laughter and clapped a hand to her own backside. Marie gave her an angry look, threw words at her in French too fast for me to catch but clearly insulting, then reverted to English.

"It's no joking matter. She was in much pain."

"All the time?"

"It came and went. In the days before she died, it was bad."

"Did she take anything for it?"

"The doctor made her up some ointment. It helped a little."

"So when she was delirious and talking about blood and people not seeing . . . ?"

"We always took care that people didn't see. It is not a polite complaint."

An unhappy thought came to me.

"Did Jenny happen to give her any herbs for it?"

Marie glared. Even talking about it seemed to be provoking her temper.

"Certainly not. She wouldn't have taken anything from Jenny. She went to a proper doctor who cost a lot of money. Besides, Jenny would have gossiped about it to all the other girls."

"So they didn't know?"

"Nobody knew, except Madame and I. Can you imagine—people seeing her onstage and thinking about . . . ?"

She threw up her hands at the impossibility of it. I saw what she meant. Fairy queens gliding on tiptoe are not meant to be subject to such humiliating ailments.

"Did Mr. Hardcastle know?"

"Now you're being ridiculous. She'd rather have died than have him know."

An idea was forming in my mind, as strange and bright as the piles of glazed straw bonnets. I think Marie was surprised when I thanked her for her time, told her I'd be back one day soon, and walked out of the room and down the stairs.

The idea grew in my mind all the long walk home across London to Mayfair and Abel Yard. When I opened the door of our parlor, Daniel's eyes turned to me from the couch. He must have seen something in my face.

"What's happened?"

"I found Marie."

I told him about the room in Southwark and the straw hats.

"She didn't kill Columbine, I'm sure of that," I said.

"Does she know who did?"

"No, but she confirmed something I suspected. The poison that killed Columbine was never in the syllabub."

"Then how was she poisoned?"

"I don't know, but I have an idea. I must go back to the Augustus tomorrow."

I was almost certain, but didn't want to raise his hopes until I had the last link in the chain.

I went upstairs and found Mrs. Martley dozing on her bed. The days of caring for Daniel had almost exhausted her. When she opened her eyes, I asked what she knew about hemorrhoids, giving them their plain name of piles. She was shocked.

"You shouldn't have them at your age. It's all that riding."

"Not I, just somebody I know. Would they make you bad-tempered?"

"From what my ladies told me, they'd make a saint bad-tempered."

"Your ladies?"

"There are some things you can't talk about to doctors. It's easier with another woman."

"Did you prescribe for them?"

"As far as I could, yes."

"What did you prescribe?"

"An ointment of dried marigold petals to reduce the swelling, and thorn apple seeds boiled in water, all pounded up in hog's lard."

"And you have to apply it to the . . . site?"

"Of course."

"Is that your own recipe, or would most people use it?"

"Anybody with any sense would. It's an old recipe, but I've never heard of a better one. Do you want me to write it down for your friend?"

"No, thank you. I shall remember it."

"Tell her to go careful with the amount of thorn apple."

Too late, alas, though I didn't say that to Mrs. Martley. She'd given me the last piece in the puzzle, and the question now was what to do with it.

All that night I lay awake, looking at the dark rectangle of sky through the window, making plans.

Chapter Twenty-six

I arrived at the Augustus at ten o'clock in the morning, but the Surrey family were there before me. Susanna's clear voice came from their dressing room:

Your crown's awry; I'll mend it and then play.

Then her mother's quieter voice murmuring and Susanna repeating the line. I knocked and was invited to come in. Mrs. Surrey was sitting at the table in her everyday clothes with a brush and a tiny pot of gold paint, regilding Cleopatra's headdress, which looked as if it had survived several desert sandstorms. Susanna was sitting on the costume basket in a yellowish-white taffeta tunic, feet bare.

"Miss Lane, is there something wrong?"

Being an actor, Honoria Surrey was alert to expressions or perhaps to tension in the way I was standing.

"I need to ask Susanna something," I said.

There was no point in pretending casualness. Mrs. Surrey wiped the paintbrush on a piece of rag and put it down, without taking her eyes from my face.

"Susanna now? David told us he'd been talking to you about stealing the syllabub for the cat. It was wrong of him, of course, but does it matter?"

"It may matter very much, but it wasn't his fault. Neither of them has done anything except what all children do, especially older sisters with younger brothers."

From the corner of my eye I could see that Susanna was giving me a hard stare.

"Neither of them?" Mrs. Surrey said.

"I have a younger brother too," I said. "When we were children, we were always giving each other dares. It got us into the most terrible trouble. I remember once Tom got stuck on a church roof and another time I went up to a very grand lady at a party and asked her if it was true she wore a wig."

A nervous snort of laughter came from Susanna.

"We usually had to bring something back to show we'd done the dare," I went on. "A sprig of mistletoe from the top of the apple tree, say, or a piece of slate from the haunted house."

"You could have cheated," Susanna said. "It could have been a sprig of mistletoe that had fallen down, or any old piece of slate."

"Yes, but you don't, do you?" I said. "There's no point in a dare, if you cheat."

Susanna and I stared at each other; her eyes were clear and challenging.

"David went into Columbine's room because you dared him," I said.

"The first time, yes."

From her voice and her look, she might have been Cordelia refusing to lie to King Lear. Love of drama was overcoming any reticence she might have.

"So when he dared you to go into Columbine's dressing room

after she was dead, you had to bring something back to show
you'd done it."

"Yes."

"Is that true, Susanna? Is that why you went in there?" Mrs.
Surrey said.

"Yes."

"And did you bring something back to show him?" I said.

Susanna held my look for a long moment, then stood up and
opened the lid of the costume hamper. She burrowed in the corner of it, came up with two objects and walked slowly toward me,
holding one in the palm of each outstretched hand. I picked up
the first one—a small china pot. It had once contained rouge, but
when I unscrewed the top it turned out to be almost empty, just a
dried-up circle of red round the bottom.

"It was like that when I took it," she said. "I haven't used any."

"Didn't you drop it when the screen fell on you?"

"No. I had both of them in my pocket."

I put it back in her outstretched palm and picked up the other
object: a glass jar, larger than the rouge pot, containing a white
ointment and less than half full. I took the lid off and sniffed. Hog's
lard, mainly, going rancid, with a musky vegetable smell under it.

"I don't know what that is," Susanna said. "I thought it might
be some kind of special makeup."

"Where did you find it, exactly?"

"They were both of them on the floor, that's why I took them."

"May I keep this one?" I said.

"If you want to."

"But why does it matter so much?" Mrs. Surrey said.

She sounded scared.

"I promise you, David and Susanna are in no trouble. In fact,
they may have done something that helps somebody very much,
but I can't tell you any more than that for the moment."

She didn't look reassured, and I could hardly blame her.

* * *

I said good-bye to them, walked along the corridor and tapped on Barnaby Blake's door.

"Come in."

He had a pile of papers on the table in front of him, pen in hand and a distracted air.

"Good morning, Miss Lane." I could tell from the weariness in his voice that he wanted to be left to his accounts. I shut the door behind me and walked up to his desk. He sighed but put the pen down. "How's Suter?"

"Recovering. You heard he was attacked?"

"From the musicians, yes. Is he angry with me for giving evidence at Jenny's trial? I promise you, I'd have avoided it if I could. I tried not to make things any worse for her than I could help."

"He thinks you did all you could—then."

"Meaning?"

"There's something else you could do for her now."

"A petition for mercy? I'll sign it, by all means, but . . ."

"More than that. We can prove now that Jenny's innocent, but we need your help."

He stared at me for a long time.

"You'd better sit down. Tell me."

I took the chair across the desk from him.

"We know who killed her and how. This person has made some mistakes so serious that it practically amounts to a confession. We've given her lawyer evidence that should be enough to overturn the verdict—but we need to be certain."

"And what is it you want me to do?"

"I want you to invite a certain person here for a business discussion."

"Who?"

"Rodney Hardcastle."

"Ah." From the tone, he'd guessed what I was going to say. "He's made mistakes, you say?"

"For one thing, we've witnessed him committing burglary to get his hands on a portfolio of Columbine's papers."

"That's not evidence of murder, though."

"And we know he married Columbine in secret just before she died."

"Married her!"

I took the marriage license out of my reticule and put it down in front of him. He looked at it, then up at me.

"Why in the world would he go and do that?"

"For her money. She was a woman of property, and she'd been buying up debts, including some important people's."

He picked his pen up again and turned it over and over in his fingers.

"So I'm to invite him to a business discussion and confront him with this?"

"Yes."

"Then what happens? Do you jump out from a cupboard and accuse him of murdering her?"

"Not far off that. Our idea is that you should show him the marriage license and hint that you know about the other things. He's not a clever man, as you know. We think he might try to bargain with you, or perhaps even lose his nerve and threaten you. Then we'll have him off balance."

"Is this Suter's idea, or yours?"

"Mine."

"Perhaps I should employ you as a dramatist. I'm not sure I care for the part of hero, though. You're asking me to confront a murderer and as good as accuse him. Suppose he produces a knife or a pistol?"

"She was poisoned. That's a different sort of crime. Besides, if Hardcastle tried to shoot somebody, he'd probably miss."

"At this range?"

"I hope it won't come to that."

"And if you're wrong?"

"I'll be hiding in the room. If it sounds as if he's becoming violent, I can rush out and help you restrain him."

Blake shook his head.

"I'm sure you're a very active young woman, Miss Lane, but I don't want to stake my life on it."

"What about Robert Surrey, then?" I tried to say it as if it had just come into my head. "He's very quick and reliable, being an actor."

He thought about it.

"Do I tell him all this?"

"No. I think all you need to say is that you're meeting a client who might be difficult and you'd like to have him on hand."

He looked around the room.

"Where would we put you both? The cupboard's not very big."

"Suppose you meet him in Columbine's dressing room? There's that big screen."

He thought about it.

"The conjuror's using the room at present, but I suppose . . ."

"Tomorrow's Sunday, so he won't be needing it."

"You want to do this tomorrow?"

"Why not? The sooner the better."

He heaved a long sigh.

"I suppose the invitation has to come from me."

"Yes. You could send Hardcastle a message asking him to meet you here at midday."

"And if he refuses?"

"He won't refuse. But I'll be here early tomorrow to make sure."

He nodded, stood up and walked to the door with me as if the weight of the world had landed on his shoulders.

"You can tell Suter that he'll owe me for this forever."

"I'll tell him."

* * *

I walked home slowly and spent most of the day helping Mrs. Martley with Daniel. He insisted on getting up and walking downstairs to the yard and back to try his legs. Kennedy came to visit before going to keep an engagement at the opera house. I waited until Mrs. Martley was out of the room and told them all I knew, what I'd guessed and how I intended to prove it. As I'd anticipated, they set up a clamor about it.

"If anybody's behind that screen, it will be me," Daniel said.

Kennedy echoed the sentiment, even more forcibly. I pointed out, none too tactfully, that if physical strength were needed, I'd have chosen Amos Legge in preference to either of them.

"We need a witness who has no personal stake in this. Apart from that, it's a matter of observation and timing, and I'm as good at that as either of you," I said. "Besides, I have a promise to keep."

Kennedy left, saying he'd be at the Augustus next day whether I liked it or not. By the time the workhouse clock struck ten, Daniel had taken one of Mrs. Martley's drafts and was sleeping, while she dozed in the chair by the fire. As I put on my coat and bonnet, Daniel turned over and his eyes opened. They were very bright in the firelight and fixed on mine. I went over to him.

"Whatever happens, thank you, Libby. I'd give the world to have you safely out of all this."

I thought, but didn't say, *All the world but one person.* It wasn't his fault.

"Sleep now. Don't worry."

I had to wait for some time on the doorstep of the Silverdales' house before a sleepy maid responded to my knock. I gave my name and said Lady Silverdale had invited me to call on her at any time. She let me in and, as before, I followed her up the carpeted staircase between candles. There were even fewer of them alight this time. Lady Silverdale wasn't expecting visitors. When we reached the top landing the maid tapped on the door.

"Miss Lane to see you, ma'am."

The door opened almost at once, onto the cave of a room and the giant telescope crouching on the edge of the night sky. As before, Lady Silverdale came to meet me wearing her own neat thatch of silver-gray hair, with the wig on the block by the door. Her daughter, Anna, carried on making notes in her island of candlelight.

"How kind of you to call, Miss Lane."

If Lady Silverdale was surprised to see me, she gave no sign of it.

"So Rodney came home safely on Monday night," I said. "I hope he managed to get the smell out of his clothes."

I made no effort to match her politeness. Her expression didn't change, but I could almost hear that quick mind whirring.

"Anna—"

Just that one word, and her daughter put the cap on the inkwell, gathered up her notes and left the room.

"We'd better sit down, don't you think?" Lady Silverdale said.

She led the way to the table with the armchairs. We sat on either side of it.

"Your son's in worse trouble than you realize," I said. "Or perhaps you do realize. Do you know what happened to him on Monday night?"

She looked at me, making no attempt to answer the question.

"We caught him breaking into a coach workshop where I live," I said. "He ripped open the seat of a phaeton that used to belong to him and ran away. He was looking for something."

"If he's done damage, I shall naturally pay for it. But unless you now own the phaeton, I fail to see what your interest is."

Her voice was as calm and low as ever, just the hint of a frown on her face.

"The same as it's always been—discovering who killed Columbine."

"I understood that poor girl had been sentenced."

"That's going to be set aside any day now. Her barrister has new evidence."

"Oh?"

"The evidence is what your son was trying to find in the phaeton—a portfolio of Columbine's very considerable property interests . . . and other things."

She said nothing for a long time. I waited, watching her face in the flickering of the candlelight.

"Why should Rodney be interested in that, and why does it change the case against the girl?"

This time, I made her do the waiting. After what seemed like a long time, she blinked.

"Did Rodney tell you he'd married her?" I said.

"Married? Married Columbine?"

The surprise sounded genuine, but then so had her claim about the earring.

"I've seen the entry in the register and spoken to one of the witnesses," I said. "She kept her marriage lines in that portfolio."

"I can't believe it."

"Ask him," I said. "Is he still with you?"

She nodded reluctantly.

"You understand the situation?" I said. "He marries her secretly, she's killed, he's desperate to get his hands on her property portfolio. As her husband, it's all his. If Jenny Jarvis's barrister had known all that at the trial, your son's name would have come out in court—and there'd have been worse embarrassments to follow."

"Do you want money?" she said.

"No. I want something else. I want you to persuade your son to put right some of the harm he's done. It will need more sense and courage than he's shown so far, but, I promise you, this is the best way I can see for him."

She looked across at her telescope and the night sky beyond it.

I could sense that she was desperate to be back among her planets set on orbits that could not be shaken by anything a mere human being could do. When she looked back at me, her eyes had changed. There was such deep sadness in them that I wished I could take the decision away from her, but knew I couldn't.

"What do you want me to do?"

"He'll have received an invitation to a business discussion with the manager of the Augustus Theatre tomorrow. I want him to accept it."

"And what else?"

"He should take a pistol," I said.

Chapter Twenty-seven

Next morning brought peals of Sunday bells, first from the Grosvenor Chapel round the corner, then echoing eastward all the way across the city as the sun came up. I had no appetite for breakfast and walked to the Augustus. Barnaby Blake was already in his office and looked as if he hadn't slept much better than I had.

"He's replied," he said. "He's coming at midday."

"Anything else in the message?"

"No. Just that one line. Do you want to inspect the stage setting?"

I said yes, and we went along the corridor to what had been Columbine's dressing room. It looked starker and less luxurious now, with the magician's various hats hanging from pegs and a long wooden rack with a variety of cloaks and coats. Columbine's couch had gone, but the screen was still in the corner. A table and two chairs stood in the center of the room, near where the couch had been.

"I'll invite him to sit down here," Blake said. "I've positioned it so that you can see him from behind the screen, but you might want to make sure."

I went behind the screen. As he said, he'd placed table and chairs carefully so that you could see them without peering round.

"Thank you. That's just right."

"Whatever you do, don't get in Surrey's way," he said. "If you're right, he may have to move quickly."

I came out from behind the screen.

"How much have you told Mr. Surrey?"

"Simply that I'm meeting a business associate who may turn violent and I'd be grateful to have him on hand."

"He agreed?"

"I think he was puzzled, but yes. Robert Surrey knows which side his bread's buttered."

"Does he know I'll be behind the screen too?"

"No. Do you want me to tell him?"

"Leave that to me, I think."

He spread his arms and hands in a gesture that said whatever might happen would be my fault. I told him I'd be back at a quarter to twelve to take up position, and then set off home. On the way I found a man standing over a brazier selling cups of hot coffee for a penny and downed two in quick succession, putting some heart into myself.

Kennedy had arrived at Abel Yard and Daniel was up and dressed with a fresh bandage round his head. Mrs. Martley had gone to church. Kennedy insisted on coming with me to the Augustus and we begged Daniel not to stir from the room until we got back.

"It will be best if you wait outside the theater," I said to Kennedy as we walked. "If he rushes out, stop him. If there's a policeman in sight, so much the better."

"I could find one and keep him talking there."

"Perhaps, but it's vital that you don't let him come in too early. It would ruin everything."

We timed our walk to be at the Augustus at a quarter to twelve. There was no point in being early. Hardcastle had probably never arrived punctually for an appointment in his life, and I wanted to avoid another discussion with Blake if I could. I walked along the cold and silent corridor, past the Surrey family's dressing room; for once there was no sound of voices coming from inside. Robert Surrey had made sure his wife and children stayed away. The door of Columbine's dressing room was shut. When I opened it, the room seemed exactly as I'd seen it earlier that morning, with the table and two chairs in the middle and the screen angled to give the best view. I'd forgotten to arrange with Blake that Hardcastle should sit with his back to the screen, but since he'd set up everything else so carefully, he'd surely think of that.

I went behind the screen, being careful not to alter the angle of it. Robert Surrey was there. He must have heard and seen me coming in and was angry.

"Blake didn't tell me you'd be here as well. Or are you his business associate who may turn violent?"

His voice was low but carrying. I gestured that he should keep it down.

"No. I'm in here with you."

He took one careful step sideways to make room for me, glaring.

"What are you and Blake plotting? My wife told me you were questioning Susanna. I resent that. Whatever's going on, the children shouldn't have been brought into it."

"I wasn't trying to bring them into it. Only—"

I stopped because there were steps going past in the corridor, from Blake's office toward the outside door. Blake must have decided to meet Hardcastle as he came in. I only hoped he wouldn't start discussions until they were sitting down.

"It must be nearly time," I said. "You'll know soon, I promise you that. Only please keep quiet and watch."

There were footsteps coming back along the corridor from the outer door, two pairs of them. For once in his life Hardcastle must have been on time. Amazing what a mother's influence could do. Then Blake's voice, sounding remarkably confident in the circumstances.

"I thought we might be more comfortable in here."

"Wasn't that her room?"

Hardcastle's voice, far less confident. The door opened. Blake walked in with Hardcastle behind him, flabby-faced and looking like a man who'd breakfasted on brandy. In spite of his annoyance, Surrey moved closer to me to have a good view.

"Please sit down," Blake said.

He was standing beside the chair facing us, which meant Hardcastle had no choice but to sit with his back to the screen. They sat and for a count of twenty or so, neither of them said anything. Blake's face was partly screened from me by the back of Hardcastle's head, but as far as I could see he was impassive.

"What did you want to see me about?" Hardcastle said.

"I think you know."

A good line. Hardcastle fidgeted in his chair. His left leg came out from under the table, showing the toe of a scuffed boot. The change of position made the right side of his coat hang down beside the chair. The pocket of it was weighted with something that looked a lot heavier than a handkerchief. I saw Surrey's eyes going to it and knew that Blake could hardly have failed to notice it on their way along the corridor. Hardcastle said nothing.

"I think you may have lost this—" Blake said.

He took a paper from his pocket and threw it down on the table in front of Hardcastle. The marriage lines.

"What are you doing with that?" Hardcastle's voice was high and alarmed.

"Do I congratulate you, then?" Blake said. "I've heard of plenty of women living off gentlemen, but not many gentlemen would stoop to living off a woman, especially a dead one."

There was a depth of contempt in Blake's voice that I hadn't expected. Beside me, I was aware that Surrey was poised for action, balancing on the balls of his feet. He motioned to me to move aside so that he could spring out quickly if needed. I stayed where I was.

"What do you mean?" Hardcastle said.

Like me, he seemed to have been caught off balance by the bitterness in Blake's voice.

"Are you going to take her name?" Blake taunted him. "The right dishonorable Mr. Columbine?"

Hardcastle made a choking noise. As far as he'd had an education, it had been a conventional one and these were fighting words.

"Dishonorable? How dare you call me dishonorable?"

Hardcastle got to his feet, pushing against the table, and moved toward Blake. Blake must have expected it. He stood up and stepped smartly sideways so that Hardcastle lurched past him toward the door, then turned, looking ready to charge. Blake faced him.

"There are worse words than 'dishonorable,' aren't there? How does 'murderer' suit you?"

From the furious expression on Hardcastle's face, Blake must have realized that he'd moved too far and too fast. As Hardcastle came back at him, Blake stepped rapidly toward the screen, stumbling in his hurry. I assumed it was to have help near at hand if Hardcastle attacked him. My main concern was to stop Surrey jumping out to protect Blake there and then. I mouthed, *Wait* at him. He might not have taken any notice, but at that moment our view changed. Blake in his hurry must have blundered against one wing of the screen, knocking it back at right angles so that Surrey and I were effectively boxed in and could see nothing.

Then Blake screamed: "Put that away. No! Put it away."

At the same time, the sounds of a scuffle, a chair falling over and Hardcastle's panic-stricken screech, higher than Blake's.

"No. No."

Then the bang of a pistol. Surrey swore and pushed me aside. The screen rocked and we both came tumbling out of it together. I had, after a fashion, expected the sight that awaited us. Surrey hadn't, but he had a clear enough view of it to be as good a witness as anyone could wish. One man was bent over, hands to his face. The other was upright, holding a smoking pistol in a hand that was rock-steady. The man bent over was Hardcastle, the one with the pistol Barnaby Blake. For a heartbeat we all stood just as we were, with no sound except Hardcastle's whimpering.

"So you tried to kill him too?" I said to Blake.

He raised the pistol. He was looking at me so he never noticed that the door from the corridor had opened. When a man-shaped meteor came flying at him and struck him a blow on the side of the head so hard that he and the pistol arced to the floor in different directions, he wouldn't even have known who hit him. I looked over his unconscious form at Daniel, who, to the best of my knowledge, had never raised a hand in anger since his schooldays, and had made up for it with this one blow.

"You needn't have worried about me," I said. "I told you it wouldn't be loaded."

It was Hardcastle's own fault that his face was so scored with powder burns that he looked as if he'd been dragged facedown along a gravel drive. I'd told Lady Silverdale that he should carry his pistol conspicuously, but unloaded. No doubt she'd passed the instructions on accurately and he'd bungled that part of it, removing the ball but leaving the wadding and powder charge in the pistol. Still, he could be forgiven for that as he'd done everything else exactly as he'd been told and had just suffered the worst shock of his life. When Blake grabbed the pistol from his pocket and fired it at point-blank range into his face, he must have thought he was dying. Now, rocking backward and forward with his hands to his eyes, he started wailing that he was going blind. Robert Surrey looked badly shaken himself but went out of the room and came back with a bowl of water and a clean rag. Barnaby Blake was still laid out on the floor with Daniel standing close beside him as if scared even now that he might escape.

"You shouldn't be here," I said to Daniel.

The sound of running feet came along the corridor and Kennedy appeared.

"There was a shot. Are you . . . ?"

"We're all right. Please go and find that policeman," I said.

"Yes," Daniel said. "It's all right. I'll look after her."

It wasn't the time to resent it. Blake started to move his head, groaning.

"What happened?" Surrey asked. "Did he panic and try to shoot Hardcastle?"

"He tried to shoot Hardcastle," I said. "It wasn't panic, though. His mind moves quickly. As soon as he saw Hardcastle had a pistol in his pocket, he decided to turn it against him. It wasn't an accident that he closed the screen so that we couldn't see."

We got Hardcastle to sit in the chair where Blake had been. Surrey gently pulled his hands away from his eyes while I dabbed them with water. They were terribly bloodshot and Hardcastle sobbed with the pain of it, but it didn't look as if they were permanently damaged. He managed a few words.

"He shot me. He grabbed it out of my pocket before I could stop him and fired it straight in my face."

"Yes," I said. "And he screamed at you to put it away, as if it were you holding the pistol. That's what we were meant to think. If he'd managed to kill you as he'd intended, his story would have been that you attacked him and got shot while he was trying to defend himself."

"But why should Blake try to kill him?" Surrey said.

"Columbine had collected a bundle of IOUs," I said. "Some of them were enormous sums, others comparatively small. One of them was Barnaby Blake's for five hundred pounds at five percent interest. It should have been settled months ago. And she owned a third share of the theater we're standing in and seemed discontented with the way he was running it."

All Blake's plans for the theater had depended on Columbine's goodwill. The conversation I'd overheard, with him trying to convince her of its bright future, had been a desperate plea for more time.

"That's why he killed her," I said. "And this is how."

I took the pot of ointment out of my pocket.

"It wasn't anything she ate or drank that poisoned her. She had an embarrassing complaint and was being treated with ointment. It was supposed to be a secret between her and her maid, but Blake made it his business to know everything that was going on in his theater. He replaced her usual ointment with a pot that had a fatal dose of thorn apple instead of a healing one. I'm sure he took what he needed from Jenny's basket. He pushed the screen over on Susanna, too. She'd almost caught him going through Columbine's things, looking for the IOU."

Surrey didn't need to know that by then it was under the seat of Hardcastle's phaeton. He must have moved with unusual speed after Columbine's death to take her portfolio of papers from her villa near Kensington Gardens, probably with the idea of securing the marriage license. When he saw her treasury of IOUs it might have looked like financial salvation to him, and his phaeton was the safest hiding place he could think of whil deciding how to exploit it. Still Hardcastle had behaved well in the end, according to his lights, so I'd decided to keep some of his secrets. I took the cloth away from his eyes.

"Can you see at all now?"

He blinked and focused on the horizontal body of Blake.

"Is he dead?"

"No, but he should be," Daniel said.

Steps along the corridor, and Kennedy's voice.

". . . hurry up, for God's sake."

He burst in with two police constables behind him. They'd been dragged from their beat, not expecting this. It took a while to convince them that nobody was dead. By then, Blake was groggily trying to sit up.

"Arrest him for the murder of Columbine," Daniel told them.

"He tried to murder me too," Hardcastle said. "Fired a pistol straight in my face."

They stared from one to the other, pondering what to do. Eventually Hardcastle's high-pitched but patrician tone had its effect.

"Can I ask your name, sir?"

"Rodney Hardcastle." Recognition dawned in their faces. Any policeman on a beat in the theater area would know about Rodney Hardcastle. He didn't leave it at that, though. "I am the son of Lord Silverdale and you'd better arrest that man for trying to kill me. Oh, and call me a cab to take me back to Mayfair, there's a good fellow."

"For the first time in my life, I'll admit that the English aristocracy has its uses," Daniel said.

It was late that night, almost midnight. He, Kennedy and I were sitting by the fire and sharing a bottle of claret. The desperation had gone from his face and voice, but reaction had set in and he could scarcely move for exhaustion. I was bone-tired too, so that even going upstairs to bed seemed a near impossibility. Mrs. Martley had retired hours ago, angry with all of us.

"Yes, I'm not sure that they'd have arrested him on our word," I said. "I'm not looking forward to having to face Hardcastle's mother, though. I hardly returned him in good order."

"Just a few scratches." Daniel dismissed him with a wave of his empty glass. "He deserved worse. Anyway, do you have to face her?"

"Probably not."

"Do you know what the best part of today was, Libby?"

"Punching Blake?"

"Not even that. The best thing was seeing the expression on Phillips's face when you put the jar of ointment on the table in front of him. I've never seen a barrister at a loss before."

"He was still cautious, though. He's not sure it will amount to proof."

"No, but he admitted that if the jury at the trial had known about the poison not being in the syllabub and about the IOUs, Jenny would probably not have been convicted. And he said it, actually said it."

In the light of all this, they can't hang her now. Charles Phillips, one of the most experienced barristers at the Old Bailey, had said the words. Daniel wanted to set them as an anthem with organ and trumpets. Phillips had been in such a hurry to go and consult people about it that he'd practically run out of the room. Daniel was to meet him again tomorrow, then they'd go together to see Jenny.

"He did warn you that they won't let her out at once," I reminded him.

"That doesn't matter. Or rather, it does, but it's nothing in the face of thinking . . . Oh God, when we left the Old Bailey after talking to him, we actually walked over the place outside Newgate where they put up the gallows. It struck me that the next time they put them up it might have been for . . ."

His voice died away.

"It's all right," I said. "It's not going to happen. Not now."

"No, thanks to you. Tell me, when were you sure it was Blake?" Kennedy said.

"When I saw the IOU, I thought it might be. Then the attack on Daniel convinced me. But I couldn't understand how he'd done it—until I saw Marie. I was following some wrong tracks too. For a while I thought it might be Surrey, in the pay of Lady Silverdale."

"From what you say, she's quite capable of it."

"Probably. Only it couldn't have been Surrey who pushed over the screen on Susanna. Quite apart from not being the sort to do a thing like that to his own daughter, he'd been in his dressing room at the time, talking to me."

"Why did the attack on me convince you?" Daniel said.

"It happened when we started seriously looking for Marie. Whoever planned it didn't want us to find her and learn about the ointment. But he was clever enough to use the old search for Rainer as bait and hire an actor to impersonate him. That meant the killer had to be somebody you'd taken into your confidence."

"I was a fool," Daniel said. "I'd really convinced myself Blake wanted to help."

"Not a fool, no. Blake was clever and took his opportunities. Perhaps the idea of murdering Columbine to solve his financial troubles only came to him after that fight onstage. He knew it would make Jenny the main suspect. He put thorn apple in the syllabub in all the confusion when Columbine was dying and made sure the policeman took the bowl away with him. He played a clever game at her trial. I daresay he bribed or bullied Jane Wood into giving evidence against Jenny, while he pretended to be sympathetic to her."

"And Hardcastle would have been his last line of defense?" Kennedy said.

"Exactly. If that pistol had been loaded and Hardcastle had died, Blake would have made sure that word about his secret marriage got out, muddying the waters all over again."

We were silent, looking into the fire. After a while, I asked the question that was in my mind, without looking at Daniel.

"When Jenny comes out, shall you marry her?"

"Yes. Shall you mind, Liberty?"

"I wish both of you joy with all my heart. You deserve it."

He got up from his chair, knelt down beside me and enclosed me in a rib-crushing, passionate hug, quite unlike the friendly or comforting hugs he'd given me in the past. I could feel him trembling and his heart thumping. The first one of its kind—and the last. He was murmuring something, his face against my hair.

"It's all over, Libby. Thank the gods, it's all over."

Chapter Twenty-eight

It wasn't quite. Ten days later I was riding in the park with Amos when a familiar figure on a showy Arab came toward us at a canter. I'd expected it, but still wasn't best pleased. For one thing, I thought it was likely to be my last ride on Rancie. The wedding of her new owner was drawing near and any day now the groom would be expecting to have her sent to his country estate. I wanted to experience every second of this bittersweet ride without distraction, even from Mr. Disraeli. For another thing, I guessed he would have spoken to Lady Silverdale and be bearing some harsh words about putting her son in danger.

He drew alongside us, raising his hat with one hand as he pulled up the mare with the other.

"Good morning, Miss Lane. I've been hearing about your exploits."

"I'm sure you have."

"A satisfactory outcome, it seems. Jenny Jarvis is to receive a royal pardon."

The news hadn't been officially announced yet, but as usual he had his sources of information.

"Yes, and isn't that foolish?" I said. "Why pardon the poor girl for something she didn't do in the first place?"

He smiled, not put out by my bad temper.

"It works faster than an appeal or retrial. You should be pleased."

"And she's still in Newgate while they go through all the legal formalities. Can you do anything to get her released more quickly?"

Since he insisted on being there, I thought he might as well make himself useful.

"I'm afraid you overestimate my powers, Miss Lane. Today I'm a simple messenger for Lady Silverdale."

"Is she very angry with me?"

He raised his eyebrows.

"Quite the contrary. She described you as an unusually resourceful and quick-witted young woman."

"Doesn't she blame me for causing her son to be hurt?"

"Why should she? For the first and almost certainly the last time in his life he's quite the hero. That's surely worth some superficial scarring and a pair of bloodshot eyes, particularly considering he was no Adonis in the first place."

"Hero? He behaved better than I expected, but that's pitching it high."

"It seems you haven't heard the full story, Miss Lane."

"Oh, haven't I?"

"How he tracked down the murderer of his wife and, at great personal risk, called him to account."

He looked at me. I tried to keep my face straight, but couldn't help laughing.

"Is that really what people are saying?"

"The whole town, I assure you. His father's so pleased he's even come back from the country."

"They've admitted that he married Columbine?"

"Once they heard about the property portfolio, they decided that she was an acceptable wife: rich and dead. I'm sure they'll marry him to somebody else pretty smartly, before the gloss goes off him."

"So it all ends happily."

I couldn't keep the sadness out of my voice, thinking of Rancie. Perhaps he thought it was for some other reason, because he dropped his teasing tone.

"And what about you, Miss Lane? What are you going to do?"

"Go on teaching music, I suppose."

"A woman can always marry. I'm sure I could find you somebody quite suitable by the end of the season."

I wondered why people would keep trying to marry me off.

"Thank you kindly, sir. But I've no plans in that direction."

"Marriage does let a woman out into the world."

"As you see, I'm out in the world already."

I waved a hand at the trees coming into leaf, the blue sky.

"And teaching girls their scales," he said.

"What else do you suggest?"

I said it sarcastically, not expecting an answer. To my surprise, his reply was serious.

"I've been giving that some thought. You have unusual talents. You don't think like an ordinary person."

"I'm not sure that anybody's ordinary."

"Is that logical?"

"No, but then a lot of things aren't."

He thought about that for a moment.

"Perhaps that's one of your strengths, Miss Lane. You have a sideways-on way of looking at things. It could be useful."

"How?"

"As an observer, a solver of problems. There are many people in London who need the kind of service you've done for the Silverdales."

"I didn't care about the Silverdales. It was for Daniel and Jenny."

"This time, yes. But supposing some of the people with problems were prepared to pay you for using your particular talents on their behalf, wouldn't that be more interesting and more profitable than teaching singing?"

Again, he'd done that trick of swinging me out and away from my normal world, to a place where things that had been unthinkable became quite possible.

"You're suggesting I should set up as a professional problem solver?"

"Yes, I am. I could even send you clients."

I laughed again, but something in my mind was saying, *Well, why not?*

"And what am I to put on my brass plate when I set up in business? 'Problem solver' hasn't quite the dignity of 'doctor' or 'attorney.'"

He laughed too.

"Who knows? 'Private intelligencer,' perhaps. I'll give the matter some thought."

Which must mean he proposed to see me again. I couldn't help feeling a surge of pleasure at that. He touched his hat and tightened the rein, preparing to turn and ride away.

"By the by, Lady Silverdale asked me to give you this. We hope you'll accept it. After all, fifty pounds doesn't last long, does it?"

He tucked a folded paper between Rancie's saddle and withers.

"I've something for you too," I said.

I'd had it ready in my pocket for the last few rides. I took out the folded paper and handed it to him. He looked at me, then down at the paper. A battle was going on in his expression, between the dandy who could never be surprised by anything and a human need to unfold the paper. Human need won. He unfolded it, took it in at a glance and couldn't suppress a smile of delight and relief.

"I am more obliged to you than ever, Miss Lane."

He raised his hat to me and whirled away. I watched him go, then unfolded the paper he'd given me. There were two short sentences. *Thank you, Miss Lane. I hope you will accept the enclosed as a token of my gratitude.* Folded inside, another paper which I had to read twice before I believed it: a draft made out to Miss Liberty Lane on Lady Silverdale's bank for the sum of one hundred pounds. I let out a yelp of surprise. The picture came into my mind of the sunny upstairs room at Abel Yard, of paying the landlord his fifty pounds and not having to move again.

Hearing my yelp, Amos came up alongside.

"Something wrong?"

"Look at this."

I showed him the draft. He took his time reading it. I thought of Disraeli's words, *After all, fifty pounds doesn't last long, does it?* So the source of the money that had kept me afloat in London so far was another problem solved. For his own purposes, Mr. Disraeli had wanted to keep me on hand.

"Very nice too," Amos said, handing back the draft. "Now, what are you looking so down in the mouth about?"

"Because it's come too late."

If I'd known that my finances would be so dramatically repaired, I'd never have let Rancie go. It had been the wrong decision, made at our lowest ebb. But the decision had been made and announced, and I was sure that, in Amos's world, it would be dishonorable to back out of it. I tried.

"I suppose once somebody's agreed to sell a horse, he shouldn't change his mind."

Amos killed off my hopes with a solemn nod.

"That's right, once you've shaken hands on a deal, it's made."

"And you shook hands for me, as I asked you?"

He looked sorrowful and bowed his head.

"It's not your fault, Amos. I told you to do it."

We rode on a stride or two. I glanced across at him and although his head was still bowed, there was a twist of a grin on his lips.

"You did do it, didn't you, Amos?"

"I suppose it must have slipped my mind."

"What?"

"No sense in rushing things, was there? I had an idea something might turn up."

"But the girl's expecting Rancie for her bride's present."

"She was, but she'll get over it. I've got my eye on a dapple-gray mare for her, pretty as paint. Suit her just as well."

The sunlight dazzled rainbows into my eyes through the tears that were rising up. I hoped the sweetest, prettiest, etc. would be as happy as a lark on her dapple-gray mare. I needn't hate her anymore. I brushed the tears from my eyes.

"By the by," Amos said, "what was that note you gave him that pleased him so much?"

I glanced at him and decided to share the joke.

"One of his IOUs."

A serious one, as it happened, with a lot more naughts on the end than my draft from Lady Silverdale. It had been in the batch that Columbine had bought. I wondered if Disraeli had known that when he was so eager to engage my services on the side of social order, but decided to give him the benefit of the doubt.

"Race you," I called to Amos.

Hardly fair, because we were five strides away before he knew what was happening, but soon the thunder of his hooves sounded behind Rancie and me as we galloped flat out westward across the park, with our shadows from the rising sun flying in front of us.

A+

AUTHOR
INSIGHTS,
EXTRAS, &
MORE...

FROM
**CARO
PEACOCK**
AND
AVON A

A Man You Couldn't Ignore

There is a man in Liberty Lane's life who makes her heart beat faster, although she knows very well that she will never have a romantic relationship with him. He and she are both clever enough to know it would be a disaster—and against her principles, if not his. But they are on the edge of dangerous ground. So am I in writing about them, because Benjamin Disraeli, member of Parliament (and, much later, prime minister) is a real historical figure. A writer of fiction has to tread carefully when dealing with one of those, especially when his life is as well documented—both by himself and others—as Disraeli's.

At the time of *A Dangerous Affair*, the real Disraeli is thirty-three years old, eleven years older than Liberty, and less than a year into what would be one of the most spectacularly successful careers in British parliamentary history. Not that anybody except himself would have predicted that at the time. To many observers he was just another young MP with big ideas, rich friends, a rather racy background and an impressive pile of debts. He was a man who took risks and a person from Liberty's background would always feel her heart go out to a risk taker.

He was also a man you couldn't ignore. We've probably all had the experience of being at some kind of social event when the talk is buzzing along nicely, all very civilized and just the slightest bit boring. Then the door opens, somebody walks in and there's a split second of silence. The talk starts again but this time it's livelier, with an edge to it, as if everybody's onstage. People shift position slightly, while trying to look as if they are still concentrating on what their companions are saying, to get a look at the person who's just arrived. The party takes off like a hot-air balloon. All his life, even before he became a famous politician, Disraeli was one of those people.

For one thing, there were his looks. As a young man, while he was making his way in society, writing fairly successful novels but mostly living on his father's money, Disraeli's great idol was Lord Byron. Disraeli dressed in what he hoped was Byronic style, his dark hair falling in long curling locks, trousers with stripes down the seams, fancy waistcoats, rings on his fingers and gold chains round his neck. With his pale face and beak of a nose, he was never a conventionally handsome English gentleman. But he was exotic and unmissable, and anyway Liberty's taste is rarely conventional. What appealed to her—as it appealed to many others—was his conviction that the world was a limitless and exciting place and he was more than entitled to have his share of it.

It was hard to resist his intelligence and wit. His first novel was published when he was twenty-two years old, and he combined novel writing with his parliamentary career. His witticisms, both in Parliament and out of it, became legendary. Even now, he commands five and a half columns in *The Oxford Dictionary of Quotations*, compared to Winston Churchill who has only three. Some of his aphorisms could have come from the mouth of Oscar Wilde, if Disraeli hadn't got there first, like: "When I want to read a novel, I write one" or "Every woman should marry—and no man." He compared his political opponents to "a range of exhausted volcanoes" and described one of them as "the arch mediocrity of a cabinet of mediocrities." When asked whether he would like Queen Victoria to visit him on his deathbed he declined because, he said, she'd only ask him to take a message to her late husband, Prince Albert.

The attraction in writing about such a character is obvious, but there are risks for an author in using genuine historical characters alongside fictional ones. One peril is simply overloading the scene with real characters. *Ah, Miss Austen, have you heard the latest about the Prince of Wales and Miss X? By the by, I must introduce you to the Duke of Wellington.* The other extreme is to avoid real characters altogether, but to my mind this loses some of the texture that you need to make the past convincing. Imagine trying to write an account of the early twenty-first century in which nobody ever mentions or thinks about a political figure, a rock star, a film actor, a notorious criminal, a famous baseball or football player. People's everyday lives are affected by what's going on round them, even if they've never met the people they talk or read about. If you ignore the famous characters of history, you lose some of the threads that make up the fabric of people's lives.

So, I am shameless in involving the real Disraeli in my fiction and writing for him dialogue which he never uttered. I do have rules, though. The main one is that if I use real characters, they must not behave much better or much worse than they did in real life. The other is that the real characters should be on the periphery of the action, rather than at its center. They may play an important part in the story, but the story is not about them.

One of the reasons I wanted to involve Disraeli is that he and Liberty are, in some ways, natural sparring partners. Politically, he is entirely on the wrong side for her. Disraeli was a Conservative throughout his life—although he had no sympathy with the old and hidebound Conservative Party that was failing to come to terms with the realities of the nineteenth century, especially how new developments in industry and the growth of great cities like Birmingham and Manchester were changing people's lives. He gave the party a shake-up that influences it to this day. Liberty comes from a totally different tradition. Her family were radicals who welcomed the French Revolution, had little liking for kings and queens and no respect for noble birth. On most social and political questions, she and Disraeli are on opposite sides. But they have one great thing in common: both are outsiders.

She has the manners and education of a lady, but couldn't help being unconventional even if she wanted to, because of her upbringing and the circumstances that have left her to make her own way in the world. Disraeli is an outsider because he was born a Jew at a time when anti-Semitism was deeply ingrained in British society. His father, Isaac D'Israeli, was a rich, scholarly and serious-minded man who decided to convert to Christianity and took the rest of the family, including young Benjamin, along with him. Although nominally a Christian for most of his life, Disraeli was always proud of his Jewish background. He saw Arabs and Jews as brothers, both children of Abraham and natural aristocrats of the desert, with a far older lineage than the English nobles who scorned Jews.

Disraeli's ambition, and his eventual success, both had an element of revenge in them, against conventional society that had looked askance at his dandyish ways, his Jewish origins and his cleverness. His progress up the ladder confounded many people. In December 1834 the political diarist Charles Greville wrote: "The Chancellor called on me yesterday about getting the young Disraeli into Parliament . . . I don't think such a man will do."

Three years later, Disraeli was a member of Parliament. His first speech there was a notorious failure. He tried too hard to impress and was howled down. Greville again: "Mr Disraeli made his first exhibition the other night, beginning with florid assurance, speedily degenerating into ludicrous absurdity, and being at last put down with inextinguishable shouts of laughter." He told the men roaring with laughter all round him: "Though I sit down now, the time will come when you will hear me." As it happened, Charles Greville lived long enough to see the man who wouldn't do become leader of the Conservative Party and Chancellor of the Exchequer, though not quite long enough to see his rise to prime minister. Even Queen Victoria herself had to change her first opinion of him, that he was "detestable, unprincipled, reckless and not respectable." He became her most trusted minister and a much-loved friend. When told of his death, she could scarcely see for tears. "Never had I so kind and devoted a Minister and very few such devoted friends."

One thing above all about Disraeli makes him a suitable acquaintance for Liberty: the effect on her career. At the end of the book, he suggests that she should set up in a profession that doesn't even exist at the time—as a private investigator. He is sure he will be able to put cases her way. Historically, this may seem the most unlikely thing about their relationship. In fact, it fits very well with the character of the real Disraeli. His success depended on knowing what people were doing and thinking, both in Britain and abroad. According to one of his biographers, Sarah Bradford, "Disraeli maintained an informal intelligence network to keep him informed of what was going on in the social, political and diplomatic world." In his novel *Coningsby*, Disraeli creates a Jewish international statesman called Sidonia, who is an idealized version of himself, and says this about his intelligence collecting: "Information reached him from so many, and such contrary quarters, that, with his discrimination and experience, he could almost instantly distinguish the truth. The secret history of the world was his pastime."

Disraeli would immediately see the usefulness of a resourceful young woman like Liberty, with knowledge of the world, an ability to speak foreign languages and unusual freedom to operate at all levels of society. As for Liberty, at the end of the book, she's thinking about his suggestion. She may be useful to him, but she'll make sure she won't be used. It will have to be on her terms because she won't surrender her independence, even to such a charismatic man as Disraeli. But she can't help being caught up in the excitement of the idea. Excitement was one of Disraeli's gifts.

Photo courtesy Karolina Webb

CARO PEACOCK acquired the reading habit from her childhood growing up in a farmhouse. Later, she developed an interest in women in Victorian society and from this grew her character of Liberty Lane. She rides, climbs, and trampolines as well as studies wildflowers.

Caro Peacock